Praise f

'Miss

'. . . some of the best examples of the British
country-house murder mystery'
Alfred Hitchcock Magazine

'Miss Wentworth is a first rate story-teller'
Daily Telegraph

'You can't go wrong with Miss Maud Silver'
Observer

'Miss Wentworth's plot is ingenious, her
characterisation acute, her solution satisfying'
Scotsman

'Patricia Wentworth has created a great detective in
Miss Silver, the little old lady who nobody notices,
but who in turn notices everything'
Paula Gosling

ALSO BY PATRICIA WENTWORTH

The Case of William Smith
The Benevent Treasure
The Listening Eye
Grey Mask
The Catherine Wheel
Miss Silver Comes to Stay
Miss Silver Intervenes
The Eternity Ring
Latter End
The Case is Closed
The Chinese Shawl
Out of the Past
The Fingerprint
The Gazebo
The Key
Through the Wall
The Alington Inheritance
The Clock Strikes Twelve
The Watersplash
The Girl in the Cellar
The Silent Pool
The Brading Collection
The Ivory Dagger

ABOUT THE AUTHOR

Patricia Wentworth was born in India and after writing several romances turned her hand to crime. She wrote dozens of bestselling mysteries and was recognised as one of the mistresses of classic crime. She died in 1961.

PATRICIA WENTWORTH

THE CHINESE SHAWL

HODDER

First published in Great Britain in 1943 by Hodder and Stoughton
A division of Hodder Headline

A Hodder paperback

15

A CIP catalogue record for this title
is available from the British Library

ISBN 0 340 108991

Typeset in Sabon by Hewer Text UK Ltd
Printed and bound by CPI Mackays, Chatham ME5 8TD

Hodder and Stoughton Ltd
A division of Hodder Headline
338 Euston Road
London NW1 3BH

ONE

LAURA FANE CAME up to London in the third week in January. A little earlier or a little later, and things might have happened differently for her, and for Tanis Lyle, and for Carey Desborough, and for some other people too. It had to be that time because of her twenty-first birthday and having to see Mr Metcalfe, who was the family lawyer and her trustee. She stayed with one of her Ferrers relations, old Miss Sophy Ferrers, who was an invalid and never went out. She gave this as her reason for refusing to leave London for some less raided part of the country, intimating with gentle firmness that since she no longer felt able to leave her house for the pleasure of visiting her friends, she would certainly not do so to please Hitler. She had had a broken window or two when the house at the corner received a direct hit, and she had taken the precaution of tying up a heavy cut-glass chandelier in a muslin bag, but further than this she declined to go.

She welcomed Laura with great kindness, and insisted that she should make the most of her holiday.

'The Douglas Maxwells have asked you for tonight. Robin and Alistair are on leave. I hope you have brought a pretty frock, my dear. Robin is calling for you at a quarter to eight.'

The Maxwells were connections – Helen and Douglas, a nice friendly couple in their middle thirties, Douglas at the War Office, Robin and Alistair both in the Air Force and unmarried. Laura had met them once or twice. She felt warm and pleased. It was a delightful beginning to her visit.

She put on a black dress, and hoped it would pass muster. Black suited her white skin, dark hair, and the grey-green eyes which were her real beauty. They were changeable and sensitive as water, taking colour from what she wore. They took the light as water takes it, and they took the shadows too. Long dark lashes set them off. They were long enough and black enough to make a shadow of their own. For the rest she had a fine, even skin, smooth and rather pale, and a charming mouth, wide and generous, with enough natural colour to have stood alone without the help of lipstick. The severely plain black frock showed a slim, rounded figure. It made her look taller than she really was, and it made her look very young – too young.

She frowned at herself in the glass. The dark hair fell curling on her neck. It might be the fashion, but it made her look about sixteen. There was a jade pendant which Oliver Fane had brought from China for his wife Lilian, a peach with two leaves and a little winged creature crawling on it. Laura pulled it out of her handkerchief-case and slipped the black silk cord over her head. Her mother had never worn it, because Oliver died that leave. The bright green fruit hung down nearly to her waist. The cord made her neck look very white. She threw her Chinese shawl across her shoulders, and felt the momentary thrill it always gave her. Oliver had brought that too, and it was such a lovely thing – black ground and deep black fringe, every inch of the ground worked over in a pattern of fantastic loveliness and all the colours of a fairy tale.

She went downstairs and showed herself to Cousin

Sophy, who put her Dresden china head on one side, opened her blue eyes very wide, and said in a plaintive voice, 'Oh, my dear – all in black!'

Laura dangled the peach.

'Not all, Cousin Sophy.'

Miss Ferrers shook her head.

'Very pretty – very pretty indeed, and quite valuable too. And the shawl – such lovely embroidery. You look very nice, my dear. It's just that black seems so – so inappropriate for a young girl.'

Laura took one of the little frail hands and kissed it.

'I know, darling – ought to be white satin and pearls, like the picture of my mother in her coming-out dress, and I ought to have golden hair and blue eyes like hers.'

Miss Ferrers smiled.

'She was a lovely creature, my dear, and she turned all the young men's heads. Your father fell in love with her at first sight. He was engaged to his cousin Agnes Fane, and it would have been such a convenient marriage because of the property, but once he had seen Lilian it was no good, he couldn't do it. People blamed him of course, and I'm afraid Agnes never really got over it. But what is the good of blaming people? It wouldn't have been a happy thing for either of them if he had married Agnes, because she was very much in love with him and she had a very jealous disposition. So what would have been the good? He didn't love her – he loved your mother. And they died so young—' Her voice went off into a sigh.

'I'm not like her at all.' Laura sounded very regretful. She would have loved to have been like Lilian.

Miss Sophy looked at her very kindly indeed.

'Just a look now and then. Sometimes it is quite strong. But of course you haven't her colouring.'

Laura bent and kissed her. And then the door bell rang, and Robin Maxwell was there to fetch her.

The old, sad story slipped away into the past. Robin was a cheerful young man determined to make the most of every moment of his leave. He never stopped talking all the way to the Luxe.

Helen and Douglas Maxwell were waiting for them in the lounge, both tall and fair, and treating Laura as if she were a real relation instead of a very distant family connection.

The rest of the party began to arrive – Alistair Maxwell with a vivacious little thing called Petra North who laughed, and chattered, and laughed again when the three tall brothers teased her. Laura thought she was like a kitten, with her little round face, and round eyes, and dark fluffy hair.

They all stood there waiting for Tanis Lyle and Carey Desborough. Laura liked his name. She remembered that she had liked it when she had seen it under a smudged snapshot two, or was it three, months ago. All the papers had carried the ridiculous picture, which really only showed a pair of shoulders seen from behind, the back of a head, one ear, and the slanting line of what looked like quite a good jaw. The snapshot was there because he had got the Distinguished Flying Cross and he simply wouldn't be photographed. The Maxwells were talking about him now. He had had a bad smash and wasn't flying again yet.

Laura thought how very alike the three brothers were. Douglas was the tallest, and Robin the fairest. His hair was really almost white, but they all had the same rather square faces, tanned ruddy skins, and bright blue eyes.

'Tanis is always late,' said Petra North. She looked at Alistair, but he was watching the door.

Robin said, 'She couldn't be in time if she tried,' and quick as lightning out came the kitten's claws, and Petra struck back with: 'She doesn't try.'

She laughed, and the dimples came out too. 'I wouldn't either if I were tall enough to make an entrance like she does. It's no good when you're five foot nothing. It simply doesn't come off, and that would be worse than anything.' She whisked round on Laura. 'Do you know Tanis? Oh, but of course you do – she's your cousin.'

Laura nodded. 'She's my cousin, but I don't know her. We've never met.'

Petra laughed.

'Oh, yes – there's a family feud – your father didn't marry her aunt, or something like that. She told me. Too medieval! I didn't know people really did that sort of thing – but of course it must have been a long time ago.' Her tone relegated Oliver and Lilian to a vague, indefinite past.

Laura felt a little embarrassed. She said the first thing that came into her head.

'She's very beautiful, isn't she?'

Petra made a little cross face. Laura had the feeling that for twopence she would have put out her tongue. The claws showed again.

'She makes people think so—' A pause, and then the one word – '*men*.' Her expression changed suddenly. 'Oh, well – here she comes. Perfect entrance, isn't it?'

It was. The floor of the lounge might have been cleared for it. There was an open lane between them and the big door, and up this lane there came the two people for whom they had been waiting.

Laura saw them as you see people in a picture. They arrested and held her attention. If at that moment she had known all that was going to happen between the three of them, she could not have felt a more breathless interest. She saw Tanis Lyle and a tall, dark man, and then she only saw Tanis Lyle, because Tanis was like that – she filled the room.

She wasn't beautiful – that was Laura's first astonished thought. She put across an effect of beauty, but it was an effect without bone and substance behind it. In that first clear moment of untroubled judgement Laura thought, 'She isn't any better looking than I am, really.' And it was true. Six or seven years older; perhaps an inch taller – or was that just the way her dress was cut; the same dark hair, but oh so beautifully done; the same very white skin; the same grey-green eyes, but greener, definitely greener than Laura's were – quite a different shape too, long and slitted, between dark lashes. She walked with the perfection of movement, but that was because there was an absolute perfection of balance. Laura thought, 'What a perfectly lovely figure.' The dark-green dress set it off – skintight to midway between hip and knee, and then flaring full. The stuff was velvet, the colour a deep, rich emerald. Just where the fullness flared the line was broken by two queer extravagant pockets crusted with a barbaric embroidery of pearl and emerald. A pearl string at her neck, fine, lustrous, perfectly matched. Pearls at her ears, and emeralds in an ultra-modern setting on the bare right hand which she was putting out to Helen Douglas.

The clear moment had gone. It never returned. As Tanis came up to her and said in her rather deep voice, 'You must be Laura – I'm so glad to meet you,' all the details, all the things which you can make into an inventory, were submerged. Because it wasn't what Tanis looked like that counted, it was what she was. She brought something with her – a vitality, an attraction.

Waves of warmth, pleasure, interest, flowed from her, changing the atmosphere. It was like champagne. Everyone felt the stimulus. All impressions were heightened, all feelings intensified.

Laura looked into the green eyes and saw them alive with interest. She felt absurdly charmed, absurdly reluctant.

And then Carey Desborough was being introduced, and she looked up at a lean, tanned face, and thought, 'Why does he look like that?' The odd part of it was that the very next moment she didn't know at all what she had seen to make her have that thought. It was something that hurt, but she didn't know what it was. It gave her a lost, shaken feeling. And then the whole thing passed, and they were going in to dinner.

TWO

LAURA HAD NEVER enjoyed herself so much in her life. There was that sparkle in the atmosphere, and everyone was so kind. They all knew each other so well, and they might so easily have crowded her out, but she didn't feel like a stranger at all.

When dinner was over they danced in the famous Gold Room. Laura danced first with Douglas Maxwell, and then with Carey Desborough. She said: 'I'm not really tall enough.'

He smiled down at her and said in a pleasant, cheerful voice, 'Oh, we'll get along.'

'Is Tanis taller than I am?'

She tilted her head and saw the smile go out. He said, with an effect of being casual: 'Oh, I don't know – I shouldn't think so.'

She danced with Robin after that. About half-way through they stood out for a moment and watched. Against the gold background the rhythmic movement had the effect of a kaleidoscope slowed down to the pace of a slow-moving melody. Laura watched with fascinated eyes. She had lived very quietly. She had never seen anything like this before. She was as thrilled as a child at its first Christmas tree. Light, colour, music, kindness made an enchanting pattern. She saw Helen Douglas go by, tall and very fair, in a dress of midnight blue. She was with Carey Desborough. Their heights matched perfectly. She saw Petra and Alistair. Petra was laughing, but Alistair looked across the room to where Tanis stood with his brother Douglas.

Robin laughed.

'Don't you want to dance?'

Laura gave a long, happy sigh.

'I want to dance, and I want to watch, and I want to talk to everyone. There ought to be at least six of me to enjoy it all properly.'

'You *are* a comic kid!'

'I'm twenty-one. I'm grown-up. I'm of age. I can squander my enormous fortune.'

'I didn't know you'd got one.'

'Four hundred a year,' said Laura. 'Three hundred of it comes from letting the Priory to Cousin Agnes Fane, so it doesn't really count, because you can't squander a house. But it gives me a lovely feeling to think that I can snatch the other hundred pounds away from Mr Metcalfe and just play ducks and drakes with it.'

'You'd much better stick to it. What sort of ducks and drakes do you want to make?'

Laura laughed happily.

'Oh, I don't. It's just a perfectly lovely thought.'

Robin's Scottish brow displayed a frown.

'It must have been awfully badly invested for you to be getting only three and a half per cent on it.'

But Laura was tired of the subject of her money. She had no idea of wasting any more time upon it. She pulled Robin out into the dance again. They went by quite close to Alistair and Petra. Laura said: 'I like her so much. Who is she? Have you known her a long time? Is she engaged to Alistair?'

Robin's frown seemed to have come to stay. He answered only the last of her questions.

'Not officially. As a matter of fact he's gone a bit off

the deep end about Tanis. She takes people that way. Not me, you know – I'm a cautious bird. When I see a net all laid out with nice little pellets of poisoned grain, I beat it for the great wide spaces.'

'Oh, Robin – how horrid of you! She isn't like that!'

'You just wait. She specialises in other girls' boy friends.'

'It sounds revolting.'

'Not a bit of it – it's all done with kindness. I've watched her at it for years. She's kind to the girl, and she's kind to the chap, and she goes on being kind to him till the girl gets crowded out, and then after a bit she gets bored and he gets crowded out too. She doesn't want any of them for keeps, you know. She just wants half a dozen of them trailing round, licking her boots, paying her taxis, and ready to cut each other's throats. She enjoys that part of it a lot.'

His tone was so savage that it rasped Laura's nerves. She looked up at him, half frightened, and saw the fair-skinned boyish face set in lines that added ten years to his age.

'I didn't think Alistair would be such a fool,' he said. And then, with a jerk that sent them both out of step, 'What do we want to talk about the woman for? She'll get herself murdered some day. She makes me see red!'

She danced next with Alistair. Interesting from the point of view of wanting to be right in the middle of these people and their emotions, but from the personal point of view perhaps a little arid, because Alistair did nothing but talk about Tanis – how wonderful she was – 'She's just been making the most marvellous film' – how beautiful, how extraordinarily kind and unselfish.

'I don't honestly believe she ever thinks about herself at all. Take me for instance. I'm just a very distant cousin, and I've never known her particularly well before. She's just been giving up her time to making my leave the most marvellous success. Why, she'd have let me fetch her tonight, only unfortunately Helen had already told Petra I was bringing her, so Tanis had to get Carey to come with her instead. I happen to know he bores her a bit. He's one of the best, you know, but that doesn't always cut any ice with women. Anyhow, that's another instance of her kindness – she's been most awfully good to him. He crashed, you know, and he's been rather a long time getting right. Tanis—' It was all Tanis.

Laura was fascinated and interested, but it did just occur to her to wonder how long the interest would last if this was Alistair's usual form, and whether he talked like this to Petra. He told her all about how much Cousin Agnes adored Tanis – 'She and Lucy brought her up, you know. They both adore her – but who wouldn't? And then she went on the stage.' Laura gathered that Cousin Agnes had been rather narrow-minded about this, and that the stage career hadn't been quite the glowing success which was Tanis's due, entirely owing to the mean jealousies and cabals which her extraordinary beauty and talent had provoked. It appeared that Tanis had glided into the pleasanter role of the gifted amateur with professional experience. Then she had been seen by Isidore Levinstein and given, first a test, and then a marvellous part in a marvellous film. She had been working herself to death on it, but now it was finished and she was resting. That was why it was so marvellous of her to give up her time to someone like him. But that was just like her – she never thought about herself. She was so different from other people that they simply didn't understand her. They were absolutely incapable of understanding such marvellous unselfishness . . .

Laura began to feel as if she was listening to a gramophone record.

It was after her third dance with Carey Desborough that he took her to sit out in one of the small alcoves off the dance floor. She saw him looking at her with an expression which she could not interpret – searching, quizzical – she didn't know. She thought there was a trace of bitter humour, and she wondered why.

'You're a cousin of Tanis's, aren't you?'

The label set off a very faint spark in Laura's mind. Her chin lifted a shade as she said, 'Yes – I'm Laura Fane.'

He said, 'You're not like her,' in a musing voice, and a whole shower of sparks went up.

'Why should I be?'

He smiled disarmingly. It made the most extraordinary difference to his face. Oddly enough, it was when he smiled that she saw how sad his eyes were – dark, disenchanted eyes. He said: 'I didn't mean that. Don't be angry. What I meant was that you're rather like her to look at – but you're quite a different sort of person.'

'I don't think I'm like her to look at.'

'Not really – just the colouring. But that's accounted for if you're cousins. It's unusual, you know. Does it run right through the family?'

'I don't know – I've never seen any of them. That's why I was so excited about meeting Tanis. I've never met any of my Fane relations except the Maxwells, and they don't really count because they take off miles farther up on the family tree, before the feud.'

'Am I allowed to ask about the feud? I've never met one at close quarters before.'

'Oh, it isn't a secret. You can't have that sort of family

split without everyone knowing, and it was a long time ago – before I was born.'

'A very long time ago!'

Laura looked at him suspiciously. He was perfectly grave. She said in a hurry: 'My father ran away with my mother instead of making the marriage the family had planned for him.'

'And they cut him off with a shilling.'

Laura showed two dimples.

'They couldn't do that. The Priory belonged to him. And anyhow there weren't any shillings except the ones he would have had if he had married Cousin Agnes. She had lots from her mother, who was quite a big heiress. She's been renting the place ever since. You see, my father was in the Navy, and he couldn't afford to live there anyhow, and nor could I, so it's just as well that Cousin Agnes wants to. I believe she simply adores the place. It is funny to think I've never seen it.'

'Why don't you go down there?'

'She's never asked me.'

Her voice sounded faintly forlorn, like a child left out of a party. He wondered how old she was. He said: 'Where do you live then? What do you do? Your father and mother—'

She shook her head mournfully.

'They died when I was five. I don't really remember them – only like a story that you've heard and you wish you could remember it.'

He thought, 'She's awfully young.' He felt what you feel towards a child – kindness – the response to an unconscious appeal. He said quietly: 'Well, someone must have looked after you.'

'Oh, yes – my mother's sister – very kind, and just a little bit strict. She sits on committees – women's welfare, and education, and all that sort of thing – and since the war evacuees.'

'And what do you do?'

'I'm secretary to a convalescent home for soldiers, and I drive the billeting officer round – she's a woman – and of course ARP – and odd jobs for Aunt Theresa—'

Carey Desborough laughed. 'And what do you do in your spare time?'

'I don't think I have any.' She laughed suddenly too. 'Oh, that's what you meant?' The dimples appeared again. 'Well, there are always odd jobs – we've only got one maid. And sometimes I go to the pictures, and I have been known to dance, but not on a floor like this.'

'The simple life!' His eyes smiled at her.

'I'm a country cousin,' said Laura. Her voice was small and meek, but the grey-green eyes had a sparkle as they met his. Then the black lashes dropped. It was quite effective, but she hadn't meant to do it. She just couldn't look at him any longer. Something behind the smile hurt her at her heart. It was a soft heart and easily hurt.

To her horrified surprise she felt herself blushing. The colour burned in her cheeks.

Carey laughed. He said in a friendly, teasing tone: 'I haven't seen a girl blush for years. How do you do it?'

Somehow that seemed to make it all right again. The sparkle returned. She said: 'I don't – it does itself. Isn't it horrid?'

'Not very.'

'Oh, but it is. It does it for nothing at all, and I never know when it's going to let me down. I used to get horribly teased about it at school.'

They went on talking while the next dance came and went. She found she was telling him all sorts of things about Aunt Theresa and the convalescent home, and their one and only bomb, and it was all quite easy and natural, and as if she had known him ever since she could remember.

'And how did you tear yourself away?'

Laura answered him quite seriously.

'Well, I hadn't had a holiday since the war started – but it's not a real holiday. I'm twenty-one, so I had to come up and see Mr Metcalfe who is my lawyer and trustee. The holiday is just tacked on.'

'Then you ought to make the most of it. How long have you got?'

'I think about a week. It depends on Mr Metcalfe.'

'When do you see him?'

'Tomorrow, at twelve.'

'Then suppose you lunch with me afterwards and we do a show?'

Laura blushed again, this time with pleasure.

'Oh, I should love to!'

THREE

FROM THE REMAINDER of the evening two things stood out. They kept coming back into Laura's mind while she was undressing and later when she had put out the light and lay there in Cousin Sophy's spare-room bed, which was so much more comfortable than any of the beds at home. The darkness made a background against which her pictures of the evening came and went. All the pictures were lovely except those two at the end, and they *would* keep coming back. She tried to send them away, to remember only how lovely it had been, but the two pictures which troubled her just wouldn't go. Tanis smiling at her and saying, 'I haven't really seen you at all. We must meet. Come and lunch with me tomorrow.' She could see herself standing there and colouring like a school-girl. 'I'm afraid I can't tomorrow.' What did she want to colour for? – and they were all looking at her. Then Carey Desborough said, 'She's lunching with me,' and that made it worse. But why – why? It was such an ordinary thing. Why was there that dreadful feeling of strain, as if she had made some terrible gaffe? Nothing could have been easier than Carey's voice. Nothing could have been sweeter than Tanis's smile. She had turned it on both of them, but especially on Carey. 'Ah, but how nice of you! It's her first visit to London – isn't it, Laura? – and we've got to give her as good a time as we can. But what about making a party of it – Alistair, and you, and me, and

Laura?' Her glance went round the circle. 'Robin and Petra too, if they're not doing anything else.'

Robin and Petra – but it was Alistair and Petra who were 'not officially engaged'. The picture kept on coming back – all of them standing there together in the lounge saying good night, and Tanis just blotting out an unofficial engagement with half a dozen effortless words and one of those brilliant smiles. Every time she looked back the smile seemed more brilliant, her own tongue-tied uncertainty more inept. Yet for the life of her she couldn't think what she should have said. She hadn't said anything – only stood there with the colour in her cheeks and a soft distressed look in her eyes. It was Carey Desborough who spoke. He laughed quite casually and said, 'Oh, I don't think so – not tomorrow. We're doing a show, and we don't want to be late.' The brilliant smile had turned on Alistair. His response was rapturous.

And then the good nights were really said. Looking back, Laura thought that Helen had hurried them a little. The party broke up, but it was Alistair who took Laura home. Laura's second picture was of Petra putting her hand on Robin's arm and saying with smiling lips, 'Wouldn't you like to take me home?' They were so close that she couldn't help knowing that Petra's fingers were not just resting lightly on the black coat sleeve but gripping the arm inside it. She moved so that she was standing between them and the others. She didn't want anyone else to see what she had seen. Alistair took her home. He never stopped talking about Tanis.

Those were the pictures. They didn't spoil the evening because it was too lovely to be spoiled, but they did spoil her remembrance of it. When she wanted to think about all the friendliness and kindness, she would hear Tanis thanking Carey Desborough for being kind to a little country cousin. Because that's what it amounted to. Laura's cheeks flamed again, all alone in the dark. He was kind. She had felt the kindness when he was talking to her. But to hear him thanked for it publicly by Tanis – well, it got worse every time she thought about it. And then all of a sudden she began to laugh at herself, because wasn't she being just the kind of silly fool that Tanis was hoping she'd be? And if she just didn't take any notice, well, Tanis wouldn't have scored after all. She had wanted to get Laura all hot and bothered, to show her up as a gauche, inexperienced young person from the country, to make Carey Desborough see her like that. Well, he hadn't taken any notice, and if Laura didn't take any notice either, the whole thing would have fallen rather flat. Petra was different – Tanis had scored there. But that was because for the time being Alistair was practically off his head, and there just wasn't anything to be done about it. She felt dreadfully sorry about Petra. Poor Petra. She began to wonder what it would be like to love someone very much, and to see him turn away from you and go mad about Tanis Lyle.

The pictures began to be blurred. Her thoughts blurred too. She slipped through the blur into a dream. The dream was not blurred at all. It was as sharp, and clear, and vivid as the image seen on the screen of a camera – sharper, clearer, and more vivid than reality. She was in a place she had never seen before, but she knew that it was a ruined aisle of the old Priory church. There was green grass underneath and a bright blue sky above. There were fallen blocks of masonry among the grass, and a lovely springing arch against the sky. She was standing at the bottom of a flight of narrow, curving steps which went up to a door in what looked like a solid wall. The sun was shining, and a great level shaft ran slanting down to Laura's feet. She was dressed in the black dress she had worn at the Luxe, and she was wearing her jade peach and her Chinese shawl. She could see all the colours in it, as bright and clear as the colours in a stained glass window. A turquoise butterfly and a grasshopper just the colour of her jade, sprays of blackberries embroidered in peach and primrose, wine-colour and all the lovely Chinese bulbs. The sun shone and a bird was singing. And then all of a sudden like a thunderclap it was dark – everything gone, colour, and sight, and sound. It was dreadfully cold. A hand came out of the dark and plucked her shawl away. Her feet were bare on the stone. She went groping up to the door in the wall, and it was locked against her. She beat on it and tried to cry out, but her voice was choked in her throat. She woke up, beating against the headboard of the spare-room bed. It took her a minute or two to realise where she was. Even after she had switched on the light she felt as if part of her had been left behind in that dark, ruined place. What a horrid dream.

She sat on the edge of the bed and looked with dismay at the twisted, dishevelled bedclothes. When she waked she had been kneeling up in bed beating on the walnut headboard. The eiderdown was on the floor, the blanket slipping. No wonder she had been cold in that horrid dream.

She made the bed, drank some water – nasty stuff London water – and then lay down again. She went to sleep almost at once, and slept without dreams until the morning.

FOUR

MR METCALFE WAS a pleasant elderly gentleman with the kind of fatherly manner which hints at authority as well as kindness. By the time Laura had shaken hands with him and emerged from the polite preliminaries she was feeling much less grown-up than she had a right to feel considering she was twenty-one and her own mistress.

'Well now, Miss Laura, I have quite a lot of business for you, and a very important proposal.'

'Proposal?' She could have killed herself for it, but she changed colour.

But Mr Metcalfe smiled indulgently.

'Oh, it's not a proposal of marriage. I hope you'll not be in too much of a hurry about that – it doesn't always answer. There are other kinds of proposals, you know, and this is really a very important one.'

'What is it?'

'Well, it deserves your very serious consideration. It is a proposal from Miss Agnes Fane—' He paused, scanning Laura's face. 'Before I tell you about it, would you mind telling me just how much you know of the breach which arose out of your father's marriage?'

Laura met his look frankly.

'I know that my father was engaged to Cousin Agnes, and that he ran away with my mother. That was what the quarrel was about, wasn't it?'

'Yes – but there was a little more to it than that. I don't know if you're quite clear about your relations.'

'Not very. You see, I've never met any of them except Tanis Lyle.'

'Oh, you know Miss Lyle?'

'I met her last night. I don't know any of the others.'

He took up a slip of paper and handed it to her.

'Well then, perhaps this will help you to get them straight.'

Laura looked at the paper with interest. It displayed a neatly typed family tree.

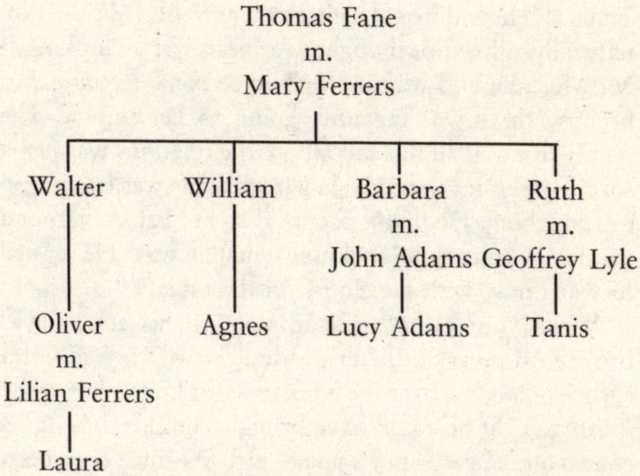

Mr Metcalfe began to expound.

'It begins with your great-grandfather Thomas Fane and your great-grandmother Mary Ferrers. If you look at that paper you will see that they had four children, Walter, William, Barbara and Ruth. Walter was your grandfather – William, Miss Agnes Fane's father. Barbara married a man called Adams. Her daughter, Miss Lucy Adams, lives at the Priory with Miss Fane. Ruth married Geoffrey Lyle. She was a good deal younger than the others, so her daughter, Miss Tanis Lyle, though a first cousin of your father and Miss Agnes and Miss Lucy, is really much nearer to you in age. Her parents died when she was a child, and she has been practically adopted by Miss Agnes Fane. She and Miss Lucy have brought her up and are quite devoted to her. Now, have you got all that quite clear?'

'Yes, quite.'

Laura was thinking that every time she met someone fresh the conversation always seemed to come round to Tanis and how devoted someone was to her. She did not, naturally, allow this thought to appear, but sat looking at Mr Metcalfe and waiting for him to come to the point, because there was certainly going to be a point. The family tree and all this talk about the relations was just a sort of preliminary skirmish. Mr Metcalfe was leading up to something. He had a proposal to lay before her, and she felt very curious to know what it was. He leaned forward now with his elbow on the table.

'When your father's engagement to his cousin was broken off a very difficult position arose. He had not a sufficient income to make it possible for him to live at the Priory even if he could have brought himself to turn his cousin out. She was not a young girl. She must have been about thirty-five – she was actually a few years older than your father – and the Priory had always been her home. Her father rented it from your grandfather – no lease, just a family arrangement – and when he died she and her mother continued there. There had been talk of a marriage between her and your father on and off for years, but nothing settled. But when Mrs William Fane died and your father came home from the Australian station, the engagement was formally given out. Mrs William had been a considerable heiress, and the whole of her fortune passed to Miss Agnes. It seemed to be a most suitable arrangement, and not only because of the money – Miss Fane was a very handsome and accomplished woman. Well, you know what happened. Your mother was a distant cousin. She came to the Priory on a visit, and your father fell head over heels in love with her. Naturally he wished to make such amends to his cousin as he could. Miss Fane had a very serious riding accident, and for some months there was no certainty that she would live. It was nearly a year before she was able to attend to business. She then asked for a lease of the Priory. Your father instructed us to give her a twenty-one-year lease from a date three months ahead. Now perhaps you see what I am coming to. You were born about a month after he gave us those instructions. The twenty-one-year lease runs out in about two months from now.'

Laura said, 'Oh!' What came next? Another lease – or something else? She said aloud: 'What does she want – Cousin Agnes? There's something she wants me to do, isn't there?'

'Well, yes, there is.' Mr Metcalfe took up a pencil and began to roll it to and fro between his fingers. A bright green pencil – the light caught it and the gold of his signet-ring.

'Does she want another lease?'

Mr Metcalfe frowned thoughtfully at the pencil. Then he transferred the frown to Laura.

'Well, no – she does not suggest a lease. In point of fact, she is anxious to buy.'

Something pricked Laura sharply. She sat up and said, 'Oh, no!' in a tone of dismay.

Mr Metcalfe laid down the pencil and stopped frowning. His manner became extremely parental.

'Now Miss Laura, this is a proposal which you would

do well to consider. It really is worth considering. Miss Fane has been paying you a very good rent all these years. She has also spent a great deal of money on the house and grounds. Most of the land, as you probably know, was sold by your grandfather. What remained, which does not amount to much more than a fairly extensive garden, was in a state of utter neglect. Miss Fane has transformed it. She has installed central heating and electric light in the house. She has never come down on your trustees for a single penny for repairs. She has made the property her first and very nearly her only interest. She is an invalid – since her accident she has never walked – and you can imagine what an interest like this has meant to her.'

'But if she can't walk—'

'She has one of those self-propelling chairs. She spends a great deal of time in the garden.'

Laura said, 'I see—' She was bewildered and taken aback. She had the feeling that she was being unfairly pressed. She turned a clear gaze on Mr Metcalfe's face.

'You mustn't talk as if I would turn her out. I would never do that.'

'Then you are prepared to consider the proposal?'

'No – I don't think so. I don't want – to sell—'

'Her offer is a very generous one. You have to consider that the rent she pays you amounts to three-quarters of your total income. She is not young, and she is an invalid. If she were to die, you would lose three hundred a year. You might let again, or you might not – that would depend largely on post-war conditions. You certainly could not hope for another tenant like Miss Fane.'

Laura gave her head a little impatient shake. The money didn't come into it – there were other things.

She said quickly: 'Why does she want to buy the Priory – after all these years?'

Mr Metcalfe had a smiling answer to that.

'My dear Miss Laura, she has always wanted to buy it, but your father wouldn't sell. He said he would never live there himself, but his son might be able to some day – anyhow, he would leave the decision to him. That was shortly before you were born, and he had quite made up his mind that you were to be a boy. As long as he lived Miss Fane made him a periodical offer. After his death she was obliged to wait for your coming of age. She now repeats her offer – twelve thousand pounds for everything as it stands.'

Laura put out a protesting hand.

'It's not the money, Mr Metcalfe. I want to know why. She's an invalid and she isn't young, and I would never turn her out. It isn't as if she had children to leave it to. Why does she want to buy the Priory?'

'Oh, she wants to leave it to Miss Tanis Lyle,' said Mr Metcalfe.

FIVE

LAURA CAME OUT on to the street and found Carey Desborough waiting for her. He had been walking up and down, and just as she emerged from the dark entrance he turned and came towards her. He had those few moments to adjust his recollections of Laura last night to Laura this morning. She was wearing a black coat over a bright green dress, and a black cap with a little shiny clasp at the side that looked like silver. He had not remembered that her colour was so bright except when she had blushed, and he wondered whether she was blushing now. He thought not. He thought that something had made her angry, and when he saw how brilliant her eyes were he was sure of it. He felt an irresponsible desire to tease her, to heap fuel on the fire, and see what happened, but she took the wind out of his sails by saying, 'I'm in a most dreadful temper. I'm not fit to go out to lunch with anyone. I shall be perfectly horrid.'

The lines round his eyes crinkled up as if he was going to smile.

'Well, I'm warned. Have you got a very bad temper?'

'It boils over. It's boiling now. But it doesn't generally last.'

'Well, suppose we walk a bit and give it a chance.'

Laura nodded.

'It would be a good plan. I really am boiling. Mr Metcalfe had a cooking fire besides all the rest of it, and there's a nice cold wind.'

'Did you say an ice-cold wind?'

Laura eyed him severely.

'You know I didn't. I said it was nice and cold. Perhaps it will cool me down. If I had to go into a hot restaurant like this I should probably burst into flame.'

Carey allowed himself to laugh. He had been wanting to for some time.

'What happens if I ask you why? Does that have the same effect?'

'I don't know. It might.' She put up a hand to her cheek and could feel it burning right through her glove. She looked at him with a hint of distress. 'I am being perfectly horrid. I'd better go home.'

He slipped a hand inside her arm.

'What's the matter? Did he upset you?'

All at once Laura could laugh. She said, 'Oh, not like that. It was just a stupid business thing.'

'Want to talk about it?'

He got another look – a very frank one this time.

'I want to, but I don't know whether I'd better. You see, I don't know how well you know Tanis.'

His face changed and hardened. He said deliberately: 'I know her very well indeed.'

Laura said an outrageous thing. She blushed for it afterwards. She even blushed for it at the time, but she said it.

'Are you in love with her? Are you going to marry her?'

The odd thing was that it didn't seem outrageous until she had said it. It was somehow vitally necessary that she should know these things, and how was she going to know them if she didn't ask him? She kept her eyes on his face and wondered whether he would be angry. And didn't care, because she had to know.

Carey said, 'You can put it in the past tense, my dear.'

'You mean you *were* in love with her?'

'I thought I was – I thought I was going to marry her. But one doesn't get beyond the thinking stage with Tanis.'

Laura said another outrageous thing. It just seemed as if all the rules about what you said and didn't say to a stranger had been blown away – perhaps on that fierce gust of anger. This time she said, 'Will she marry Alistair?'

Carey seemed to have scrapped all the rules too. A stranger – there was nothing strange between them. They were answering each other's thoughts.

He said, 'She won't marry anyone – not yet – not for a long time – not as long as she can get what she wants without paying for it.'

Laura's voice came back in a whisper.

'What does she want?'

She never took her eyes off him. His face was expressionless and controlled.

'Oh, to see us all make fools of ourselves – to be the candle and watch the moths come up and burn their wings. She hasn't got any use for them after that. She's a bright candle, isn't she?'

Laura didn't answer him – she hadn't any voice. She didn't know what was happening to her, but it hurt – it hurt horribly. Not for herself, but for Carey. The hurt came into her eyes and made a shadow there like the shadow of a cloud on water.

He said quickly, 'Don't look like that. It doesn't matter any more. Do you hear – there isn't any Tanis. As far as I'm concerned the candle's out.'

Laura took a soft breath. She said on that breath, 'She hurt you – dreadfully—'

And Carey said, 'It's gone. It doesn't matter any more.

It never really mattered at all, because she doesn't matter.' And then he laughed suddenly and said, 'Look where we've got to!'

They were in a narrow street with a mews opening on to it on one side, and a high building on the other, full of blind, bricked-up windows.

It was no use Laura looking, because she had no idea where they were or how they had got there. She hadn't even realised that they had stopped walking. She discovered now that they were standing on a narrow, dirty pavement just opposite the entrance to the mews. An errand-boy went by on a bicycle quickly, but otherwise the place seemed quite deserted. She said in a bewildered tone, 'Where are we?'

'I haven't the slightest idea.'

When they had emerged into a recognisable road and found a taxi Laura began to wake up. It felt just like that – as if she had been asleep and had one of those dreams which don't make sense, but which leave you still charmed when you wake up and have odd snatches of remembrance coming through the waking up, like the half-remembered snatches of a tune. She sat back in her corner and wondered at herself, and wondered why she wasn't ashamed of the things she had said. It had all started with her being angry, but being angry didn't account for it.

She saw Carey watching her, and before she knew she was going to speak she said, 'Why did we say those things? I *don't*—'

'Nor do I.'

'Then why did we?'

'Don't you know?'

She shook her head.

'It frightens me. I can't stop. I'm doing it now.'

His eyes were smiling into hers.

'What are you doing?'

'Saying things.'

'Instead of just thinking them?'

She nodded. Her eyes really had a frightened look.

'I've never done it before.'

'I haven't either – not like this. I shouldn't be surprised if it meant that we were falling in love.'

She changed colour, but the change was to white, not red. She looked for a moment as if she had been shocked right out of her senses. There was a rushing sound in her ears like water, like great waves. And then Carey saying her name urgently.

'Laura – what's the matter?'

'I – don't – know—'

Then he saw the colour come back and her lips begin to tremble.

'Laura – are you all right?'

She said, 'Yes.'

He was holding both her hands.

'Would you mind if I fell in love with you? Because I'm going to.'

She made a very great effort. She shut her eyes for a moment and thought hard about how she had been brought up, and what Aunt Theresa would say. It was all quite mad. She opened her eyes again and pulled her hands away. Then she said in a voice that was not as firm as she had hoped it was going to be, 'Please don't talk like that.'

'Why?'

'Because it's quite mad.'

She heard him laugh.

'Don't you like it?'

Laura didn't say anything. She knew just what she ought to say, but the words wouldn't come.

He went on.

'I've shocked you, offended you. Is that it?'

There were still no words.

'Because if I have, you might be honest enough to tell me. You're an honest person, aren't you? Well, then, you've only got to look me in the eye and say you don't want me to fall in love with you.'

Laura's tongue was suddenly loosened.

'What would you do if I did?'

He said, 'Fall a little deeper.'

And at that inopportune moment the taxi drew up.

SIX

PERHAPS THE MOMENT was not so inopportune. Everything had gone at racing speed – a race without rules, without bounds. Laura at least was thankful for the halt. She went into the cloakroom and did the best she could with her face, but a powder-puff has its limits. She could, and did, tone down the carnation in her cheeks, but there was nothing to be done with the shining look which met her in the mirror, or with the new soft line of her lips. She considered what the powder-puff had effected, and decided that it was a pity. The colour had been very becoming. She found she was smiling, and before she could change her mind again she pulled a handkerchief out of her bag and was wiping the powder off. Then she went out and found Carey in the hall.

He took her down a flight of steps into a small irregularly-shaped room which seemed to be quite full of people, but when they had threaded their way among the tables, there was the one he had reserved, set right into the corner. They sat facing one another across it.

Laura discovered that she was hungry – frightfully hungry. And the food was extraordinarily good – hors d'oeuvres, and a fishy thing, and a sweet with layers of coconut and chocolate frozen hard, and a hot chocolate sauce.

Carey made a charming host. He looked at her as if he loved her, but he talked of all the things which Laura liked talking about – safe, interesting things which had nothing to do with the race which had taken them so far and at such a break-neck speed.

It was over the coffee that she told him why she had been angry.

'My cousin Agnes Fane wants to buy the Priory and leave it to Tanis. I don't know why that made me so angry, but it did. One minute I was sitting there just polite and interested, and he was telling me all about the feud and the relations, and the next minute I felt as if I was going up in a puff of flame exactly like a firework. It was a horrid feeling.'

'It must have been.' His voice was sympathetic, but his eyes laughed.

'I've got a temper – I told you I had – but I've never been so – so unreasonably angry. It's rather frightening, because I did feel as if I could have done anything—' She paused, and then repeated the last word. '*Anything*.'

He saw that she had turned quite white, and that she really did look frightened. He said in a steadying voice, 'What did you do?'

Her colour came back again with a rush.

'I just said that I wouldn't think of selling, and when he tried to persuade me I listened for a bit, and then I got so boiling that I couldn't any more, so I came away.'

Carey said thoughtfully, 'So he tried to persuade you—'

Laura nodded.

'He's Cousin Agnes's lawyer too. He knows her awfully well. Aunt Theresa says he wanted to marry her. Anyhow, they're very old friends, so of course he would be on her side.'

'He oughtn't to have a side.'

Laura laughed.

'Why, he couldn't help it. He's known her for simply

ages. He's fond of her – you can see he is. I'm horrid, but I'm not so horrid that I would expect him not to be fond of her, and not to try and get her what she wants. It's all quite reasonable, you know. I can see that now I've stopped boiling. Tanis has been like her daughter – it's quite natural she should want her to have the Priory. And as Mr Metcalfe says, I couldn't live there myself, because I've only got a hundred a year besides the rent Cousin Agnes pays me, and if she died nobody might want it, or if they did they mightn't give me as much. It's all quite reasonable.'

'But you're not going to sell?'

'I don't feel reasonable about it at all,' said Laura.

He poured her out another cup of coffee. Then he said in a tentative voice, 'You're fond of the place?'

She shook her head.

'I've never seen it. There are photographs which belonged to my father – I used to get a sort of thrill from looking at them and thinking, "It doesn't matter who lives there. It's mine really – it belongs to me." And I used to plan what I would do with the rooms. Most of the furniture belongs to Cousin Agnes, but there are some old bits that have been there ever since the house was built. I used to plan curtains and chintzes, but of course it was just a game. Aunt Theresa always told me I couldn't possibly live there unless I married someone with enough money to keep it up, and she always finished up by saying I wasn't in the least likely to do that.'

He looked up, began to laugh, and then was suddenly grave again.

'Is she making you a good offer?'

'Twelve thousand pounds. Mr Metcalfe said it was very generous.'

'It's a fancy price. You know, you ought to go down and see the place. Can't you do that?'

'I couldn't unless Cousin Agnes asked me.' She hesitated, and then came out with, 'I think she's going to.'

'You'll go?'

'I don't want to.'

'Don't be silly! Of course you must go! For one thing, it will smash this feud business, and for another, don't you see, you may simply loathe the place, and then it's too easy.'

'Suppose I don't loathe it – suppose I fall passionately in love with it?'

'That's quite easy too – you dig in your toes and wait for a handsome husband and three thousand a year.'

'If he had three thousand a year he'd probably be hideous.'

'Then you'd have to go on waiting.'

She looked at him with the frank, confiding look he liked so much.

'Do you know the Priory? Shall I like it? Have you been there?'

'Oh, yes, I know it quite well.'

'Shall I like it?'

'I don't know, my dear. Anyhow, you ought to go down if Miss Fane asks you.'

Laura nodded reluctantly.

'I suppose I ought.' She brightened. 'Perhaps she won't ask me.'

The afternoon went by. They saw a play, but in each of them the current of thought and feeling ran too strong to leave any but the most surface attention free. Each was too conscious of the other to know what was passing on the stage. There was light, and colour, and music. The players came and went and said their lines. The curtain rose and fell. And all the time the unseen current ran like a race.

They came out into the dark and found a taxi. Blackness shut them in.

Carey said suddenly, 'They don't know whether I shall be able to fly again.'

Something in his voice brought Laura out of her dreams. She said in the quick, soft way she had, 'Oh – why?'

'That crash – it's done something to my sight. I can't judge distances any more.'

'You'll get all right – I'm sure you will.'

'I may. It's one of those things they don't know about. It's hell.'

She put out her hand and found his.

'You'll get all right – I know you will.'

They sat like that with the dark going by them. Neither of them spoke. When the taxi stopped and they were standing under Cousin Sophy's porch, he broke the silence to say, 'No one knows except you.'

Laura didn't say anything. She put out her hand again in a groping gesture. It brushed his arm, and suddenly he was holding it to his face, kissing it.

'Laura! Laura!'

She reached out and held him.

'Don't mind like that! Oh, Carey, *please*!'

'I'm a fool – I've no right—'

She shook him a little, or tried to.

'You're not to talk like that! I won't have it! You've got to be sensible and give yourself a chance. Why, it isn't any time yet. You've been worried – strung up. You *haven't* given yourself a chance.' But in her heart she was saying, 'Tanis hasn't given him a chance.'

She came very near to hating Tanis then. It was like

coming near to the open mouth of a furnace. The heat rushed out. It took her breath and blinded her. She shrank in the wind of it, and was afraid.

Carey felt her tremble. She put up her face to his, and when he touched it it was wet. She said through tears: 'Please, Carey, *please*! It's going to be all right.'

SEVEN

COUSIN SOPHY WAS on her sofa in the drawing-room in a panoply of shawls. There was one from Galloway in shades of blue and green. It was really more of a rug than a shawl, and was dedicated to covering her to the waist. 'I took such a fancy to it when I was travelling with my dear father, and it has worn remarkably well – such pure wool, and of course only vegetable dyes. It always reminds me of the colour of the sea and the hills – such a wild coast – just the same blue and green.' There was another shawl at the slender waist, a wisp of violet and grey, and a grey silk shawl with a knotted fringe for the frail shoulders. There was also a supplementary one of heavy pale blue wool, crocheted by Miss Sophy herself, and one rather smaller in white wool to put over the head when a window was opened to air the room.

From all this shawlery Miss Ferrers extended a pair of eager, fluttering hands.

'Oh, my dear Laura – I am so glad! Have you enjoyed yourself?'

Laura said, 'Yes, very much.' She had the feeling that she stood in a cloud of joy – a glowing cloud, bright with the sun.

'I am so glad you have come in, and so glad you have enjoyed yourself too. But oh, my dear, Agnes Fane has been telephoning. She wants you to go down there – tomorrow, I think. She says Tanis Lyle is taking down a party of young people, and she thought it would be a pleasant way of making your acquaintance.'

The brightness failed suddenly. Laura didn't know why. She felt cold without it. The little fluttering hands were reaching out to her. She went forward to the sofa and sat down on the edge. Cousin Sophy went on talking in an excited thread of a voice.

'I think you ought to go, my dear. She was very nice about it. Rather grand in her manner, but then Agnes always was rather grand. I knew her very well when she was a girl, before the quarrel. I am older than she is of course – let me see – ten – no twelve years older. But the Ferrers and the Fanes saw a lot of each other at that time. My grandfather John Ferrers and Mary Ferrers who married Thomas Fane and was Agnes's grandmother and of course your father's too, were brother and sister, so Agnes and I are second cousins. And she was very polite, asking about my health and saying she was afraid I must feel the cold weather and the bombs, which everybody doesn't trouble about when it's a long distance call. My dear father always said that when everybody had a telephone nobody would have any manners, because there wouldn't be time for them. And of course he was perfectly right, because by the time it has clicked on and clicked off, and you're not sure how many minutes you've had, and you're not sure if you've said what you were going to say, even the politest person is apt to find that they are being a little abrupt.'

Laura smiled. She loved Cousin Sophy, and it was restful not to have to talk. You didn't have to with Cousin Sophy. She loved an audience, and sooner or later she got everything said.

'I haven't seen Agnes for twenty-two years, but her voice hasn't changed. She must be fifty-seven – or is it fifty-eight – I'm really not quite sure – but her voice hasn't changed. She had a contralto singing voice too, very deep and striking, but my dear father considered that she had too dramatic a style for an amateur. He had no objection to singing as a drawing-room accomplishment – it was still fashionable when I was a girl – but there was something about the way in which Agnes sang *Infelice* and Tosti's *Goodbye* which he considered inappropriate to the family circle or a concert at the village hall. I remember she used to look very handsome and proud when she was singing, and she always looked at your father, which was just a little embarrassing, because – well, you won't know either of those songs, my dear, they've really gone quite out of fashion. But they were – well, I don't quite like to say so, but there really isn't any other word for it – quite *passionate*.'

Laura had a sudden picture of Agnes Fane singing passionately to the Vicar, the village, and Oliver Fane. It came across the years, sharp, and bright, and painful with an old pain which had never been forgotten.

Cousin Sophy flowed on.

'My brother Jack used to say, "If Agnes rides such a high horse she'll be getting a fall one of these days." He was inclined to be in love with her, and it would not have done at all, because they both had terrible tempers. They were always quarrelling and making it up. And then one day they quarrelled and they didn't make it up. And Jack was killed in the last war, so if she had married him Agnes would have been a widow all this time. But of course she never really thought of anyone except your father.'

It was just on seven o'clock when the new young parlour-maid opened the door and began to say, 'Will you see Miss Lyle—' She had been specially told to say ma'am by Beecher, Miss Sophy's maid, who had been with her for thirty years, but she never got it out, because Tanis Lyle walked right past her into the room.

'You will, won't you, Cousin Sophy?' she said in a clear, ringing voice, and before there was time for anyone else to speak, there she was, touching Miss Sophy's hand and slipping out of a fur coat.

Laura found herself taking the coat like a lady-in-waiting. Lovely fur – so light and soft. She put it down over a chair and turned to see Tanis, bare-headed, in a short, slinky black dress. Immediately she felt that her own dress was too bright a green, too thick, and much, much too countrified. She had a perfectly clear conviction that no matter what she wore, Tanis would always make her feel like that, and that if she lay down under it now she would never get up again. 'After all, I do live in the country,' she told herself, and felt better.

Cousin Sophy was speaking.

'Well, my dear, we dine at half-past seven, because I have to go to bed early. Mary may not like to ring the dressing-bell. I am afraid it sounds very inhospitable, but Beecher will be waiting to dress me, and it does not do for me to be hurried. It upsets her dreadfully.'

Tanis stood there, smiling down at her. She looked younger, less sophisticated. The smile was a charming one.

'But, Cousin Sophy, of course I wouldn't dream of keeping you. Perhaps I could go up and talk to Laura while she dresses. I am full of messages from Aunt Agnes, and this seems to be the only time. I had to go to the Theobalds' cocktail-party, and I'm dining out.'

When Beecher had been rung for and Laura and Tanis were on the stairs together, Tanis laughed softly and said, 'Does she really dress for dinner?'

Laura nodded.

'Oh, yes. She puts on what she calls a tea-gown, and a white China crêpe shawl instead of the grey one, and Beecher does her hair with little curls at the side. It's the curls that take the time. They're sweet.'

They came into the bedroom. If Laura had ever disliked anything in her life, it was the prospect of having to dress with Tanis watching her. But she wasn't giving in to it. Tanis was an underminer, but people can't undermine you if you don't let yourself be undermined.

Tanis sat down on the bed, pulling the pillows round to make herself a back.

'Well, Aunt Agnes said she'd been ringing Cousin Sophy up, so I expect you know she wants you to go down and stay at the Priory.'

Laura was hanging up her coat. Without turning round she said, 'Yes.'

'She's been trying to get me all the afternoon, but of course I was out. I had to ring her up as soon as I got in. She's set her heart on your coming.'

Laura unhung the dress she was going to wear – her old black velvet. She knew exactly what it was going to look like to Tanis, and she told herself she didn't care. She hung it over the rail of the bed and took off her hat.

Tanis was looking at her with an effect of eager charm.

'I do hope you're going to come.'

'It's very kind of Cousin Agnes.'

'Oh, no, it isn't. It's what she ought to have done years and years and years ago. What's the good of quarrelling? And then to keep it up all this time – as if anything in the world was worth a fuss like that! Too archaic! Of course I'm very fond of the aunts – by the way, they're only cousins really, but I've always called them aunt. They like it, God knows why. It's about the most hideous word in the English language, but it pleases them, and I'm all for pleasing people when I can.'

She produced a platinum cigarette-case with a diamond initial, offered it to Laura, who said, 'Not while I'm dressing,' and then lighted a cigarette herself. A little curl of smoke went up between them.

Laura went over to the wash-stand.

'One gets filthy in London. Don't you want to have a bath?'

Laura would have liked to say, 'Yes, I do,' but to strip, to be naked and defenceless before an enemy – that touched something very old, very primitive. She said, 'There won't be time if you want to talk. I can't keep Cousin Sophy waiting. I can have one when I come to bed.'

The water splashed in the old-fashioned flowered basin. Tanis waited until she came back to the dressing-table. Sitting there, Laura could see the reflection of the bed, her own black dress thrown across the foot, and Tanis against the fat white pillows at the head. The smoke went up between them. The cigarette described a sudden graceful movement.

'Well, Laura, I hope you're coming.'

Laura said, 'Why does she want me to come?'

'I suppose because she thinks this idiotic quarrel has gone on long enough.'

Laura felt that she had been ungracious. She said, still looking into the mirror, 'It's very nice of her – I do feel that. It isn't easy to put a stop to something that has been going on for a long time. I do think it's very nice of her.'

'Then what's the matter with coming?'

Laura swung round on the low chintz-covered stool, comb in hand, black hair ruffled.

'You know she wants to buy the Priory?'

Tanis's lids came down and veiled her eyes. She said, 'Well?'

'I don't want to sell,' said Laura bluntly.

The lids rose. The eyes looked out, very much alive, very green.

'Well?'

A note of distress came into Laura's voice.

'Of course I wouldn't ever turn her out – I couldn't do that. But I don't want to sell unless I simply have to. I may have to – I don't know – in which case it would be better for it to go to Cousin Agnes. But I haven't made up my mind. I want to think it over.'

The green eyes went on looking at her. A faint smile came, and slipped away.

'Well?'

'Don't you see, if I go down there I'm afraid Cousin Agnes will think I'm saying yes, and I haven't made up my mind. It wouldn't be fair to let her think that I was going to say yes.'

There – she had got it out, and it was easier than she had expected. The sense of dealing with an enemy had gone. She felt ashamed that it had ever been there between them. She turned back to the glass and straightened the ruffled hair. Tanis's reflection smiled with a sudden bewildering charm.

'Scrupulous person, aren't you? Well, you've got it off your chest. Now listen! You can come down without prejudice. It won't commit you to anything at all. It won't be a meeting between a prospective buyer and seller. It won't be anything except the aunt wanting to see you and put an end to the quarrel.'

The smoke between them had spread into a faint blue haze. Laura thought, 'I've been a beast. They want to be friends. I must go down.' She jumped up and came to the foot of the bed. As she picked up her dress she said gravely and frankly, 'Thank you, Tanis – if it's like that, I should like to come. Shall I ring Cousin Agnes up?'

'Yes – she'd like that. We can go down tomorrow afternoon.'

Laura pulled her frock over her head. If she was careful she could do it without disarranging her hair. She emerged successfully and was smoothing down the long, straight blackness, when Tanis said, 'It ought to be quite a good party. We'll get the end of the Maxwell boys' leave, and there'll be you, and me, and Petra, and Carey.'

Laura turned back to the glass. Her heart beat hard. The dress needed a brooch. She picked up an old-fashioned circle of pearls and fingered it. Tanis's voice came from behind her, lightly, sweetly.

'Carey's a charmer, isn't he? But don't take him seriously. He's taken a fancy to you, but he's never serious. It's just the way he's made – if he likes a girl he can't help making love to her, but it doesn't mean a thing.'

Laura was pinning her brooch. The little white circle looked nice against the dead black velvet. The dress might be an old one, but it was very becoming. She turned round and said in the same grave way that she had spoken before, 'You're not engaged to him, are you, Tanis?'

Simplicity is always disconcerting. Tanis was disconcerted, but not for any time long enough to be measured. In a flash she was adjusted, and striking back with a suave, 'Well, not exactly.'

Laura looked at her. Her eyes said steadily, 'What's the good of saying that sort of thing to me?' Then she turned to the door.

'Shall we go down? I think Cousin Sophy will be ready.'

EIGHT

LAURA RANG UP the Priory as soon as the meal which Miss Sophy still called dinner had been disposed of. The stately repasts of the eighteenth century, the heavy banquets of the Victorian age, had dwindled to a cup of clear soup and a lightly-poached egg surrounded by spinach. The ale, the strong waters, the fine claret, the Madeira which had made the journey round the Cape, the sherry, and the port, were gone away to a flagon of orange-juice and a jug of barley-water. The transition to the dining-room was too risky for an invalid, so there was a comfortable low table drawn to the side of the couch in the drawing-room. But Miss Sophy still dined.

As soon as Mary had removed the last traces of the meal the business of telephoning began. Miss Sophy superintended. It was the most interesting thing that had happened for a long time. It was a *rapprochement* – it was the end of the family feud. Oliver's daughter and Agnes! Miss Sophy's colour rose and her eyes shone. She fairly fluttered with excitement.

Laura would much rather have waited until Cousin Sophy had gone to bed. She could have borne to wait for ever. She felt an extreme reluctance to call across that twenty-year gulf and hear Agnes Fane answering her. It was naturally not the slightest use to feel like that. She put through the call while Miss Sophy poured out reminiscences, and almost at once, before she was expecting it, there was a voice on the line – what Laura would mentally call a suet-pudding voice.

'This is the Priory. Miss Adams speaking.'

Cousin Sophy's hearing was very acute. She plucked Laura's sleeve and whispered, 'Your Cousin Lucy—'

Laura said, 'It is Laura Fane, Cousin Lucy,' and waited.

There was a sound as if the receiver had been jerked. The voice said, 'Oh—' just like that, without any expression. Laura found it rather daunting. There was a pause, a murmur of voices too low to be caught. She thought the receiver had been set down or muffled.

Cousin Sophy whispered, 'Don't take any notice of Lucy. She is a very stupid woman.'

And then another voice was speaking in a deep, firm tone. If Laura had not known that this was Agnes Fane she would not have been quite sure that it wasn't a man.

'Is that Laura?'

Laura said, 'Yes, Cousin Agnes – it is Cousin Agnes?'

The deep voice said, 'Yes.' And then, 'I hope you are coming to stay with me.'

Laura thought, 'She knows I'm coming. Tanis must have rung her up.' The voice was dominant and assured, a voice that was accustomed to being obeyed.

This feeling persisted through her polite thanks and Miss Fane's reply. The conversation was as short, as formal, as devoid of emotion as if there had never been a passionate Agnes who had sung *Infelice*, and a reluctant Oliver who had loved somebody else.

Miss Sophy heaved a sigh as Laura rang off.

'Well, my dear, that's over. And a little disappointing, don't you think? Things so often are, you know. When your father ran away with your mother they were having a fête at the Priory – Primrose Day – no, it couldn't have been that because it was in the summer, really a very hot day – but it was something to do with the Primrose League. Very inconsiderate of Oliver and Lilian, but of course they were very much in love, and when young people are in love they don't think of anyone except themselves. The grounds of the Priory are very beautiful, and Agnes was pouring out tea under the big cedar, when one of the footmen, a very foolish young man, brought her Oliver's note on a salver. Of course he never meant her to have it like that – it was a most stupid mistake. But she opened it, and read it, and put it away in her bag, and went on talking to the Lord Lieutenant and pouring out tea. No one would have known there was anything wrong. But when everyone had gone she took her horse, Black Turban – such a curious name I always thought – and rode out on him. And when she didn't come back they sent out a search party, and there she was at the bottom of the quarry, and the poor horse was dead.'

Laura was speechless. She gazed white-faced at Cousin Sophy, whose pretty pink colour had not faded at all. It was just an old story to her, but to Laura it felt like all the terrible and unhappy things and all the unkindness in the world brought to a focus.

Cousin Sophy stroked her hand with a soft fluttering touch.

'Don't look like that, my dear. It was a long time ago and if Oliver had gone on with the engagement and married her, they would both have been most unhappy, because Agnes was always very intelligent, and she would have known quite well that he didn't really love her.'

Miss Sophy went to bed at half-past nine. At a quarter to ten the telephone startled Laura from her book. She picked up the receiver, and heard Carey Desborough say, 'Can I speak to Miss Fane?'

'Oh, Carey!'

She sounded warm and pleased, and all at once she hoped she didn't sound too pleased. That was the worst of the sort of things Tanis had said – you pushed them out of your mind and tidied it up, and then you found some lurking trail of slime.

Carey was asking, 'Are you alone?'

'Yes. Cousin Sophy's gone to bed.'

'My head spy told me she went at half-past nine. Laura, are you going down to the Priory?'

'Yes, I am.'

'Tanis said so. She doesn't tell the truth unless it suits her, so I thought I'd rather have it from you. Because I'm not going unless you are.'

The little trail of slime caught the light in Laura's mind. She said easily, 'Thank you. What a lovely compliment!'

'It wasn't a compliment – just a plain statement of fact.'

Laura said nothing. It was absurd that a voice travelling along a wire should reach the strings of your heart and shake them.

The voice said her name insistently.

'Laura—'

'Yes?'

'Have you see Tanis?'

'Yes. She came in just before dinner to fix up about going down to the Priory.'

'I thought so. What did she say about me?'

'About you?'

'Yes, darling – me. I know she said something. What was it? She didn't by any chance warn you against me, did she?'

'Why should she? I mean, is there any reason why she should warn me?'

Laura was rather pleased with this. Then she heard Carey laugh.

'She did – I knew it! Kind cousin warns débutante.'

'I'm not a débutante!' said Laura, revolted.

'Compared with Tanis you are, my child. I'm sure she did it with the utmost charm and delicacy. What did she say?'

Laura's voice changed. She stopped trying to be light and indifferent, and spoke with simplicity.

'She said you were never serious.'

There was a pause.

He said, 'I see—' And then, 'She didn't by any chance say or suggest that I was engaged to her?'

'She said, "Not exactly".'

There was an angry laugh.

'What a convenient phrase! Laura – listen. I asked Tanis to marry me six months ago. I was under the impression that she had accepted me. A month ago when I came out of hospital I found out that I was not the only man who was under that impression. She said then that she couldn't imagine how I had got it. She had never intended anything of the kind. She didn't want to marry anyone, but why not be friends? Well, I was fool enough to agree. Since then I've been gradually coming to my senses. When I met you last night—' He paused, while they both gazed astounded at the fact that it was only last night that they had met.

Laura found the receiver shaking a little in her hand. She heard him say, 'It doesn't seem possible,' and she heard herself say, 'No.'

He gave an odd, eager laugh.

'Well, thank God it happened! Laura, when I met you it was like coming out into the open air. I woke right up, and I shan't go to sleep again. Now, about tomorrow. I've got some petrol. Let me drive you down.'

'Tanis suggested that I should go down with Petra North.'

She heard him whistle.

'That means she's annexed Alistair.'

'I think I'd better go with Petra really.'

'I'll take her too, and we'll collect Robin. I'll fix it. I'll be round for you about half-past two. Is that all right?'

Laura said, 'Yes.' It was rather pleasant to have it all taken out of her hands.

'All right. Wait a moment, don't hang up. About this business of my not being serious, an important announcement follows immediately. Are you listening – Miss Laura Fane?'

Laura said, 'Yes.'

'Well then, my intentions are serious, honourable, and dreadfully premature. Good night!'

NINE

FOUR PEOPLE AND their suit-cases were a tight fit in Carey's car, but they piled in, Laura behind with Petra, and the two men in front. It was Laura who had insisted on this arrangement. She wanted to talk to Petra, and there would be more room for the luggage. But the real reason was that she couldn't – no, she really couldn't, sit there in front with Carey under the eyes of a girl who was losing her lover. She felt most desperately sorry for Petra, who appeared, vividly made-up, in a scarlet leather coat and a green and scarlet bandeau round her dark curls. Her eyes were the unhappiest things in the world, but she laughed and chattered nineteen to the dozen until they were clearing London, when she fell silent and sat staring at the long, straight road.

In front of them Carey and Robin were deep in Air Force shop. To all intents and purposes the two girls were alone. Presently Petra looked sideways and said, 'She's gone down with Alistair.'

Laura didn't say anything, but she had a very speaking look. The air was suddenly full of kindness.

Petra bit a scarlet lip.

'I expect you know all about it – everybody does. And I expect you're wondering why I go tagging after them.' There was a note of defiance in the voice which hardly rose above a whisper. Laura was reminded of the kitten again – a kitten at bay, ready to scratch and fly. She said, 'No.'

Petra looked past her.

'You don't waste words – do you?' She laughed. 'I'm a fool to play her game. She loves an audience, and I'm helping to provide her with one. Do you know why?'

Laura nodded gravely. 'I think so.'

'He's dreadfully unhappy too.' Petra looked at her. Her eyes dazzled with tears. She put out a hand, clutched for a moment at Laura's, and let it go. She looked away and nodded. 'She tortures him. I can't bear it. I could give him up if she really wanted him, or if there was any chance that he'd be happy. But she doesn't want him – she doesn't want anyone, except to play with, and make fools of, and pull them about on a string. She's had enough of being married.'

Laura exclaimed, '*Married?*'

'Didn't you know? It was when she was on the stage. She married an actor, a man called Hazelton – he used to be quite well known. They kept it quiet for a bit, and then she found out he doped or something. I expect she drove him to it. Anyhow she was through with him, and she got a divorce. The aunts threw a thousand fits, and then settled down to being thankful she'd got rid of him. It's about six years ago now, and no one ever mentions it. I expect you were at school and they kept it from the child.' There was a delicate darting malice in voice and look, but no sting.

Laura laughed, and said, 'I expect they did. What happened to the man?'

Petra shrugged.

'Oh, he's around somewhere. Someone told me he'd cropped up again. As a matter of fact he was at the Luxe last night. He came up and spoke to her.

'What did she do?'

'Oh, nothing – got rid of him – it's the sort of thing

she's particularly good at. I wonder what he thinks about it all. He used to go about saying he'd get even with her some day. He's got it in for her all right. I know someone who used to know him awfully well. She says he's like the elephant – you know, the never-forgets touch – and that some day he'll make Tanis wish she hadn't. But people don't do that sort of thing six years afterwards – do they?'

'I shouldn't think so.'

Petra laughed.

'I wish someone *would* do her in! I can't think why they don't. I can't think why I don't myself. I'd like to, but there would be nobody left to hold Alistair's hand.' Her laughter ran up to an odd high note.

It was Laura's turn to put out a hand.

'Oh, *don't*!'

Petra dropped to a low murmur.

'That's why I go tagging round. Sometimes, even now, he wants me. If it wasn't for this damned war, I might get a little proper pride together and let him want, but you can't do it when you never know which time is going to be the last.'

Laura didn't say anything at all. The men's voices went on all the time, loud, cheerful, argumentative. They seemed to be discussing a gadget sponsored by one Nicolson which Robin thought well of, while Carey considered it rotten. They were obviously perfectly happy to go on arguing about it.

Petra made a sudden movement. She whisked open her bag, got out her compact, and busied herself with repairs. Presently she said, 'I've really got a bit too much on, haven't I?'

Laura nodded.

'Just a bit, but it's awfully well done.'

Petra made a face like a cross kitten.

'That's the snag – it gives you confidence, but if you overdo it, it gives you away. I've put on so much that Tanis will know why.'

'Take a little off. Not the lipstick – you'd only make a mess of that . . . Yes, that's a lot better.'

Petra snapped the compact to.

'You must think I'm pretty odd, talking to you like this after only seeing you once. I wouldn't believe it myself. It's not the sort of thing I do as a rule, but I suppose I've got to the point when I've got to talk or blow up, and – you're easy to talk to.' She laughed suddenly. 'A stranger is really much the best person, because they don't give you advice like a relation would straight away. Don't you hate your relations?'

Laura laughed and said, 'No.'

'I do. They're full of good advice, and it's all the same – "Let him alone till he comes to his senses." And the reason I hate them is that it's damned good advice . . . Let's talk about cooking. Can you cook?'

'Can you?'

'A treat! I do an omelette that would make a French chef turn green.' She reached forward and poked Robin in the back. 'Don't I?'

'Don't you what?' He looked over his shoulder with an interrupted air.

'Don't I cook beautifully? Aren't my omelettes the cat's whiskers?'

'I hope not – it sounds foul.' He turned back to his conversation.

Petra put out her tongue at him.

'Well, they *are*!' She flung Laura a gay smile. 'Don't men like talking about the most extraordinary things?'

TEN

LAURA'S FIRST SIGHT of the Priory was etched indelibly upon her mind. There was no sun. The clouds hung low. The January day was darkening already, though it was not four o'clock. They came up a drive between sombre evergreens and under leafless trees, and then out upon a great rectangle of gravel with the house on its farther side – a grey house with a central block and two wings enclosing a paved courtyard with a fountain in the middle, and the right-hand wing was the ruined Priory church. She looked at it with all her eyes, letting down the window and leaning out.

The ruined arch of the east window faced them as they turned into the court. Sky and trees showed briefly through the empty windows. The effect was startling and graceful. The ruins were grey and clean and bare, but the house was dark with ivy and festooned with the light dry stems of Virginia creeper and the twisted limbs of a huge wistaria whose branches ran right up on to the roof and sprawled there.

Carey turned round as he stopped the car and said, speaking to her for the first time, 'Like it, Laura?'

She met his eyes. Her eyes were shining.

'I love it!'

'Love at first sight? How unreliable!' His look teased her, asked a question.

Laura said, 'Dreadfully. But I always know at once – don't you?'

And then they were all getting out, and she had a moment to stand and look at the ruins before the door opened and they were coming into the hall with a big fire of logs blazing on the hearth and a broad stairway running up out of the shadows beyond. Coming out of the daylight and the cold, she thought the hall was like a cave – dark – warm – enclosed. There was a little light from the three narrow windows set rather high on either side of the door, but where it met the firelight it seemed to fade, and the shadows had it their own way.

Then all in a moment there was light – bright, warm, and glowing. It came from high up, where crystal sconces were held above the line of the dark panelling. The stairway, rising by a dozen shallow steps and then dividing to sweep up to right and left, sprang into view. Tanis Lyle was coming slowly down from the right. She reached the half-landing, smiled, put out both hands, and ran down the rest of the way. In a high-necked cinnamon jumper and a rough tweed skirt to match, she was the country hostess to the life. If her entrance had been planned, it was certainly very effective. If it had not, she was the darling of coincidence. Laura had not the slightest doubt that it had all been planned to the last detail, from the sudden burst of light, to the suggestion that it was Tanis who was welcoming her guests, and welcoming them with the greatest possible charm.

Laura found herself crossing the hall with a guiding hand upon her arm.

'The aunts are longing to see you. Come along before the others disentangle themselves. The drawing-room is at the back. It looks south and west across the garden. Aunt Agnes adores her flowers, and it has all been planted so that she can see as much as possible without going out.'

'Doesn't she go out at all?'

'Oh, yes – every day. As soon as it's warm enough she'll be in and out all day in her chair. She has one of those self-propelling ones, and she's really very clever with it.'

She opened a door as she spoke, and brought Laura into a long room panelled in white, with violet curtains already drawn across the three windows facing west and the two at the far end which looked to the south. The effect under the light of electric candles set in old gilt sconces was sombre and unusual, but it was relieved by chintzes gaily flowered in purple, blue, and rose, and by the Persian rugs of which the prevailing shade was a deep-toned rose melting into ruby.

There were two women in the room, sitting on either side of the rather chilly-looking marble hearth with its white pillars rising to support a narrow slab which might appropriately have adorned a tomb. Upon this slab there stood two bronze horses with lashing tails, and a black marble clock. But at the moment Laura was not really aware of anything except Agnes Fane, who sat watching her approach from an invalid chair.

There were no shawls or mufflings, no appearance of invalidism, about the fine erect figure. She wore what any other lady might have worn in her own house at tea-time, a dress of some wine-coloured woollen stuff and a loose corduroy coat of the same shade. She had pearl studs in her ears, a string of pearls at her throat, and a fine ruby on the third finger of her right hand.

She put this hand out slowly as Laura came up. It took hers, and was cold to her touch – very cold. The dark eyes under their strongly-arched brows were lifted in a long regard. Laura thought them as cold as the hand which had just relinquished hers.

She returned the look with an interest which heightened her colour and brightened her eyes. She did not know what she had expected, but whatever it was, Agnes Fane was different – quite different.

She was a very handsome woman – handsomer now than she had been when she was young. The high, dominant features, the proud carriage of the head, sat better on the woman in her fifties than they had ever done on the girl. She had the same fine, white skin and springing dark hair as Tanis and Laura herself, but there were deep lines about the eyes and mouth – lines of pride and suffering – and the hair was frosted. It framed her face in waves, beautifully arranged.

With skin and hair the resemblance ended. The features were of a bolder type, the face narrower, the line of cheek and jaw a harder one, and the eyes under their beautifully modelled brows a very deep brown, instead of Tanis's green darkening to grey, and Laura's grey brightening into green.

'How do you do, Laura?'

The voice was the voice of the telephone, grave, and deep, and rather cold. Something in Laura admired its dignity, its restraint.

There was a polite enquiry for Theresa Ferrers, and then Tanis was introducing her to Lucy Adams.

Laura saw a plump woman of middle height and middle age. Cousin Sophy's remark sprang unbidden to her mind – 'Lucy always was a very stupid woman.' For stupid was just what cousin Lucy looked. She had a flat, well-cushioned face of no particular colour, small blinking grey eyes, and a very palpable auburn front. She wore grey, of all colours the least becoming. A gold-rimmed pince-nez hovered uncertainly on her nose. It was attached to the right-hand side of her bodice by a fine gold chain and a gold bar brooch. Her noticeably thick ankles were encased in grey woollen stockings, and her feet in rubbed black glacé shoes with ribbon bows. She shook hands frigidly with Laura and turned at once to Tanis, her voice gushing and her manner exuberant.

'But where are the others? I am simply longing to see them. Fetch them in, and – oh, yes, I will just ring the bell – for I'm sure they must all be simply dying for their tea. The car wasn't open, was it? Oh, no, of course not – in January. Even Carey wouldn't do that, though I remember his bringing you down on a *very* cold autumn day with everything open, and I told him he ought to be more careful – and so he ought.' She turned towards Laura with a jerky movement. 'Do you know Carey Desborough – but of course you came down in his car, didn't you?'

Laura said, 'I met him last night,' and thought how strange that sounded.

Tanis took her up to her room after that. They took the right-hand turn of the stair and came by way of a short gallery to a corridor with doors on either side.

'Aunt Agnes is at the end there, on the left. Her room is over the drawing-room. Her maid, Perry, has the dressing-room, and Aunt Lucy the room beyond. I'm opposite Aunt Agnes, next to the octagon tower. It is the only bit of the old house left. That's the door, at the end of the passage. It's very convenient for Aunt Agnes, because, owing to the octagon shape and the very thick walls, they've been able to fit in a lift between my bathroom and the tower. It just takes her chair, and there are doors through to my sitting-room and the drawing-room on the ground floor. She can manage it all herself, which is what she likes to do with everything. Here you are – I hope you will be comfortable. Petra is just beyond you. There's a bathroom between the two rooms – you won't mind sharing it with her, will you? Aunt Agnes has put in bathrooms wherever she can, but it doesn't quite run to one for every room. Miss Silver is over on the other side of the house, and so are Carey and the Maxwells. She's a girl friend of Aunt Lucy's. They were at school together. She started life as a governess – and does she look like one! Just wait till you see her! I believe she's a detective or something now. Completely useless, I should think, but not a bad old thing. You'll see her at tea. Her name is Maud! Can you find your way down all right?'

Laura said she could. As a matter of fact, only a mentally defective person could have failed to do so. She was very glad to be left alone. Her first overwhelming feeling that here was a house which she could love and which was friendly to her had given way to a lonely sense of estrangement. It was only the outside of the house which had any welcome for her. The inner self, the presence which lives in every habitation, was formidably antagonistic and aloof.

The room in which she found herself, with its pale blue chintzes patterned with ivory scollop shells, was a stranger's room. It was charming, and it charmed her, but it had nothing to do with Laura Fane. Like all the rest of the house, it rejected her.

She went to the left-hand window and looked out. The curtains had been drawn. She put one of them back, noticing that it had been lined with black sateen to make it light-proof, and wondered whether they had had any raids down here. She looked out upon the courtyard. The dusk was gathering fast. There were shadows everywhere. The line of the ruined Priory church ran out on her left, with the last of the light coming over and through the shattered arches. She stayed looking at it for as long as she dared. Then she tidied herself in a hurry and went down.

ELEVEN

THE DRAWING-ROOM was full of people having tea. Lucy Adams was pouring out from an immense silver teapot. Laura went up to take her cup, and was introduced to 'my friend Miss Silver'. She beheld a little middle-aged person with small, neat features and a great deal of mouse-coloured hair neatly disposed in a coiled plait at the back and severely restrained by a net in front. She received the impression that it was never let out even at night. She thought, 'You couldn't possibly take her for anything but a governess.' Only it was a governess of the early Edwardian days, or perhaps something earlier still. Aunt Theresa had possessed Victorian books, and Laura had been brought up on them.

Miss Silver, like Cousin Lucy, wore glacé shoes with bows, and strange thick stockings. She was dressed in one of those flowered garments which saleswomen press upon unresisting elderly ladies for summer wear. In Miss Silver's case it consisted of a dark-green dress lavishly patterned with a kind of Morse code of dots and dashes in orange, magenta, and green. The accompanying coatee was mercifully of a plain dark green. The collarless neck had been filled in with a twist of cotton lace, and was fastened by a heavy oval gold locket-brooch bearing in seed pearls the entwined initials of Miss Silver's father and mother, now some forty years deceased.

Laura had not time to do more than say how do you do before she was directed to a chair which had apparently been kept for her beside Agnes Fane. She was received with a surface tinge of graciousness and questioned about her work, her interests, her friends. It was a little alarming, because she had the strongest feeling of being explored, weighed, brought up for judgement.

Presently Agnes Fane was talking of Tanis.

'She has been very glad to meet you. I am pleased that you were able to come down. It seemed such a good opportunity as the Maxwells and Petra were already coming, and of course Carey Desborough – but we hardly count him as a visitor. He is the son of a very old friend, and we hope he and Tanis will be announcing their engagement very soon. I don't know if Tanis told you, but there is really no reason why there should be any secret about it.'

Laura's colour rose and failed. She had the sudden sickening sense of just what a trap she had walked into. No wonder her reluctance had warned her not to come. Whatever happened now between her and Carey was going to look like a repetition of the old story. *And that's how Tanis meant it to look*. Lilian Ferrers had taken Oliver from Agnes Fane. Laura saw herself being pushed on to a lighted stage where she was to re-enact her mother's part. Whatever happened, Agnes Fane wouldn't believe that it wasn't Tanis who had been out-witted and betrayed. The realisation was the matter of an instant.

'We're so fond of him,' said Agnes Fane – 'and so very anxious that Tanis should marry and settle down. I don't at all like this talk of Hollywood. It would be a great grief to Lucy and myself. She's been like a daughter to us, you know, and we would like to see her children here.' The dark eyes were bent on Laura. A sudden and quite charming smile changed the line of the lips. 'I promised that I wouldn't talk business to you – or no, I do not think I did promise anything of the sort, for after all that is why you are here, is it not? And I believe in frankness. It has never been my way to hint or beat about the bush. This has been my home since I was a child, and it has been Tanis's home since she was a child. It is my dearest wish that it should be her children's home.'

She was still smiling as she finished speaking. It was the smile of the great lady who needs only to allow her wishes to be known.

'And now I would like to talk to Alistair Maxwell for a little. Will you tell him?'

When Alistair had been reluctantly detached from a group of which Tanis was the centre, Laura found herself being invited to a seat beside Miss Silver. When she had taken it she was looked at – kindly, firmly, thoroughly. It was exactly like arriving at school and being inspected by the headmistress. She felt that she might at any moment expect to be put on her honour and told that she must aim at being a credit to the school. Instead Miss Silver said in a precise, pleasant voice, 'I knew your father and mother.'

Laura flushed into warmth.

'Oh, did you?' Her voice meant more than the words.

Miss Silver nodded.

'I was in the neighbourhood when they were here before their marriage. I was still engaged in the scholastic profession at the time, and I had a young charge at Fairholme Lacy, which is only a couple of miles from here. Your mother was friendly with my employer's sister. I saw a good deal of her, and of your father. You are like them both.'

'Not my mother.'

'Not her colouring of course – she was so fair. But

there are expressions – when you smile – and the turn of your head and the tone of your voice are exactly hers. I hope Miss Fane will show you the portraits which Amory did of her and your father. You could not very well ask to see them, but she may show them to you. They are in her bedroom.'

Laura caught her breath. In her bedroom – through all those years of resentment – hanging there for her to see by night and by day . . . She said in a low voice, 'How strange!'

Miss Silver nodded.

'For some people, but not for Agnes. She had commissioned the three portraits, and they are considered very fine.'

'Three?'

'He painted her too. Her portrait is hanging between those two end windows. You can see it without moving.'

Laura looked past the tea-table, past Tanis and Robin, past Carey Desborough who was laughing with Petra North, to the wide ivory panel which separated the two south windows with their heavy folds of violet brocade and their deep pelmets edged and fringed with gold. The canvas was long and narrow set in a frame of tarnished gilt. It showed Agnes Fane bare-headed and in riding-clothes, coming down a flight of steps. A light switch dangled from one hand, and in the other she held an apple. The whole thing looked so natural that Laura was carried back a generation. This was Agnes Fane – this tall, handsome, imperious creature, coming down the steps to feed her horse Black Turban perhaps, whom she had ridden over the quarry.

Laura looked quickly away. She was very pale. Her thoughts clamoured. Why does she do it? Lilian and Oliver in her bedroom to look at always, and this picture here for everyone to see. It was a parading of something which should have been hidden, a wearing of tragedy as if it was a garment thrown on carelessly and worn for all the world to see. And with what pride, what stubborn determination, through how many bitter years. It hurt – it hurt dreadfully. To say something, she spoke falteringly.

'It's – a wonderful portrait. We have copies of my father's and mother's at home. I don't know who did them.'

There were a great many questions she would have liked to ask, but Miss Silver picked up a brightly-flowered knitting-bag from the floor beside her and got up.

'I promised to show Agnes a new knitting stitch,' she said, and moved away towards the invalid chair.

Laura joined Petra and Carey, but she had no sooner done so than Petra whisked round and went to meet Alistair, who had given up his place to Miss Maud Silver. It was the last thing that Laura would have planned, but having the opportunity thrust upon her, she had an overwhelming impulse to make use of it. She said low and quick, 'Carey, it's dreadful. Cousin Agnes has been talking to me, and she thinks you and Tanis are engaged.'

He laughed, but his eyes were angry.

'How do you know she thinks so?'

'Because she told me. She said you would be giving it out almost at once.'

'Oh, will we? She'll have to think again!'

Laura's hands held one another tightly.

'You mustn't speak to me, or come near me, or – anything. Don't you see how dreadful it is? Whatever happens, don't you see, it's going to look as if I had come between you – just like my mother did. *Carey—*'

He said quickly, 'Don't get worked up.' Then, raising

his voice, 'You can see the end wall of the Priory from those windows. Come and have a look.'

Laura said, 'But it will be dark—' She was frightened and bewildered.

Carey took her by the arm.

'That's the best way to see a ruin. There's always some light from the sky. Come along!'

Lucy Adams turned her head to say, 'It's much too cold to go outside.'

Carey sent her a laughing, 'Oh, we're not going out.' He took Laura to the end of the room and, parting the curtains of the left-hand window, made way for her to pass between them. It was so quickly and publicly done that she could think of no way of holding back. He followed her and dropped the curtain behind them. They were alone, with darkness veiling the world beyond the window. An icy chill struck inward from the glass. Carey said, still in that raised voice, 'You must give your eyes a minute or two, then they'll begin to see again.' He dropped to something that was only just sound. 'You're not to worry – do you hear? It's going to be all right.'

'I don't see how.'

His arm was round her shoulders.

'Well, I do. Tanis has got us into the mess – she must do something about it. I'll have it out with her – tonight if I can.' His voice rose again. 'Are you beginning to see anything? There's the west end of the church on your right. A little later in the year the moon shines through what's left of the rose window. It looks very fine.'

Dark shapes began to emerge from the general gloom – the high shape of a broken wall, and a black heaped mass of trees. Carey's arm held her close, and felt that she was trembling. His hand came under her chin, and his lips came down on hers in a long kiss. When he let her go he said in a hard, determined whisper, 'That's to remember me by. I'd kill anyone who came between us. You're mine, and don't you forget it.'

The next moment she was holding the curtain again and they were coming back into the room.

Laura felt dazed and shaken. She had the sensation of having been caught up in a sweeping tide which without any will or volition of her own was carrying her along. She had neither the wish nor the power to resist. She could not look at Carey, but she had to face the room. She saw Petra standing alone, looking at a book which she had taken up. With a feeling of relief she joined her.

TWELVE

CAREY DESBOROUGH WALKED straight up to Tanis and said bluntly, 'Can I see you for a moment? There's something I want to talk to you about.'

She and Alistair were over by the piano at the north end of the room. She threw him a queer look and said, 'I was just going to sing.'

Carey said nothing. His eyes, angry and determined, held hers.

She said with a laugh, 'I suppose the house won't fall down if you have to wait.'

'It might. Come along – you can sing afterwards.'

They went out together. Alistair stared gloomily after them. Agnes Fane watched them go and turned to Miss Silver with an approving smile.

'A handsome couple, Maud.'

Miss Silver gave a slight deprecating cough.

'Very handsome,' she said in a dry little voice.

'And just what do you mean by that?'

Miss Silver's needles clicked above a cloud of pale pink wool.

'Oh, nothing.'

'Maud!'

Miss Silver looked up placidly.

'Well, I would not call them a couple.'

'And pray, why not?'

'Because I see no signs of their being in love with one another.'

Miss Fane smiled in a superior manner.

'Perhaps, my dear Maud, you will allow me to know a little more about that than you do.'

Miss Silver smiled too.

'I do not think so. You are too much interested – wishes are apt to be misleading. Let us change the subject. My niece Milly Rogers is expecting another baby. I was most fortunate in finding this pretty pink wool in Ledlington.'

Miss Fane surveyed it with disfavour.

'You should be knitting comforts for the troops.'

Miss Silver's needles clicked.

'Babies must have vests,' she remarked in a mild but stubborn tone.

Tanis Lyle led the way into the charming small sitting-room which had been her own from the time she had left school. The walls were panelled in some pale modern wood. The furniture was modern too – couch and chairs wide-armed cubes; pale green curtains; green cushions; pale coverings to match the walls; a clever use of ice-green glass for the fireplace and the pelmets – the whole thing an admirable setting for Miss Tanis Lyle.

She had switched on the light in a heavy block of glass beside the couch, but Carey, following her, pulled down another switch. A bowl in the ceiling sprang into brilliance and flooded the room with light. She looked over her shoulder as if she were going to speak, but she said nothing, only turned, held out both her hands, and smiled. It was the smile which had enchanted many men. It had enchanted Carey once, but it would never enchant him again. She said, still smiling, 'Well, darling – what is it? Don't you want to kiss me?'

Carey smiled too. He had an extraordinary sense of

freedom, of release. Laura had set him free. He was completely and satisfyingly immune. He had no more desire to kiss Tanis than he had to kiss Lucy Adams – impossible to put it more strongly than that. He could say in quite a friendly tone, 'I want to talk to you.'

There was a green gleam between the black lashes. She went over to the couch, leaned against one of the wide ends, and said, 'A bit cave-man, aren't you, dragging me out of the drawing-room like this? What is it all about? My idea was that you wanted to make love to me and simply couldn't wait another moment. Obviously a mistake. Now it's your turn.'

'Tanis, I want to talk to you.'

'Yes – you said that before. You'll end up boring me.'

He came and stood over her, his eyes grimly amused.

'Oh, no, I'm not going to bore you – you'll be quite interested. Look here, Miss Fane seems to be under the impression that we're engaged.'

She looked up at him.

'And aren't we, darling?'

'No, darling, we are not. You made yourself particularly clear on that point when I came out of hospital.'

She shook her head.

'I don't remember about that.' She laughed. 'Who told you what Aunt Agnes thought – Laura?'

Carey blundered.

'She told her we were engaged.'

'Meaning that Aunt Agnes told Laura, and that Laura told you. Quick worker, aren't you, Carey? Well, where do we go from there? Do *I* tell anyone?'

'You tell Miss Fane that we are not engaged.'

'Really?'

'And that we have no intention of being engaged.'

'Do I?'

'And that we are, in fact, nothing but very good friends.'

'Are we?' Her eyes blazed suddenly with green fire. 'Is that all?'

'I think so. I should like you to do it at once. We are all in a false position.'

Tanis straightened up.

'You mean that Laura is in a false position. That is what you mean, isn't it?'

'I said all of us.'

'But you meant Laura. And of course, my dear, how right!' Her face lit up suddenly with a smile which had no enchantment this time, but a kind of vivid mockery. 'How completely, entirely, delightfully right! Laura is for it – she is the vamp who has separated two loving hearts! It's a marvellous situation, isn't it? And won't the aunts just lap it up! It should go down particularly well with Aunt Agnes, you know. "Be thou chaste as ice and pure as snow, thou shalt not escape calumny." That's what I learned at my school of dramatic art. And how true! In other words, darling Laura's name is going to be mud. And she won't even have had her fun first – or will she?'

The dark colour rushed in Carey's face. He stood rigidly still for a moment, and then pushed his hands down into his pockets. His eyes stared at her with a kind of raging contempt. There was a furious tension between them. 'You'll go too far some day,' he said.

Tanis went on smiling.

'Meaning that you'd like to murder me?'

'It would be a pleasure.'

The words had a quiet edge to them. They got under Tanis's skin. Anger, passion, jealous rage, were so much incense at the shrine of her vanity. Contempt pricked her. Her smile went rigid. Her eyes stared.

He swung round and went to the door, but with his hand on it he turned again and came back.

'Look here, Tanis, what's the good of all this? Losing our tempers and having a slanging match doesn't get us anywhere. We've had some good times together, haven't we? And you don't want to marry me any more than I want to marry you, so what's the use of stirring up trouble?'

Tanis still had that queer fixed look. It came to him that there was something familiar about it – familiar, and rather horrible. He had seen a cat look like that, watching a bird that had got away. Something about the rigid pose and slitted eyes brought the likeness too vividly to mind for comfort.

She said quite slowly and clearly, 'You have a nerve, Carey, haven't you – even if you've lost it for flying.'

Her voice stopped, and everything stopped with it. There was a moment of deadly silence before he said, 'Thank you, Tanis, I think that's about enough. Don't you?'

This time he went out of the room and shut the door.

THIRTEEN

WHEN ALL THE events of that evening were raked over and sifted out, there was to be a curious changing of values. Some things that had appeared important at the time just slipped away and were lost. Some which had hardly been noticed came under a magnifying glass. A few things remained as they had seemed. It mattered to no one that Laura and Carey had kissed behind the curtains, because no one but they themselves was ever to know of it. The fact that the door between Tanis's sitting-room and the ground-floor room of the octagon tower had been carelessly closed by the maid who had been in to draw the curtains was to assume a terrible importance. The bit of gossip which Petra North brought hotfoot to Laura when she was dressing for dinner maintained its significance.

There had been some music. Tanis had sung. She had a lovely limpid voice worthy of better music than the dance tunes which she sighed or crooned to her own flashing accompaniment. It was all very clever, very finished, very modern.

Miss Fane looked across the room and said in her deep-toned voice, 'That's enough of that horrible stuff. Sing something civilised for a change.' Whereupon Tanis, smiling, struck a familiar chord and sang *Who is Sylvia?* with great sweetness and delicacy.

Then to Sylvia let us sing.
For Sylvia is excelling.
She excels each mortal thing
Upon this dull earth dwelling.
To her let us garlands bring.

As the words tripped out, Miss Fane's eyes rested upon the singer, and not hers only. Alistair Maxwell, propping the wall, fixed her with a gaze of such intensity that it was plain enough that, for him at least, here was Sylvia with each excelling grace.

It was after this that the party dispersed. Miss Fane went to her room, and Laura thankfully to hers with the immemorial excuse of a letter to write. The dressing-gong had sounded, when there was a knock on the door, immediately followed by the appearance of Petra North.

'Can I come in? Laura, guess who's here! But you won't – not ever – I'll have to tell you!' Her grey eyes were round and dancing. 'You know, we were talking about Jeff Hazelton. Tanis's husband, only of course he isn't now – well, he's here!'

Laura looked up from the stocking she was changing, leaving it half on, half off a pretty bare foot.

'How do you mean *here*? They haven't made it up, have they?'

Petra leaned on the rail of the bed.

'Of course they haven't – they're divorced. But I didn't mean here in the house – I mean down in the village.'

Laura pulled up her stocking and fastened it.

'What is he doing here?'

'Staying at the Angel.'

'How do you know?'

Petra straightened up and did a couple of dance steps.

'Aha! Wouldn't you like to know!' She gave quite a

good high kick. 'Did you know I once had a dancing part in a play with Tanis? Not professional of course, but I don't dance badly. I did have leanings towards the stage, instead of which I put in umpteen hours a day sorting out the most revolting clothes for the bombed.'

Laura fastened the second stocking.

'Is that what you do?'

Petra nodded mournfully.

'Grim – isn't it?'

'Are the clothes really revolting? What a shame!'

'Anything's revolting when you've been sorting it for umpteen hours.' She took a flying jump on to the bed by Laura and caught her hand. 'Don't let's talk about it – I'm having a holiday. Let's talk about Jeff.'

Laura couldn't help laughing.

'But it was you who changed the subject.'

'That was only to get you all worked up. You don't know the rules. Now we go back to you asking me how I know about Jeff.'

'Well, how *do* you know?'

'Because Robin told me.'

'And how does Robin know?'

Petra let go of her hand and settled herself against the rail at the foot of the bed.

'Well, after you went upstairs Carey and Robin dragged Alistair off for a walk – and about time too, if you ask me. They said they wanted exercise, so they went the long way round to the village and fetched up at the Angel. And there was Jeff, drinking himself blind – he does, you know.'

'I thought you said it was dope.'

Petra's face sharpened.

'I told you Tanis said so. She did. I didn't say anything. But everyone knows he drinks – there's no light under a bushel about that. Well, there he was, all lit-up and talking big about why should he be out in the cold when there was a party up at the Priory, and he wasn't an outcast, was he, and things like that. Robin says he wouldn't put it past him to come along up and crash the gate. Don't you hope he does?'

Laura looked appalled.

'Oh, *no*!'

Petra jumped up, laughing and mimicking her.

'Oh, no! Oh, no! Oh, yes, yes, yes, yes, *yes*! Don't be such a mimsy, Laura! Wouldn't you like to see Tanis taken down a peg or two? Wouldn't you like to see her up to her knees in mud? Wouldn't you like to rub her face in it?'

'I'd simply hate it,' said Laura frankly, 'and so would you. And we're both going to be late if we don't hurry up and dress.'

She got down in time to see Miss Fane make her entrance. The door to the octagon room stood wide. She could see a background crimson curtain, and then out through the doorway, alone and unassisted, came Agnes Fane in her self-propelling chair. She wore a long robe-like garment of black velvet with fur at the neck and wrists, and she had changed the pearls at her ears for long ruby and diamond drops which winked and caught the light. The rugs were so arranged as to leave an open lane of parquet. Just short of the hearth there was a left-hand turn. Miss Fane took it dexterously and came to rest in the place which she had occupied at tea-time. A tall, thin woman in grey stepped into the room for a moment and stepped back again, closing the door.

Laura approached a little timidly. It seemed to her that in this house for one right thing you might do or say there were a hundred wrong ones, and that any one of the hundred might do irreparable harm. It was a thoroughly unnerving thought.

But Miss Fane was pleased to be gracious.

'Tanis will show you the house tomorrow. It is better seen by daylight. I always think a room without the view from its windows is like a blind person, and to be more practical we have not completely blacked-out some of the rooms which are not in use. There are only a few, now that we have evacuees in the north wing . . . Oh, didn't Tanis tell you that? She's not very pleased about their coming, but they are really no trouble at all. These things are just a matter of arrangement. There are a dozen of them – two families, really very nice people – and we have been able to fit them in very well. The servants' quarters are in the north wing, you know, with the kitchen and offices on the ground floor and a separate staircase. I have fitted them up a kitchen of their own where they can cook on oil and not be in Mrs Dean's way. It works perfectly.'

Laura thought, 'Anything she arranged would work perfectly.' There was so much poise, so much certainty about Agnes Fane. It was quite easy to believe that everything in her household would be ordered with unsparing efficiency.

The others came in – Tanis in a gold house-coat, her eyes very green; Lucy Adams in one of those black satin dresses which look as if they had been slept in for years; Miss Silver in brown velveteen; the three men; and, flying in as the sound of the gong was dying away, Petra in sealing-wax red with her lips and nails made up to match.

After dinner Miss Fane and Miss Adams played chess and Miss Silver knitted. The rest talked, played games, and talked again, with the exception of Alistair Maxwell who sat silent and moody with his eyes on Tanis Lyle. Petra talked enough for half a dozen. Her colour rose, her eyes shone, and, egged on by Robin and Carey, she gave them flashing imitations of the great lady who was the very nominal head of her Clothes for the Bombed; the anxious, nervous little secretary who did everyone's work and got nobody's thanks; the stout lady who explained in embarrassing detail just how she felt and what she looked like when the blast of a bomb blew her clothes 'clean off of her – and me in my you-know-whats, and blimey if Jerry didn't send another one along and strip me bare!'

She had got to the meek little man who wanted to know if they could help him with a rabbit-hutch because he was all broke-up, when the door opened and the butler was seen to be standing there. If the word could be used in connection with anyone so solid and respectable, Dean was flurried. Without coming into the room he fixed an entreating gaze on Tanis and said across the space which separated them, 'If I might speak to you for a moment, miss—'

She got up and had almost reached the door, when there appeared beyond it a tall, shaking figure. Head slumped forward, long hair falling dishevelled across a brow glistening with sweat, Jeffrey Hazelton stared over Dean's massive shoulders at the girl who had been his wife.

He made a forward lunge. Dean stood his ground, and in a moment Tanis had reached the door.

'How do you do, Jeff?' she said, and then, 'That will do, Dean – you needn't wait.'

The group she had left saw the butler step aside, saw her put a hand upon Hazelton's shaking arm, and saw no more. The door closed.

The ladies in front of the fire continued their game of chess. Miss Silver knitted. The door being in line with the hearth, she was the only one of the three far enough out in the room to have seen Mr Hazelton's brief appearance. She knitted, but her eyes remained fixed upon the door, and she had afterwards to unravel a couple of rows.

Petra said in a breathless whisper, 'That was Jeff Hazelton!' and all of a sudden there was a loud crash from the hall – the sound of a shot and the ring of breaking glass. Lucy Adams, the white queen in her hand, looked up, drew a sharp breath, and screamed at the top of her voice. Miss Silver dropped her knitting and reached the door only a shade after the three men, Laura and Petra behind her.

The hall was brightly lit. It smelled of smoke. A barely discernible hint of blue hung on the upper air. One of the ring of lighted sconces was missing. There was a glitter of shivered crystal on the parquet floor, thin slivers that looked like ice, and scattered grains like sugar. Tanis was standing in the middle of the open space, and, holding to the left-hand newel-post of the stair, Jeffrey Hazelton swayed and shook with a pistol hanging limply from his hand.

'Told you I'd do it – and I've – done it – haven't I? Who says – I can't shoot straight?' He raised the pistol and described a wavering half-circle, finishing up with a straight enough aim at Tanis. 'Shoot you – before I – let anyone else – have you. What's divorce? I say you're my wife! Anyone says you're not – I'll shoot him – greatest of pleasure.'

Alistair Maxwell made a thrust forward, but Carey and his brother Robin pulled him back.

Tanis said sweetly, 'Don't be a damned fool, Alistair!'

She began to walk towards the stairs. 'And don't you be a fool either, Jeff! We all know you're a crack shot without your breaking Aunt Agnes's glass. I thought you said you wanted to talk to me. Well, I'm not talking to anyone who's flourishing around with a gun – I don't like them.'

She was within arm's length of him, when he let go of the newel, reached out, and caught her by the shoulder. Leaning there, shaking, he brought the pistol up and pressed the muzzle hard against her breast. Six people watched him do it. Three of them were young, active men, and they might just as well not have been there at all. Worse. It needed only a movement, an outcry, even a caught breath, to bring catastrophe. The shaking finger halted on the trigger, but jangle those driven nerves and it would fall. Even Alistair, blind with passion, knew that.

Tanis lifted her eyes in a steady look.

'Well, Jeff? Don't you want to talk to me?' She smiled a little and put up her hand to the one which held the pistol. Her fingers moved on it caressingly, her voice dropped and changed. She said, 'Jeff darling – how *silly*!' and all at once he broke. His hand wavered and went limp. The pistol fell. He put his head down on her shoulder and began to sob in a lost, bewildered way.

'Tanis – Tanis – *Tanis*!'

And then they were on him. He made no resistance at all. There was no need for any force. A broken creature, saying Tanis's name over and over between heart-breaking sobs.

Carey bent to pick up the pistol. As he straightened himself he came face to face with Tanis standing on the bottom step, the tall newel behind her, a look of triumph on her face. Her gold dress shone. Her green eyes glinted. She had never been so nearly beautiful. The poor sobbing wretch whom Robin was shepherding back to the Angel was nothing more to her than the occasion for this triumph. She had had her big scene with him, and she had played him right off the stage. *Nunc plaudite*, as they used to say in the old comedies – and now for the applause.

They went back into the drawing-room, and she got it in full measure. Lucy Adams was hysterical in endearment, and Alistair suddenly full of words with which to praise and exalt her. If Agnes Fane was pale and stern, there was a high pride in her bearing as she turned to Carey with the brief comment, 'Tanis does not know what fear means.' Then, in a lowered tone, 'What has been done with him? There must not be any scandal.'

'There won't be any. Robin will see him to bed. He's going to get old Jones to come over and give him something to put him to sleep. Then we'll go down in the morning and pack him back to town. I take it Dean won't talk.'

Agnes Fane said, 'No,' and then, 'Thank you, Carey.'

She turned to Tanis, who had taken the pistol from Carey and was balancing it on the palm of her hand as she talked.

'Tanis, put that thing down! There has been quite enough playing with firearms. I suppose it is Mr Hazelton's property, but he is certainly not fit to be trusted with it. It had better be locked away.'

Tanis said, 'It's mine.'

'How is it yours?'

'He had a pair. This one is mine. He gave it to me.'

Miss Fane looked down her nose.

'What a singular present! Do you mean to tell me that Mr Hazelton has probably got the other one?'

Tanis laughed.

'I should say certainly.'

'Then it's most unsafe.'

'Oh, he won't do anything now – he was all in. All right, Aunt Agnes, I'll put it away.'

She went out by the door to the octagon room, and through to her own sitting-room.

Laura thought, 'She's very, very brave. I ought to admire her, but I can't. That poor creature had been her husband, and she doesn't care – she doesn't care a bit.'

Petra, beside her, hummed under her breath:

Then to Sylvia let us sing,
For Sylvia is excelling—

Her cheeks were scarlet and her eyes brightly mutinous.

Alistair was saying, 'Where she's so marvellous—'

And then Tanis was back again, and Agnes Fane broke in in her deep voice.

'What have you done with it?'

'Put it in my bureau, darling.'

FOURTEEN

LAURA UNDRESSED AND got into bed. It had been the longest day she had ever known. She seemed to have travelled a thousand miles from the Laura Fane who had come up to town to stay with Cousin Sophy and see her solicitor, not much more than forty-eight hours ago. That there were other longer days ahead waiting to drag out interminable hours of anxiety and pain, she fortunately did not know. She had had a deliciously hot bath, she was relaxed and warm. The thought of Carey was like something shining in her heart.

She was about to stretch out her hand and switch off the bedside light, when there was a knock at the door and Tanis Lyle came in. With a brief, 'I thought you wouldn't be asleep yet,' she crossed to the foot of the bed and stood there in a long black dressing-gown over pale green pyjamas. They were the sort of pyjamas which suggested the bedroom scene in a West End play. Laura, who had never imagined that they existed in private life, gazed at them entranced. The dressing-gown was also very intriguing – a tailored garment of heavy, dull silk with a gold and green curlicue on the pocket which was probably intended to be a monogram.

'What is it, Tanis?' she said and Tanis Lyle came round the bed-post and sat down with her back against it.

'Just a talk,' she said. 'There's always such a crowd, and I want to talk to you about Aunt Agnes and the house. She's mad keen to buy it – you know that.'

Laura sat up straight against her pillows. She really did feel that this was the last straw. It was bad enough to have quasiparental pressure brought to bear upon her by Mr Metcalfe in his office, and to have Cousin Agnes being pathetic in the drawing-room about wanting to see Tanis's children grow up at the Priory, but to be pursued at midnight and cornered in bed when you couldn't possibly get away was really the limit.

Her eyes brightened and her colour rose as she said, 'Yes, I know she wants to buy it – but I don't think it's any good talking about it, because I haven't made up my mind. You can't do a thing like that in a hurry. I've got to think first.'

'And talk it over – oh, not with me, but shall we say with Carey Desborough?'

There was certainly no beating about the bush with Tanis. Whatever the situation might be, she was right in the middle of it. In a way it made things easier, because you knew where you were.

Laura kept a steady look and said, 'Why do you say that?'

'It's true, isn't it?'

'What makes you think so, Tanis?'

Tanis laughed.

'You needn't fence, my dear. For the moment, and for what it's worth, Carey seems to have fallen for you. It won't last – his affairs never do – but here and now he's gone in off the deep end, and you won't get me to believe that he hasn't told you so.'

Laura had turned rather pale. She said, 'I'm not trying to make you believe anything.'

Tanis swung a bare foot from which the soft black slipper had fallen.

'Well, that being that, suppose we get down to brass

tacks. As I was saying, Carey has certainly told you that he has fallen for you, but I don't suppose it has occurred to him to tell you that he has quite a big income. Old Desborough was in iron and steel. There used to be pots of money, and I believe it's still quite a tidy sum – in fact, our Carey is a catch. It's one of the things he's modest about, so I don't suppose he's mentioned it.'

Laura said, 'No.' She had a bewildered, driven feeling.

'In fact, you were prepared to love him for himself alone. Too romantic! What a pity he's engaged to me.'

Laura said nothing. Her eyes spoke for her. Wide and indignant, they gave Tanis the lie. And Tanis laughed.

'My dear, do you really believe every word he says? Anyhow the point is that if I say we are engaged, everyone will believe me, and the aunts will swear to it. If Carey backs out, there will be the most awful stink, and your name, my dear, will be simply and utterly mud. I don't think you're stupid, so you can probably see that for yourself. You come in from outside, you smash up my engagement just as your mother smashed Aunt Agnes's and what do you expect – that people will receive you with open arms? All right, you just go ahead and try! Only don't say I didn't warn you.'

'Tanis!'

Tanis bent down to retrive her shoe, soft and black like the coat, with the same green and gold monogram. She slipped it on and turned a sudden smile on Laura.

'Don't go up in smoke. There's a way out – if you'll take it.'

For a moment Laura had been angrier than she had ever been in her life before. Now suddenly she was cool. She thought, 'She did that on purpose – she *wanted* to make me angry. Why?' She got the answer to her own question – 'You don't think when you're angry. She's got something up her sleeve. She doesn't want me to have time to think.' She said, 'I don't know what you mean.'

Tanis nodded.

'Not yet. But you will – I'm going to tell you. If you and Carey mean business you're in a jam, and I'm the only person who can get you out of it. As it happens, I don't mind doing a deal. You and Carey want my help. If I go to the aunts and tell them that Carey and I made up our minds months ago that we'd hate being married to each other, there won't be any stink. They won't like it, but they'll have to lump it. Well, I'm prepared to do that if you'll do something for me.'

Laura thought, 'What's coming? What's she going to say? I don't like it. What am I going to say?' For the moment she said nothing, only kept her eyes on Tanis, sitting straight up against the white pillows in her pink night-dress.

'You don't ask what it is? Well, it's this Priory business. You can have Carey if—'

'If I sell the Priory to Cousin Agnes.'

Tanis leaned back. Her eyes were wide and smiling. Her lips smiled too. She said in a gracious, easy voice, 'Oh, no, my dear – it's not that way at all. You can have Carey if you promise *not* to sell.'

It was so unexpected that Laura's rising anger just fell down flat. Astonishment left her with nothing to say but a primitive, childish, '*What!*'

Tanis was smilingly pleased to explain.

'I don't want Aunt Agnes to buy the Priory. I'd much rather have the twelve thousand pounds.'

Laura said, 'Oh—' She thought, 'I'm behaving as if I was half-witted. I suppose she knows what she's driving at. She can do the talking herself.' She waited with an air of grave expectancy which exasperated Tanis to the very quick of her bones.

'Well?' she said a little sharply. 'Is it a deal?'

Laura shook her head.

'I want to know why.'

Tanis laughed.

'Cards on the table? All right – I don't mind. But I should think it was fairly obvious. The aunts want me to settle down. They want to bring the brat here and bring him up at the Priory—'

Laura said, 'What brat?'

'Didn't you know that Jeff and I had produced one? That's what gave the show away. Rotten luck, wasn't it? Well, anyhow, there he is, up in the north with Jeff's sister who is married to some ghastly parson. I haven't seen him since he was about a month old, but Aunt Agnes keeps in touch. She's getting keener and keener about the wretched brat – I believe she thinks he's like your father. That's why she's dead set on my marrying Carey. You see, it's all right for Mrs Desborough to have a son by a former marriage, but when it comes to Miss Lyle and her little boy, Aunt Agnes mercifully blanches. So I've been able to stave it all off up to date, but if she bought the Priory she'd never let up until she got Bill here and me married to someone, just to put us on the County map. You don't know what she's like when she's set on anything. I've a pretty good will of my own, but I'm simply not in Aunt Agnes's class. Besides she's got the whiphand of me over the money. She knows perfectly well that if it comes to the pinch I won't risk being cut out of her will.'

Laura went on looking at her. She was horrified, fascinated, and intensely interested. Her face showed only a grave attention. It would have given Tanis a lot of pleasure to smack it. It was not civilisation that restrained her, but a determination to get her own way. Laura, slapped, would certainly prove recalcitrant. She therefore exercised considerable self-control, and after a silence which Laura showed no sign of breaking returned to the charge.

'Well, there you are – if she can't have the Priory, she'll let up on getting me married and having the brat. Is it a deal?'

Even then Laura did not speak at once. She continued to look thoughtful. At last she said, 'I don't like it, Tanis.'

'What do you mean?'

'I don't like any of it – going behind Cousin Agnes's back, and – and – making a bargain. I *don't* like it.'

Tanis got to her feet. The movement was a graceful one – all her movements were graceful – but it came a thought too quickly upon Laura's words.

She said, 'Squeamish – aren't you? Better think it over. If you sell you'll get twelve thousand pounds and you won't get Carey – unless you like to steal him and take the consequences like your mother did. If you don't sell, even the aunts can't say very much, for after all the darned place does belong to you, and I'll smooth out the Carey business. Think it over. I'm going to bed.'

Laura lay awake a long time in the dark. There was a high wind moving outside. The casement which she had set open creaked. She could see the shape of the window where she had drawn the curtain back. The wind and that faint creaking sound ran like an accompaniment below her thoughts and kept them moving to an odd reluctant rhythm. Carey – the Priory – Tanis – the child who was somewhere up in the north – Lilian and Oliver – the little boy who was like Oliver – Agnes Fane, with her heart set on him – threads shifting, tangling, lacing, and interlacing . . . Only one way with a tangle – cut it out and start all over again. Drifting into her thoughts the phrase, read somewhere or heard – 'Atropos with the shears' . . . The drift went on and took her into sleep.

She dreamed she was walking with Carey in the ruined church. The air was dark. Someone was crying. They went among the fallen stones towards the broken altar at the east end. It was their marriage, but she wasn't dressed as a bride. She was wearing her black lace dress and the Chinese shawl. It was very cold. She put out her hand to find Carey, and he wasn't there. She was alone with that desolate weeping—

She woke, shuddering, and it was a long time before she slept again.

FIFTEEN

NEXT MORNING TANIS took her round the house. There were a great many rooms, a few of which were permanently unused, and others only in occasional use as guest-rooms. The north wing besides accommodating a staff of five also found place for two families of evacuees. Each family had a large room fitted with bunks as a dormitory, and a smaller one which they could use as they liked. There was a bathroom at their disposal upstairs, and a bathroom and a kitchen below.

Laura met Mrs Judd, small and wiry, coping cheerfully with communal life in the country and controlling an aged grandmother and four lively children with brisk efficiency. She also met Mrs Slade, a limp person with a mother-in-law, three children, and a flapper sister. The mother-in-law was bedridden but dynamic, the flapper sister as pert as they come, the children spoiled and vociferous. Mrs Slade, whose husband was at sea, yearned for Rotherhithe with its crowded, noisy streets, and confided in all and sundry that if it came to a choice between being bombed and having to do another winter in the country, she was going back and she didn't care who knew it.

Tanis was not disposed to linger. She took Laura down the back stairs, and remarking, 'You won't want to see the kitchen and all that sort of thing,' led the way back to the hall.

'You've seen the dining-room. Aunt Agnes has a sort

of office in this room opposite. She only uses it for business. You can look in if you like – she won't be there. It's all filing-cabinets and things like that. Too bleak.'

They went through the hall to the drawing-room.

'You can see the view now, such as it is. It's quite good in the summer when the roses are out, but it's grim at present.'

The three west windows looked upon a paved terrace which ran the whole width of the house. Beyond were rosebeds, dark against the clipped green turf. Beyond the beds there was a wide green lawn with a magnificent cedar, the whole enclosed by a yew hedge, tall and black, with arches cut in it here and there. It was not the best of days for seeing a garden. The wind had dropped. The sky was grey. A mist obscured the distant view.

Laura moved on to the south window from which she and Carey had looked last night. The west wall of the Priory church ran level with the inner wall of the drawing-room, and the terrace turned the corner to meet it, forming rather a charming little courtyard. Pressed into the angle between the church and the house, and partly built into the latter, was the octagon tower running up to a pepper-pot roof topped by a weather-cock. The ruin, seen in the daylight, was very picturesque. The stone traceries of the rose window had by some miracle remained intact. A yellow jasmine bloomed against the wall. Across the tower a great camellia spread its shining emerald leaves. It was thick with bud. Near the middle of the bush a half-expanded flower shone like a scarlet jewel. Laura was enchanted. The place was a magical place. If she could only have been there alone—

She turned reluctantly from the window and followed Tanis to the door through which Miss Fane had made her entrance the night before. Open, it disclosed an empty room with a polished floor, whose octagon shape showed only on the side towards the church, the right-hand side being flattened off to take the lift. On the left two archaic lancet windows flanked by straight crimson curtains looked into the church, and between them, partly concealed by the velvet folds, was a stout oak door with a heavy iron lock and hinges.

Tanis pushed aside the curtains, turned a portentous key, and pulled the door towards her. It opened without a sound. Somehow Laura had expected the hinges to groan and the key to grate in the lock, but there wasn't a sound. She was to remember that afterwards.

She moved, and found herself at the top of eight or nine steps leading down into the church. Immediately she had the feeling that she had seen this place before. Only there was something wrong about it. She ought to be standing down there on the rough grass looking up at the steps. It came to her that she had dreamed about standing at the bottom of the steps, and that the dream had frightened her.

Tanis was saying, 'The drop to the church is a bit of a surprise, isn't it? But the house is built on a plinth to make room for cellars underneath. The seventeenth century was great on cellars.'

As she spoke, the telephone bell rang. She stepped back and went through the door which had faced them as they came from the drawing-room, leaving it open behind her. Laura caught a glimpse of pale unusual panelling and sea-green curtains – windows looking to the front of the house and into the church. She stood where she was, not liking to follow, and heard Tanis say in a warm, pleased voice, 'Oh, Tim – it's you!'

She moved towards the drawing-room, but before she could reach the door Tanis was speaking again.

'Oh, yes, you're going to see me. Come over and dance tonight. We've got a houseful . . . Yes, of course I mean Sylvia too. Better come to dinner. I expect the food will go round, and if it's rabbit you won't know, because Mrs Dean camouflages it till nobody can swear they're not eating pheasant or anything else she likes to call it. Actually, I believe, we've really got pheasant, so now you can just keep guessing . . . Well, you'll be over at eight? . . . That will be divine. Love to Sylvia.'

She rang off, and found Laura in the drawing-room.

'How tactful! But I never talk compromising secrets with the door open. That was Tim Madison. He and Sylvia are dining, and we'll dance afterwards. He's Navy – waiting for a board to pass him fit for sea again after being bombed or torpedoed or something. He's practically all right again. Irish, and the most perfect partner.'

'And Sylvia?'

Tanis shrugged.

'His wife. That's the trouble with sailors – they will marry.'

'Don't you like her?'

Tanis laughed with genuine amusement.

'I should adore anyone Tim had married.'

SIXTEEN

TANIS WENT AWAY, and with suspicious promptness Carey walked in.

'Go and get a coat and I'll show you the ruins.'

He saw her hesitate. She said, 'I don't know—'

'I do. Go and get that coat. We've got to talk, and it's quite a good excuse.'

She ran upstairs feeling a little as if she was playing hide-and-seek. But it was no good, she had got to talk to Carey. Quite as passionately as Mrs Slade, she longed to be back in London where nobody noticed where you went or whom you met.

In the passage outside her bedroom she almost ran into Miss Adams, who was emerging from her own room opposite. Stopping to apologise, she found herself unwillingly engaged in conversation. Since Cousin Lucy quite obviously disliked her, it was impossible to guess why she should wish to converse. It was equally impossible to escape.

In the cold tone which was in such marked contrast to her usual way of speaking, Miss Adams began with what might have been either a question or a statement.

'Tanis has been taking you round the house—'

Laura assented, and Lucy Adams went on.

'It's a fine house, and interesting to those who value its associations, but of course it is not a cheap house to run, especially nowadays.'

Laura supposed not.

'Very expensive – very expensive indeed. And maids are so difficult to get in the country. This is my room. I think you haven't seen any of these rooms. I will show them to you.' There was a suggestion of effort in voice and manner, as if she had set herself an uncongenial task and meant to carry it through.

Laura beheld a room which she found distressingly pink. Victorian furniture, grave and heavy, appeared at variance with rose-coloured Axminster on the floor and rose-coloured damask at the windows. There was a pink bedspread which was a little out of key, and rose-flowered china which reminded her of the set in Cousin Sophy's guest-room. There was some kind of flowered paper on the walls, but almost every inch of it was covered by innumerable sketches, photographs, and engravings of famous pictures. Millais' *Huguenot* hung above the mantelpiece in a frame of yellow maple. From it Laura's bewildered eye wandered over every sort of picture in every imaginable sort of frame. The furniture vied with the walls in supporting photographs of every relation and friend Lucy Adams had ever had. Above all there were pictures of Tanis as a baby, Tanis as a child, Tanis in her teens, Tanis as a débutante, Tanis up-to-date.

Laura got no further than the threshold. The room repelled her. She murmured something, and Miss Adams knocked on the next door and then opened it. The tall, thin woman in grey whom she had seen for a moment the night before looked up from her fine sewing. She had a long nose and pale bitten-in lips without colour. There was no colour about her anywhere. The eyes she turned on Laura were sharp and pale.

'This is your Cousin Agnes's maid, Perry. She has been with us – for forty years, is it?'

'Forty-one, Miss Lucy.'

Laura came forward to shake hands, but somehow Perry's hand was not there to shake. That appraising stare and some slight inclination of the head were her limit of response. Laura thought of Carey waiting below. She had a sense of time prolonging itself indefinitely in this unwilling company.

But Miss Adams turned to the door on the right.

'Agnes has gone down, so I can show you her room.'

Laura felt a reluctance beyond her power to conceal. She hesitated, began to say something, and was caught in the tide of Miss Lucy's offence.

'*Really*, Laura! Perhaps you will allow me to know what Agnes would wish. But since you are so scrupulous, I will tell you that she *asked* me to show you these rooms.'

Laura coloured faintly, murmured something which never really got into words, and followed a stiffly erect Miss Adams into a room as unlike her own as it was possible to conceive – fine old furniture; rich, quiet colours; no fuss, no frills, no photographs; walls covered with a heavy cream paper; marble mantelpiece supporting a modern atmospheric clock; and, hanging above it to the right and left of the chimney-breast, Amory's portraits of Lilian Ferrers and Oliver Fane.

Laura had grown up with the copies, but here in the space and austere dignity of Agnes Fane's room the originals rather took her breath away. She felt soothed and charmed by their beauty, and then deeply and painfully moved. What had kept the portraits there? Was it courage, pride, stoic endurance, or the perverted instinct which sets pain above pleasure and presses it home to the self-tortured heart? For twenty-two years Oliver and Lilian had hung where Agnes Fane must see them morning by morning and night by night, they in their youth and strength, the world before them – this world or another – lovely and pleasant in their lives and divided for so short a time by death. And Agnes, barren and a cripple, deserted and betrayed – how had she looked at them through all the mornings and evenings of those twenty-two years?

Lucy Adams's voice struck in coldly.

'They are valuable portraits, but I do not care for oil paintings in a bedroom. They are Agnes's property of course. They do not go with the house, but if you sell the house, they will remain here. It would be very much to your advantage to accept Agnes's very generous offer. I hope you will do so.'

Laura was embarrassed, and under the embarrassment angry. Cousin Lucy had no business to try and corner her like this. It wasn't fair.

'I don't know – I don't think – please, Cousin Lucy, need we talk about it?' she said in a hesitating voice.

There was a sharp offence again – very unpleasant and trying. As soon as she could Laura escaped.

She found Carey very impatient indeed.

'You've been hours!'

'Cousin Lucy caught me.'

He took her to the octagon room and down the steps into the ruined church, where the place was rough with fallen masonry, but up the middle of what had been the nave there was a clear, grassy path. As they walked on it together Laura thought, 'It's what I dreamed last night – Carey and I walking up the aisle to be married.' She said quickly, 'I dreamed about us last night. We were being married – here. Only I was in my black lace dress and my Chinese shawl.'

'I'd love you to be married in that.'

She laughed.

'I'm afraid it wouldn't do.'

'Laura, when will you marry me?'

She looked up, and down again. Something in his voice had shaken her heart. She said, 'You don't know me.'

'I love you.'

'But you don't know me, Carey.'

She was looking up at him again, letting him see what was in her eyes and reading love, amusement, tenderness in his.

'Don't I, my sweet? I think I do. Shall I tell you what I knew after half an hour at the Luxe? I knew that you were kind, honest, and just – dreadfully honest, scrupulously just. I knew that you were very, very sweet, and I wondered if you were going to be sweet to me. I knew that you couldn't tell a lie to save your life, or act one that would deceive a month-old baby. You didn't talk very much, but you thought quite a lot. The things you were thinking showed in your face and in your eyes. It's the nicest way of talking I know. When are you going to marry me?'

She said very soberly, 'I don't know.' And then, 'Tanis came to my room last night. She said she would tell Cousin Agnes that she wasn't engaged to you and never had been, if I would promise not to sell the house.'

Carey whistled.

'*Not* to sell it?'

Laura nodded.

'She doesn't want it. She doesn't want to live here. She'd rather have the twelve thousand pounds. She said so.'

'Just what did she say?'

Laura told him. When she had finished, he said, 'Well, it's not really very surprising. I can see her point of view all right. This place is all very well as a background with Miss Fane to run it. It's no bother to Tanis – she can come down whenever she likes, bring a party whenever she chooses. But she doesn't want to make it her life work. She wants to go to Hollywood.'

Laura looked unhappy.

'I don't know what to do. I can't bear making a bargain with her behind Cousin Agnes's back.'

'No – I see. But nobody's going to make Tanis live here if she doesn't want to. She'd sell the place as soon as Miss Fane was gone.'

Laura said, 'I don't know what to do. I wish I had never come here.

SEVENTEEN

WHEN LAURA HAD left her, Lucy Adams remained in her cousin's bedroom. She was looking up at the portraits, when the door from the dressing-room was pushed open and Perry stalked in. She came up close and said in an angry whisper, 'Well, what did I tell you, Miss Lucy? She's not a Fane for nothing, nor a Ferrers neither – not in her looks nor in her ways! "She'll be glad enough to sell the house" was what you said to me. And what did I say to you, Miss Lucy? "Fanes isn't as easy as that", that's what I said and you can't get away from it. And I haven't lived with them going on forty-one years without knowing. "Don't you count no chickens, Miss Lucy," I said, "or maybe you won't hatch none." And now there isn't any maybe about it. She won't sell, and you'd best be making up your mind to it.'

'She didn't say that she wouldn't sell,' said Lucy Adams in a vacillating tone.

Perry's long nose twitched in a sniff.

'She didn't say that pigs wouldn't fly neither. There's things that don't need saying. She didn't say she wouldn't sell! "Need we talk about it, Cousin Lucy?" – that's what she said, as I couldn't help hearing, seeing you'd left the door on the jar – and I don't know what more you want than that. Them that's willing to sell is willing to talk.'

'Oh, I don't know.'

'You can put won't for don't, Miss Lucy. There's none so deaf as those that won't hear. We'd best make up our minds to it and be ready to turn out when Miss Laura gives the word.' She stalked out of the room without waiting for answer.

About ten minutes later Miss Adams, who had returned to her own bedroom, heard a very perfunctory knock which was immediately followed by the entrance of Perry in a state of repressed triumph.

'If I could trouble you, Miss Lucy—'

Lucy Adams was startled and annoyed. She had been caught with her front off, and Perry had eyes like gimlets. From now on every time Perry looked at her she would be seeing, not the decorous auburn waves, but the sadly widened parting which they concealed.

'What is it, Perry?'

'Well may you ask! Seeing's believing, and when you've seen with your own eyes what I've seen, perhaps you'll believe me. When Miss Agnes told me she was asking Miss Laura to come down here, I said to her then, "Miss Agnes," I said, "who brought the trouble into this house – Miss Lilian Ferrers. And if you ask Miss Lilian's daughter here, it's my belief you'll be asking trouble again." '

Miss Adams fixed her front with a couple of hasty pins, and said in a flustered voice which she tried to make repressive, 'What is it? Really, Perry, you startled me very much.'

Perry stood aside from the door.

'You come with me, Miss Lucy, and you'll see for yourself. Nobody's ever called me a tell-tale yet, but seeing's believing. If you'll just step into the octagon room—'

They came into it together, Perry a step behind. Like the room downstairs it was empty of furniture, with a bare floor and the lift on the inner side, but instead of the oak door and the lancet windows of the ground floor there was one large recessed window with a deep window-seat cushioned in red damask to match the curtains.

'Look for yourself, Miss Lucy!'

Lucy Adams came up to the window and looked out. What she saw had been familiar to her all her life. The whole length of the ruined church lay before her, but about a third of the way up the nave Carey Desborough was standing with Laura Fane. They stood by a broken pillar with the grass under their feet and the grey sky overhead. They were not speaking. They were not standing very near together. They were looking at each other. And if they had been strained heart to heart, lips meeting in some ardent kiss, their love could not have been more plainly shown. It was there as a presence, as a fact. It flowed from them and surrounded them. It was in the look that each had for the other. It was tenderness, confidence, passionate gladness, a wellspring of hope. There was no need of word, or touch, or kiss.

Perry said with that note of austere triumph, 'You can see for yourself, Miss Lucy. Miss Lilian all over again – that's what she is!'

A faint familiar sound checked the words upon her lips. She turned, stepping back a pace. Lucy Adams turned too, with the hurried movement of a child caught doing some forbidden thing.

The sound was the sound of the lift gate opening. Agnes Fane's chair came out. She drove it straight to the window, passing between her cousin and her maid without a look at either of them. Sitting there, controlled and upright with a crimson leather cushion at her back, she could see what they had seen. Carey and Laura had not moved. The tranced moment held them.

Agnes Fane looked for as long as you might draw a

breath. Lucy Adams held hers. Her face twitched and she put up her hand to it. But Agnes Fane showed nothing at all. She looked, and then she put her chair into reverse and, turning, went through the open door, across the passage, and into her own room.

EIGHTEEN

IN THE LATE afternoon as the dusk began to fall, Laura escaped to the garden and walked there. She had a longing to be in the cold air and to be alone, and she had a fancy to walk just once, just by herself, in this place which had belonged to so many Fanes and now was hers. She could not feel – she wondered if she would ever feel – that the house belonged to her. It was full of alien thoughts, alien lives – thoughts which rejected her, and lives in which she had no part. But a garden was different. It slept its January sleep, but its thoughts and dreams were its own. They belonged to something older than Agnes Fane – older than any of the Fanes who had walked here, touched its surface with their whims, and passed away. She thought there might be something for her in the garden if she looked for it.

She found grass that was green in a sheltered spot about a sundial scarred with lichen. She could not read what was written on the dial. The words had lapsed into the dumb stone again. She found snowdrops in a drift under a leafless tree. It was cold. She went bare-headed with a coat over her green dress. She found a holly clipped to the shape of a peacock. She found great trees, and thought what they must look like in their summer green.

She was on a path which twisted through the heart of a shrubbery set with rhododendrons, cypress, holly, and all manner of trees and bushes that would be sheeted with bloom in the spring – syringa, lilac, thorn, laburnum, currant, forsythia – when at a turn of the path she came suddenly upon the sound of voices. There was a man's racking sob, and then Petra speaking in a tone muted to utter tenderness.

'Oh, my darling – do you love her so much?'

For the moment Laura was too startled to move. She could not see where Petra was. She could only guess that she and Alistair must be somewhere in the shrubbery, and it was certain that they thought they were alone. She came back from her shocked moment and turned to go. Alistair's voice followed her, suddenly loud.

'Sometimes I think I hate her!'

She put her fingers to her ears and ran breathlessly back along the path until it cleared the trees.

It was when she had gone up to dress for dinner that Petra knocked at the door and came in.

'Was it *you*?' she said without any preliminaries. 'In the shrubbery – just before tea?'

She had been gay and vivacious downstairs. Now she looked pale and determined.

Laura said, 'Yes.'

Petra's face relaxed.

'I thought it was, but I couldn't be sure. I didn't think anyone else would have run away. How much did you hear?'

Laura answered quite simply.

'I heard you ask him if he loved her so much, and I heard him say sometimes he hated her. Then I put my fingers in my ears and ran. I'm terribly sorry, Petra – I didn't mean to listen.'

Petra smiled. It was just a flash, there and gone again.

'I don't mind *you*. It's better when someone knows.'

Laura hesitated. Then she said, 'Do you want to talk about it?'

Petra nodded.

'Yes – it helps – if it's the right person.'

Laura opened her lips to speak, and then shut them again.

Petra laughed at her.

'Go on – say it!'

Laura said it.

'Alistair said he – hated her sometimes. But he is always saying how marvellous she is.'

The red sprang vividly into Petra's cheeks – red flames, and her eyes very bright above them.

'Don't you see, he's got to think her marvellous, or he's sunk. He *minds* about me – about hurting me – about our engagement, and the way he's behaving. He can't just do it and not care. He minds dreadfully. So he's got to think how wonderful and marvellous and beautiful she is, or else there's nothing left. And sometimes he can't hold on to it, and then I've got to be there – I've got to. It isn't because I can't take it, or because I'm trying to keep him – it's for him. She does something to men – they go crazy – something gets wrenched, twisted.' She was very pale again, her voice low and rapid, her eyes on Laura's face. 'Laura, sometimes I'm frightened of what he might *do*—' The last word failed as if her breath had failed. Then with a sudden flashing change she flung her arms round Laura's neck and gave her a light, laughing kiss.

'You're *nice*!' she said, and ran out of the room.

NINETEEN

PETRA CAME IN in her scarlet frock, and the two girls went down together.

'I'm glad you're wearing the same dress again too. But it wouldn't really matter what either of us wore, because Tanis would make it look like something off a bargain counter, anyhow.'

Laura considered the gay little figure and laughed.

'It would be a marvellous bargain counter.'

'Soothing syrup! It's all very well for you, with that lovely Chinese shawl. But you wait – Tanis will go all out tonight. The Madisons are coming.'

'Yes, she told me about them.'

Petra's voice sharpened.

'Did she tell you she was smashing up their marriage, and that Sylvia is pretty well off her head with jealousy, poor kid?'

'No.'

The Madisons arrived early. They came into a room which contained neither Tanis nor Agnes Fane. They seemed to know the Maxwells and Carey Desborough very well. Laura was the only stranger. By the time Petra had explained her Miss Fane was making her entrance, very fine indeed in ruby velvet with the twinkling earrings, and a great ruby and diamond jewel at her breast.

Laura had time to consider the Madisons. She saw a stocky man with a sailor's walk, a hot blue eye, and a perfect conflagration of red hair. He hadn't a tenth of

Alistair Maxwell's good looks, but when he came into the room something came in with him – something daring, resourceful, stick-at-nothing. The nearest Laura got to it was, 'He looks like a pirate.' The little Sylvia was quite eclipsed. She was young, and she had no manner to cover her obvious unhappiness. She had been pretty in a blonde, fragile way, and she would be pretty again when she was happy again. Her looks were not of the kind to stand a strain. She wore a pale blue dress which was neither smart nor very well cut. The colour, which had once been flattering, now emphasised a pallor which she had done nothing to mitigate.

Laura's eye, travelling from her to Petra North, approved her defiant scarlet and the make-up which accompanied it. If you must wear the willow, it is better to carry it gallantly.

Tanis Lyle came in. She wore a white chiffon frock. It was of a breath-taking simplicity, and, as Petra murmured, it had probably cost the earth. It was a young girl's dress. Tanis, wearing it, was a young girl again, her hair in simpler waves, a string of pearls her only ornament. They were all to remember her like that.

She came smiling to the Madisons, laid a caressing touch on Sylvia's shoulder, and bent to kiss a pale averted cheek. Laura had never seen her kiss anyone before. It went through her mind as sharply as a knife that the kiss was a weapon, as surely as the knife itself would have been. The hand, with its emerald and diamond ring, stayed for a moment where it had rested. In that moment Tanis raised her eyes to meet Tim Madison's.

Laura felt rather than saw the spark which leapt between them. She wanted to do something, say something. But it was the entry of Lucy Adams which broke the tension. Flushed with hurry, on the edge of being late, clanking with chains, bangles and assorted brooches, she plunged into the midst of the situation without the slightest idea that it existed.

'How do you do, Sylvia? Are you quite well? You're looking dreadfully pale. You should drink more milk and go to bed early. You really look quite run down. She's quite lost her colour – hasn't she, Tanis? Mr Madison, you should make her go to bed quite early, and she should have a cup of milk at eleven, and another the last thing. You mustn't let her lose her colour, you know. I remember it was the first thing I noticed about her when she came here.'

The gong sounded in the hall as Miss Silver made a composed and unhurried entrance, knitting-bag in hand.

After dinner they rolled up the rugs and danced in the drawing-room. Tanis had all the latest records, and the floor was good. Laura danced with Carey. Tomorrow she would be gone. All day long she had been counting the hours, but now for a little while in Carey's arms she could have wished them to stand still. She said in an almost soundless voice, 'I'm going back to Cousin Sophy tomorrow.

'I'll drive you up.'

'Better not.'

'I'll drive you and Petra then.'

Laura nodded.

'That might do.'

Tanis danced with Tim Madison. Three dances – then one with Carey. And then Tim Madison again. Carey, with Sylvia Madison, saw Miss Fane look up and frown, then back to her game of chess again. Miss Silver had finished her baby's vest and was starting another. Alistair and Petra had disappeared. Laura was dancing with Robin, whom she liked very much. They were laughing.

Sylvia said in a small, tired voice, 'I didn't want to come. He made me.'

'Would you rather not dance? We can go and sit somewhere if you like.'

She shook her head.

'It wouldn't be any good – I should go on seeing them. I do, nearly all the time, you know. I think it's worse when it isn't real, because then I feel as if I'm going queer in the head. Do you think I am?'

'No – of course not.'

'Sometimes I think I must be. I hear them talking – when I'm quite alone. That's why I came tonight. It's better than being alone.'

Carey was desperately sorry for her. 'It won't last, you know – it's just a flare up. Stick it out. She doesn't really want him,' he said very kindly.

They were moving to the rhythm of the dance. Her next words came on a faint fluttered breath.

'He comes up here – to see her – at night—'

'Nonsense!'

'No – it's true. Not last night, because I wouldn't go to bed. He wanted me to, and I wouldn't. We had a *dreadful* row. That's why I'm so tired. It kills me to have rows with Tim. I shall go to bed tonight, and he'll come up here to her.' Her thread of a voice had taken on a kind of dreamy finality. She might have been talking in her sleep.

'My dear girl, you're all in. Get him to take you home early, and go off to bed with the cup of hot milk Miss Adams was prescribing.'

Sylvia said faintly, 'We won't talk about it any more.

Can you think of something to say? Tim's looking at us. I don't want him to be angry. I get frightened.'

Carey began to tell her about Laura.

'The place belongs to her, but I don't suppose she'll ever live here. It's too big. This sort of house was out-of-date after the last war, and when this war's over we'll all be doing quite different things and living quite different lives. The old country house tradition has been dead for a generation. There's nothing left of it except a ghost or two. Laura—'

His voice changed on her name, and Sylvia caught him up.

'Laura – are you in love with her?'

His face changed too, softening, breaking into a smile as he nodded.

'Dead secret. Don't tell anyone.'

She looked up at him, her blue eyes suddenly wet.

'*You've* got away. I'm glad.'

It was a little after this that Alistair came back into the room alone. He had the look of a man under a heavy strain. Even to Laura's inexperience it was obvious that he had been drinking, but instead of being flushed he was exceedingly pale. He walked straight up to where Tanis was standing with Tim Madison and said in a voice which anyone could hear, 'When are you going to dance with me?'

She gave him a fleeting glance, green and bright between black lashes.

'You haven't asked me.'

He said, 'That's a lie!' And then, 'I'm asking you now.'

Her fingers closed about Tim Madison's wrist. She said '*No!*' to him in an emphatic undertone. And then, with her sweetest smile, she said it to Alistair, 'No, thank you, darling.'

Just for a moment the thing hung in the balance – it might blow up, or it might not.

The moment passed. Alistair turned and went out of the room, walking as if he were drunk. Between the opening and the shutting of the door Laura, at an angle to it, caught a glimpse of Petra's scarlet in the hall beyond. The door shut heavily.

As Robin Maxwell put on another record, Miss Fane caught Carey Desborough's eye and beckoned imperiously. He came round to the far side of her chair between her and the fire, because Miss Silver was on the nearer side. She turned, and as he bent towards her she said, not whispering but low and deep, 'Have you and Tanis quarrelled?'

Carey smiled.

'What makes you think so? I was dancing with her just now.'

'Once,' said Agnes Fane. Then, with a further drop of the voice, 'You should be dancing with her now. Mr Madison never leaves her alone. He's making her conspicuous. Go and get her away from him! Whom are you dancing with?'

He thought, 'She knows perfectly well.'

His hand had been at Laura's waist and the music starting when she beckoned him.

He said, 'Laura,' and felt the dark eyes searching him.

'You're very friendly with her all of a sudden.'

He said, 'Yes.'

The dark eyes held his. They were stern. He felt a fixity of purpose, an inescapable will.

He was dismissed.

He danced with Laura, and was solaced. They moved to music which was in their hearts. The moment was a brief, enchanted one.

He danced with Tanis, and was at once aware of a change which took him a long way back in time, and longer still in mood. That hers was heightened, quickened, was plainly to be seen. She had an air of victorious expectancy. It was not for him – he knew that with relief – but it brought a return of her old smiles and glances, a softening of the voice. If he had not been in love with Laura he might have been in danger. Her hand pressed his.

'You're not angry with me? We're friends?' she said.

Carey laughed.

'Excellent friends. That's what you've got to tell your Aunt Agnes.'

She nodded.

'Yes, of course. We mustn't quarrel, must we? We've had good times – let's remember them. But, *darling* – you won't let Laura stick me with this place, will you? She'll listen to you. I'd die if I was tied up here, or else I'd bust the whole place wide open with some frightful scandal.'

'You're doing that now.'

She looked up, vividly amused.

'I know. It's marvellous, isn't it? But that's just what I mean – you dance three times with a man and you're damned in a place like this.'

'Three times—' He smiled agreeably.

That pleased her too. He thought to himself, 'Good Lord – has she gone off the deep end about the fellow?'

She said in a melting voice, 'Poor Tim! There's nothing in it, you know – just Irish fireworks. Too amusing – while it lasts—' Her voice went suddenly down and away.

The music stopped. She stood leaning against him, her hand still on his arm, and shivered.

Carey said, 'Cold?'

Her fingers tightened and clung, then let go. She stepped back, smiling and shaking her head.

'Somebody walking over my grave,' she said.

TWENTY

THE EVENING ENDED. Alistair had not returned. Petra came back to the drawing-room about twenty minutes after Laura had seen her in the hall. She stood for a moment with Carey and Laura, and said lightly, 'Alistair's walking it off. He'll come back like a lamb. How bad was it? Did he make a scene?'

Carey said, 'It might have been worse. He called Tanis a liar, and marched out of the room when she wouldn't dance with him. I don't think Miss Fane heard what he said.'

'Someone's bound to tell her,' said Petra briefly. 'Let's look on the bright side. They've had some awful row, and he's fit to cut her throat. Perhaps they won't make it up.' She gave a small forced laugh and added, 'What a hope!'

The Madisons made their farewells and went out into a cold windy night. 'Blowing up for rain, but it won't come before morning,' was Tim Madison's comment as a swirling gust came in at the open lobby door. He took Sylvia by the arm, and they went off together to walk the quarter of a mile between the Priory and their cottage.

By ones and twos the others said good-night and went upstairs, Robin Maxwell last with Alistair, who walked in without explanation or apology at a little after one. The house quieted. There were no sounds except the wind like a rising tide coming out of the distance and thundering by, rocking the straining trees, beating against the ruined church, dying to a moan, and then hurling itself against the house in some tremendous gust of sound.

Laura slept, her last waking thought relief because the visit was over. She would look back on it and remember only that Carey and she had found each other. And everything else – the strain, the old cousins disliking her, Tanis – would all be forgotten. She did not know that they would never be forgotten by her, by Carey, or by anyone else.

She woke some time late in the night, coming suddenly broad awake, and remembering that she had left her Chinese shawl downstairs. It seemed so odd to wake up like that and remember it, when she had not thought about it at all before she went to sleep. She had come upstairs with Petra, but they had not talked. She had undressed, and got into bed, and gone to sleep without ever remembering the shawl. And now it filled her mind, urgently and to the exclusion of everything else. She thought, 'How silly – but I shan't go to sleep again unless I go down for it.'

She got out of bed without putting on a light, because the curtain was drawn back from a partly-opened window. It blew in the wind, the casement creaked. But the thunderous gusts had ceased. The gale had passed. There was no more now than a high wind blowing. She found her dressing-gown and slippers, put them on, and came out into the corridor. A light burned dimly at the far end.

Laura went the other way, towards the stairs, holding the banister rail and feeling before her with a slippered foot. Once round the turn, there was a glimmer of light from the hall.

She considered where the shawl might be. The drawing-room . . . No – she had had it after they all came out of the drawing-room, because she remembered Robin looking at it and saying something about one of the embroidered butterflies. He was keen on butterflies and he knew this one's name. Well, if she had had it in the hall, why hadn't she taken it upstairs? It came to her that she had left Robin standing beside the newel, turning the embroidery this way and that, butterfly hunting, while she said good-night to Lucy Adams and Miss Silver. And then Petra had caught her by the arm with a quick, 'Come along, Laura!' and she had gone up without giving another thought to the shawl, because she was afraid that Petra had suddenly come to the end of what she could bear – ghastly under her make-up, and a hand shaking on Laura's arm. The shawl just went right out of her mind.

And now she could think of nothing else. She thought how odd that was. But when she came to the newel where Robin had stood, the shawl wasn't there. It wasn't anywhere in the hall. She switched on the lights and looked everywhere. It wasn't in the hall, and it wasn't in the drawing-room. Robin must have put it somewhere. He might have taken it upstairs. She began to feel rather silly, hunting for a shawl in the dead end of the night, and quite sure that it wouldn't go down at all well with Cousin Agnes and Cousin Lucy.

She switched off the lights and began to climb the stairs. The big hall clock struck three. She regained her own room with relief.

There is something strange about being the only person awake in a sleeping house. It is all right if you are in your own room, but to go out and wander in untenanted places while those to whom they belong are withdrawn in sleep is the loneliest thing in the world.

She stood inside her door and closed it softly. Standing there in the dark for a moment before she turned away, there came to her, faint but unmistakable, the sound of another closing door.

TWENTY ONE

AT TWENTY MINUTES past eight next morning Dean, the butler, came out of the north wing and entered first the dining-room and then Miss Fane's study in order to draw the curtains and admit the slow, cold beginning of the day. It was still so dark that he switched on the dining-room light and left it burning. The actual moment when the black-out regulations allowed of an uncurtained light was 8.24. He considered that summer time extended to the winter was doubtless of use to people in towns who hoped to get home before the nightly air-raids began, but that it was very inconvenient not to be able to open up the house before pretty near half-past eight.

Continuing on his way, he came to the hall. He crossed it and opened the door of Miss Lyle's sitting-room, switching on the light as he did so. The room sprang into view, the wide window facing him and the two other windows which looked towards the front of the house all curtained in pale silvery green. The heavy folds hung straight and still. But from somewhere there was a cold wind blowing, and it didn't take him more than a moment to tell where it was coming from. The door to the octagon room stood in at an angle, and through the half-open doorway the wind was blowing.

It was at this moment that Dean became alarmed. Because there oughtn't to have been anything open in the octagon room. The windows had been closed all day, and the door had been locked when he made his round after Mr and Mrs Madison had gone and Mr Alistair had come in. With the idea of burglars in his mind, he cast an anxious glance about the room, and noticed that the top drawer of Miss Lyle's bureau had been pulled out. He went over to look at it and saw, tumbled into the corner upon a pile of letters, a small automatic pistol. He considered it to be the pistol which Mr Hazelton had so carelessly fired off in the hall the other night, breaking a sconce which was going to be very difficult to replace. Drunk, of course, but that wasn't any excuse for frightening ladies and destroying property. As he had told Mrs Dean at the time, 'If a gentleman can't behave like a gentleman when he's drunk, well, to my way of thinking he's no real gentleman at all.'

He frowned at the pistol and thought Miss Tanis was a bit too casual, leaving firearms about like that. Suppose there'd *been* a burglar, or one of those German parachutists – well, she was making them a present of it, as you might say.

He left the curtains and went through into the octagon room. The wind met him. The door to the church stood wide. The grey daylight came in, and that cold wind blowing. He stood at the top of the steps and looked down. Something was lying there. The steps ran down to the angle between the house and the west wall. The shadow made it difficult to see – it was still nearly half an hour before sunrise – but something was lying there. No, someone. A woman. He began to feel cold and a little sick.

He went down the steps, going slowly because he was afraid – only going at all because it was his duty, and he had always tried to do his duty.

He came to the floor of the church . . . Yes, it was a woman. It was Miss Tanis, and he thought she was dead.

She was wearing those black pyjamas which had always rather shocked his sense of what was right and befitting in a young lady, and her black dressing-gown over them, and she was lying on her face with her right arm flung out as if she had pitched forward off the steps.

His mind felt stupid and stiff. It went through it to wonder whether she had walked in her sleep, and so fallen. He wondered whether she had broken her neck.

And then he saw the hole. A small round hole in the silk of her coat a little below the left shoulder-blade. Everything inside him seemed to turn over. He went down on his knees because they were giving way, but after a moment he reached for the out-flung hand and lifted it and felt the wrist for the pulse which he knew very well would not be there. As soon as he touched her he knew that it would not be there.

He laid the hand back on the grass and got stiffly to his feet. His duty sustained him. It was his duty to notify the police that Miss Tanis Lyle had been murdered, and when he had done that, to break the news to the household.

He went back up the steps into Tanis Lyle's sitting-room and rang up the Ledlington police.

TWENTY TWO

THE FIRST STUNNING shock was over. The dreadful routine which waits on murder ran its accustomed course. Police surgeon, fingerprint expert, official photographer, played their parts and went away. Finally, all that was left of Tanis Lyle went away too, in an ambulance.

The superintendent from Ledlington, Randal March, sat in Miss Fane's study checking over the statements which he and Sergeant Stebbins had been taking. He was a tall, good-looking man in his middle thirties, with a pleasant, cultivated voice and a manner in which authority was agreeably veiled. The eyes, the line of the jaw, the set of the head, asserted its presence, but the pleasant veil was there – for as long as he desired it to remain.

Miss Maud Silver, entering the room, was very warmly received. She addressed the superintendent, to Sergeant Stebbins's edification, as 'My dear Randal', and enquired affectionately after his mother and his sisters. In fact, compliments were exchanged. Sergeant Stebbins was sent to interview evacuees who might possibly have heard the shot, and Miss Silver took a chair.

In the days when she was a governess she had been governess to Randal March and his sisters. Her friendship with the family had been maintained. Some three years previously Randal March had had to confess that he owed his life to her skill and acumen in the rather horrible case of the poisoned caterpillars. And they had been very closely associated in the autumn of '39 over the mysterious Jerningham affair. But in spite of these up-to-date contacts his first sight of Miss Maud Silver invariably carried him back to the days when she was the unquestioned dispenser of law and knowledge to an inky little boy with a marked distaste for acquiring information or for doing what he was told. In spite of this distaste he had learned and he had obeyed. Respect for Miss Silver had entered into his soul. He found it there still.

As she took her seat and extracted some pink knitting from a brightly-flowered work-bag, he reflected that the years which had made him a superintendent of police in a country town had apparently left her quite unchanged. She must have been much younger in those old schoolroom days, but she had not seemed any younger to him then than she did now. She had always been terrifyingly intelligent, conscientious, sincere, religious, dowdy, and prim. She retained a pristine passion for knitting, and for the poetry of Alfred, Lord Tennyson, and his contemporaries. She was a perfectly kind and just human being and a remarkably good detective.

With a mind hovering between old and well-merited respect and an amusement which in no way detracted from it, he sat back in his chair and responded to enquiries about his family.

'Margaret is in Palestine with her husband. She managed to get out there at the tail end of '39. The little girl is with my mother.'

Miss Silver nodded. 'She is very like Margaret. Mrs March kindly sent me some snapshots.'

'And Isobel has joined the ATS. In fact, you may say that I am the only member of the family who is not in the Army.'

Miss Silver coughed in slight reproof.

'The enforcement of law at home may, I think, be considered quite as important to our war effort as anything that Isobel or Margaret may be able to do,' she remarked. Then, changing the subject briskly, 'This is a terrible affair. I am very glad to have an opportunity of talking to you.'

'And I to you. I have most of the statements now, and I should be glad to know how they strike you.'

Miss Silver knitted in silence for a minute. Then she said, 'I was sorry to miss you the other morning when I was in Ledlington. The note I left for you informed you that I was staying at the Priory. I think I must now tell you that I am here professionally.'

'*What?*'

In that faraway schoolroom Miss Silver would have reproved this unadorned ejaculation. She let it pass.

'This is of course in confidence. Miss Fane would not wish it to be known.'

Randal March looked concerned.

'But I'm afraid I must ask you—'

'Oh, yes – I was about to explain. Lucy Adams is an old schoolfellow of mine. I used to visit here when I was a young girl, but after I had entered the scholastic profession my time was so much occupied, and my interests so very different from Lucy's, that the acquaintance – it was hardly a friendship – faded away. We had met no more than a dozen times, I suppose, in the last twenty years when I came down to stay with dear Lisle Jerningham and she very kindly asked Lucy to tea. Lucy appeared to be much interested in my change of profession, and later that evening I was rung up by Miss Fane. She asked me to come over and see her, which I did next day – there is quite a convenient bus. She told me that small thefts of money had been taking place in the house, and that suspicion was being cast upon the evacuee families she had taken in. She was extremely anxious that the matter should be cleared up. She asked me whether I would undertake it professionally. I did so.'

Randal March smiled.

'And solved the problem?'

Miss Silver said, 'Yes,' in rather a grave tone of voice.

He looked at her shrewdly.

'Not one of the evacuees then?'

She shook her head.

'Oh dear, no.'

He was conscious of a rising interest.

'Are you going to tell me who it was?'

She laid down her knitting for a moment and looked at him.

'I think so, Randal – I think I must. But it is for your information only.'

'What do you mean by that?'

'I mean that you are not to make a police court case of it – it is not to be dealt with in that way. If there had not been a murder in the house, I should not have mentioned it, but after what has happened I do not feel justified in withholding any information however remote.'

He said, 'You're quite right. You had better tell me. I won't use the information unless it bears upon the murder. Who is the thief?'

Miss Silver got up and went to the door. As she opened it, Miss Fane's maid, Perry, went past, carrying a small tray. The smell of coffee floated in. Randal March saw the tall, stiff figure in grey go by.

Miss Silver closed the door and came back to her seat. In a very much lowered tone she said, 'Perry.'

'You mean that that was Perry who went by? Miss Fane's maid, isn't she?'

'No, I don't mean that at all, Randal. I mean that Perry is the thief.'

'What! I thought she'd been here for donkey's years.'

Miss Silver took up her knitting again.

'Oh, yes – forty-one years of devoted service. She worships Agnes Fane.'

'And pilfers from her!' He looked and sounded incredulous.

Miss Silver coughed.

'It is not quite so simple as that. She does not like having the evacuees here. The thefts were planned to lay them under suspicion and to bring about their removal.'

'What a mind! Are you sure?'

'Oh, yes. But I have not told Miss Fane. I should have done so today, because, having accepted the engagement, I should have felt it to be my duty. But I had no expectation that she would believe me. She has an extremely rigid type of mind.'

Randal frowned.

'I haven't seen her yet, or Miss Adams. I suppose you have. How are they taking it? They were devoted to the poor girl, weren't they?'

The term struck Miss Silver as incongruous. With time at her disposal she could have moralised upon the theme – Tanis Lyle with the ball at her foot come down to that pitying 'poor girl'.

She gave a faint dry cough. 'I have not seen Lucy – I believe that she is quite prostrated – but I have just come from Agnes Fane. Shall I tell you how I found her?'

He said, 'Yes,' in a voice which showed a trace of astonishment.

She paused briefly to take up a stitch, and then continued. 'She was writing a letter to her solicitor.'

'To her solicitor?'

Miss Silver nodded.

'He is a Mr Metcalfe, an old friend of the family. But she was not writing to him as a friend. Her letter pressed him to push forward without delay the negotiations which he is carrying on with Miss Laura Fane for the purchase of this property.'

Randal March was really startled. He said, 'My dear Miss Silver!' and there for the moment words forsook him. She nodded, and went on knitting.

After a short pause he said, 'Well, you've answered my question. Devoted!' He gave a short laugh. 'It hardly seems to be the right word – does it? I suppose it's about three hours since she heard of her niece's death!'

Miss Silver raised her eyes to his face.

'You must not misunderstand me, Randal. It would be perfectly true to say that Agnes and Lucy were devoted to Tanis Lyle. They built their hopes on her. She meant everything to them that they had missed themselves. Especially to Agnes. To her, I think, she also represented a weapon.'

'What do you mean?'

Miss Silver paused for a moment. Then she said, 'How much do you know about Agnes Fane?'

'I suppose what everyone in the county knows – that she was jilted by her cousin – that she rode her horse over Blackneck quarry and has been a cripple ever since. It's too dramatic a story to be forgotten, isn't it?'

'Yes. It has never been forgotten. Agnes has never forgotten it.'

'It must have been a long time ago.'

'Twenty-two years. I was staying in the neighbourhood at the time. I knew Mr Oliver Fane and the girl he eloped with – a Miss Ferrers. She was a cousin also. They were very charming people. It made a terrible split in the family. From that time I believe that Agnes has had but one idea – to acquire the property, which would have been hers if she had married Oliver Fane, and to divert it from his daughter to Tanis Lyle.'

'The daughter being Laura Fane, the girl who is staying here now?'

'Yes. She is just of age, and she has not seemed very much inclined to sell. Agnes asked her down here in the belief that she would be able to influence her. She is a woman of strong will and inflexible purpose.'

Randal March made a sudden movement.

'Now, just why are you telling me all this?'

'My dear Randal!'

Miss Silver's tone expressed reproof, but he shook his head.

'You have an ulterior motive. What is it?'

Her needles clicked.

'It is a very simple one. A violent crime has been committed. As I am familiar with the background against which the motives and actions of everyone in this house must be viewed, I thought it my duty to give you some impression of it.'

He said, 'I see—' And then, 'Miss Fane is still set on purchasing the property? Why?'

'To divert it from Laura Fane. You know that Tanis Lyle had been married? There is a child, a little boy of six. If she could buy the Priory, Agnes would adopt him and bring him up to succeed her.'

Randal March looked at her meditatively.

'Surprising thing human nature – isn't it? Yes, I knew of the marriage. The husband is, of course, this Hazelton fellow who figures in the shooting affair of the previous night. I've got five statements about that – Desborough, the two Maxwells, Laura Fane, and the butler, Dean. Now what have you got to say about it?'

TWENTY THREE

MISS SILVER GAVE him her account of Jeffrey Hazelton's brief meteoric eruption into their midst. It was lucid and remarkably to the point. Randal March, with the sheaf of statements in his hand, glanced sometimes at them and sometimes at her. When she had finished he said, 'H'm – yes. No difference of opinion as to the facts. What did you make of the fellow? Was he really dangerous? Or showing off? Or just too drunk to know what he was doing?'

Miss Silver considered.

'All three, I should say,' she said then.

'Would you like to amplify that?'

She took a moment. 'He is still very fond of her, and he has a grievance. I gather that he has been seeing a certain amount of her lately. He spoke to her the other night at the Luxe. I believe he asked her to dance, and that she refused. It would have made her rather conspicuous, though I do not know that she would have cared about that. He evidently followed her down here. The Maxwell brothers saw him drinking at the Angel some time before dinner. Then a good deal later he came up here. He was drunk, and obsessed with his feelings and his grievance. He was out of his own control and on the edge of a collapse.'

'You think that he might have shot her then?'

'Undoubtedly. He had the pistol actually pushed against her chest and his finger shaking on the trigger.

If she had shrunk away from him, or cried out, or done anything to stimulate his nervous excitement, he would, I am quite sure, have shot her then. She behaved with great coolness and presence of mind.'

'And you don't admire her for doing so. Will you tell me why?'

Miss Silver dropped her knitting in her lap and looked at him.

'I never saw anyone show less feeling,' she said. 'Even a stranger would have experienced some pity for Mr Hazelton – he broke down so completely, sobbing, and saying her name over and over. And she had not a thought for him. She was excited, pleased – almost openly triumphant. I considered it a very painful exhibition.'

Randal March laid down the papers he was holding.

'Your sympathy seems to be entirely with the criminal,' he said drily. 'Rather unusual for you, isn't it?'

Miss Silver picked up the pink infant's vest she was knitting, measured it carefully against her hand and wrist, and began to cast off. She said then in a quiet, serious voice, 'I should be very much surprised to learn that Mr Hazelton was the criminal.'

Superintendent March did not exactly start, but he came very near to doing so.

'I should have thought it was sufficiently obvious.'

Miss Silver coughed and said, 'My *dear* Randal!'

He laughed, but he changed colour.

'Well, you know that nine times out of ten the obvious person really is the criminal.'

She repeated the cough.

'I would not put it as high as that myself. But even with one chance in ten I consider it inadvisable to close the mind to other possibilities by assuming one obvious person's guilt.'

Incontinently his mind went back some twenty-six years. In the dock – in this case his father's study – Randal March aged nine and a month or so, accused of stealing plums from old Gregory's orchard and very much the obvious criminal. Miss Silver, then as now, declining to accept the obvious, sticking it out, proving her point, bringing Isobel, the real culprit, to repentance, getting him off – all in the primmest, driest manner imaginable, without fear or favouritism.

He turned an affectionate and respectful look upon her now.

'You'll admit, I suppose, that Hazelton is a suspect. I'll be interested to know why you won't consider him as the murderer.'

She cast off a couple of stitches.

'I think he might very easily have shot her on Wednesday evening. But he was seen off to London next day by Mr Desborough and Mr Robin Maxwell. I do not find myself readily able to believe that he returned that same evening, induced Miss Lyle to admit him to the Priory, and then shot her in the back – she was shot in the back, was she not?'

'Oh, yes. Why do you think he wouldn't do it?'

The pink stitches were dropping evenly and methodically from the needles. Miss Silver said, 'He was very fond of her, very much in love with her. It would have required some strong stimulus to make him shoot her. She would have had to be facing him – quarrelling, or arguing, or resisting him. I feel quite sure that he would not have shot her in the back.'

As she spoke, the door opened. The maid Perry stood there. Seeing her full face for the first time, March found her one of the least attractive of the female sex. Such a flat, ironed-out figure. Such a fleshless, bloodless face. And those pale eyes.

She kept a hand on the door, long, thin, and bony, and said with a certain acid restraint, addressing the superintendent, 'Miss Fane will see you now.'

If he expected a 'sir', he didn't get one. He never would from Perry. The police were the police. They had their work to do, and it was better not to get on the wrong side of them, but they were, and remained, the dirt beneath the feet of Miss Agnes Fane.

'Thank you. I will come up in a moment. Miss Silver will show me the way. You need not wait,' he said in a pleasant, authoritative voice.

When she had gone and the door was shut, he said, 'I haven't been able to find anyone yet who heard the shot. I must have everyone asked whether they heard it. When we go up I want you to go in to Miss Adams and just ask her that one question. Will you do that?'

Miss Silver broke off her wool, passed the end through the last stitch, and drew it tight. She put the needles and the completed vest into her knitting-bag and rose to her feet.

'Certainly, my dear Randal.'

They came up the stairs and turned into the corridor.

'In the rooms on the right,' said Miss Silver, 'are, first, Laura Fane, then Miss North, with a bathroom between. Then Miss Lyle, another bathroom, and the octagon room, which, as you see, juts out into the corridor. On the left there is first a bathroom. Then Lucy Adams, another bathroom, a small room occupied by Perry, and Agnes Fane's room, which is much larger than any of the others. Of all the people in the house she is the most likely to have heard the shot, since her room has two windows looking that way. It is, in fact, barely possible that she did not hear it, whereas Lucy is very unlikely to have done so. There are three rooms between hers and the side of the house where the murder was committed, and I happen to know that she would not dream of having a window open at night at this time of the year. But if you wish me to ask her whether she heard anything, I will do so.'

'If you don't mind.'

Miss Silver tapped at the door and, receiving no articulate reply, opened it and went in, leaving it ajar behind her. She found herself in a confusing pink dusk, the curtains being completely drawn across both windows. As she advanced towards where she knew the bed to be, a voice came to her choked with sobs.

'Who is it? I can't see anyone – I *can't*!'

Her eyes adjusting themselves to the semi-darkness, Miss Silver made out the bed and, prostrate upon it, Miss Adams, her face half-buried in the pillows. She said in a kind, firm voice, 'I am not come to disturb you, my dear Lucy. I am sure you know how much I feel for you in your grief. The superintendent has deputed me to ask you a question. He has no wish to intrude upon you, but it is his duty to find out whether there is anybody in the house who heard the shot. Perhaps you will just tell me whether you did hear anything.'

Miss Adams sobbed into the pillow. A hand was laid gently but firmly upon her shoulder.

'Come, Lucy, you have only to say yes or no. Did you hear anything?'

The head turned. The eyes blinked against tears. The weak voice said, 'Not a shot – how could I – the windows were shut – I didn't hear any shot—'

Something in the faint, wavering emphasis upon the twice-repeated word made Miss Silver say quickly, 'You didn't hear the shot? Did you hear anything else?'

As soon as the words were said they seemed absurd, for what else was there to hear?

Lucy Adams became still and rigid under her hand. Then she pushed the hand away with violence.

'I can't talk about it – I can't! You mustn't ask me! I can't tell you – I can't tell anyone!'

Miss Silver came out of the room and shut the door behind her.

'You heard what she said, Randal?'

'Yes – no shot – but something else. It seems to have had a very upsetting effect. I wonder what it was.'

Miss Silver said without any noticeable expression, 'She is greatly upset. It has been a severe shock. But she will be better tomorrow. You can question her then.'

TWENTY FOUR

RANDAL MARCH FOUND himself a good deal impressed by Miss Agnes Fane. She was sitting in a large armchair beside her bedroom fire. The curtains were drawn back and the light came in. There was none of the disorder or dishevelment of grief. She sat upright and composed, her hair in its accustomed waves, a string of pearls relieving the plain black of her dress.

He received a slight inclination of the head and a request that he would be seated. She understood that he desired to see her, but she was afraid that she could do very little to assist the course of justice. Her voice was deep and strong. She spoke with authority and condescension. But though she carried it with an air she was plainly a woman who had received a very great shock. She held her head high, but the tension of the throat muscles were to be discerned. The hand which had laid down the pen at his entrance now rested upon the wide arm of her chair. The finger, slightly curved, had an appearance of rigidity. One of them wore a very fine diamond solitaire.

He put his question and received his answer.

'No – I heard nothing.'

His eyes went to the two south windows, one on either side of the bed. They came back to her expressionless face.

'You are a sound sleeper, Miss Fane?'

There was a faint flicker of a smile.

'A very poor one, I am afraid. So poor that I am sometimes obliged to take a sleeping-draught. I did so last night. I am an invalid, you know.'

She might have been claiming some prerogative. He felt a slight unwilling amusement. Pride, yes – but pride in her own disability? He thought Agnes Fane had been made for better things than that.

He rose to go, but she detained him with a lift of that rigid hand. The diamond flashed.

'Has he been arrested?'

'There has been no arrest as yet. May I ask whose arrest you were expecting?'

A spark like contempt came into her eyes. He found it galling.

'Whose arrest? Why, the murderer's. Has no one told you that Jeffrey Hazelton would have shot my niece on Wednesday night if she had not saved herself by her own courage and presence of mind? He is, of course, not responsible for his actions and should have been placed under restraint. I am very much to blame for not having insisted on it.'

'You think Mr Hazelton returned here last night, and that it was he who shot Miss Lyle?'

Again the contempt which set him definitely in the moron class.

'I should say it was obvious.'

He said a little stiffly, 'Mr Hazelton has naturally not been overlooked. He will have to give an account of his movements after leaving here. I am expecting a call at any time now. You may be quite sure that everything is being done, Miss Fane. But the surgeon's report and that of the ballistics expert will have to be taken into consideration.'

She regarded him for the first time with interest.

'If the bullet had been fired from the pistol which was taken from Jeffrey Hazelton on Wednesday night, the expert would be able to prove it. That is what you mean?'

'Yes. A bullet is marked by the rifling. No two firearms would mark a bullet in quite the same way.'

Her face changed.

'That proves nothing in this case. He may have shot her with that pistol, or with another one. It proves nothing. He had another.'

'Yes, I remember – Desborough mentioned that in his statement. Miss Lyle said so – didn't she?'

'Yes.' Her hand clenched on the arm of the chair. Before he could speak she said in an insistent voice, 'Mr Desborough was engaged to my niece. Did he mention that in his statement?'

If Randal March was surprised he contrived not to show it. It had certainly not occurred to him to regard Carey Desborough in the light of a bereaved lover. In their short interview he had displayed the gravity and concern of a friend, but nothing more.

He said, after what he hoped was not a noticeable pause, 'No, he didn't mention that. Was there an engagement?'

'Yes – they had had an understanding for some time. The engagement would have been announced shortly.'

After a moment he said, 'Why do you tell me this, Miss Fane? Are you suggesting jealousy as a motive for the crime? Was Mr Hazelton known to be jealous?'

She said, 'I don't know.' And then, 'My niece obtained her divorce for infidelity. Mr Hazelton had no rights where she was concerned.'

Well, he had obviously had feelings. There was no more to be said. He took his leave.

As he passed thc maid Perry's door it opened and she came out. Her pale eyes dwelt on him with a flicker of something which he thought was dislike. She said in her acid voice, 'I'd like to have a word with you if it's convenient.'

TWENTY FIVE

CAREY AND LAURA walked across the field when the day had slipped into afternoon. As far as the light went, it might have been any time between dawn and dusk – low cloud, no visible sun; no colour in sky, or grass, or hedgerow; a desolate greyness everywhere. It was cold. Not with the stinging cold of wind or frost which whips the blood to the cheeks. The wind was all gone, there was no frost. The path was soft and miry. A chilly damp which might be fog by nightfall oozed from the ground and clung about them. But it was better than being indoors. Here at least they could be alone together and could speak freely.

'It's frightful in the house – like being shut up in the dark, you don't quite know what's there.' Laura's voice was still hushed, as if it hardly realised its freedom. 'I wouldn't mind if one could be any use to anyone, but one can't. They'd be thankful to be rid of us. How long do you think we shall have to stay?'

'For the inquest – and the funeral. The Maxwells' leave is up on Sunday night. If the inquest isn't tomorrow, I suppose they'll have to come back for it. I don't know how long these things take.'

'Nor do I. It will be a good thing for the Maxwells to get away. Alistair looks awful, doesn't he?'

'A dozen murders and he's done them all. It's just as well everyone's so sure it's Hazelton. Petra and Robin have dragged Alistair out. I don't envy them their walk.

But it's no use his mooning round, setting everyone talking.'

'No – they had to get him out. But I don't know about us – I've got a feeling that we oughtn't to have come.'

'What harm is it doing anyone?'

She managed rather a piteous laugh.

'*Darling* – there are such heaps of things that don't do any harm and you can't do them, because it simply isn't worth upsetting people like Cousin Agnes and Cousin Lucy. I don't think we're really supposed to go out before the funeral. Aunt Theresa's like that, so I know.'

Carey said something sharp and short. He added that they would have to go to the inquest anyway, so as well be hanged for a sheep as a lamb.

'Anyhow, there's no sense in our all being boxed up there together till we go off our heads.'

Laura nodded.

'Carey, it's frightful – isn't it? I don't mean just about Tanis, but what it does to everyone else. If you speak, you feel as if someone was listening at the door. Perry *does*, you know – Petra says she's practically caught her at it. And Cousin Agnes frightens me.'

Carey slipped an arm through hers and held it close. Comforting to feel that strong arm and the rough thickness of his coat.

He said, 'Have you seen her?'

A little shiver ran over her as she said, 'Yes.'

'When?'

'Just now, when I went up to get my coat. Perry came and knocked on my door and said Cousin Agnes wanted to see me. And there she was, with boxes of things she had had sent out from Ledlington – mourning, you know. And she gave me a black dress – I've got it on – and said she would be glad if I would wear it. She said she didn't expect me to go into mourning for a cousin whom I scarcely knew, but she thought it would be better for me to be in black as long as I was at the Priory. She thought I should have to stay for the inquest, and that she would appreciate my presence at the funeral. It was all frightfully grand and condescending. And right at the end she said that this wasn't of course the time to talk about business, but she would like me to realise that her plans with regard to the Priory were unchanged.'

'She didn't!'

'She *did*.'

'She still wants to buy it? Now – after this?'

He felt her shiver again.

'It's frightful, isn't it?'

'It's a bit inhuman. What will you do – let her have it?'

'Oh, *yes* – anything she wants! And I'm thankful she wants it. We couldn't live there, could we – not now – not ever?'

He said in a meditative voice, 'I suppose not—' And then, with a lively change of manner, 'It doesn't matter where we live, does it? But let's plan it. There isn't any Hitler and there isn't any war and we're getting married next week – what sort of house shall we have?'

The cold, dark current which was carrying them sank away out of sight. Their raft of make-believe hid it for one of those short enchanted hours which make amends for all. That it was still there, that its tide rocked the very fabric of their happiness, that its spray would presently chill them to the bone again, they knew, but for the moment they did not greatly care. There was so much to give, to learn, to share – all those inner treasures of the heart which are increased by such a giving.

They made a wide circuit and were coming home, when a solitary walker passed them at no more than a twenty-foot distance. It was Tim Madison, walking fast and furiously, hands deep in the pockets of a Burberry. He was bare-headed. The red hair flamed. His chin was thrust out and his face lifted. His eyes, blank and blue, stared at the sky. He looked like a blind man, or a man walking in his sleep. He went past them without a sign and on down the reaches of the field.

Carey said, 'Poor devil – he's taking it hard.'

TWENTY SIX

'YES, RANDAL?'

Miss Silver advanced into the singularly bleak room which was so much more like an office than a lady's study. The floor, doubtless for the convenience of Miss Fane's invalid chair, was quite uncarpeted, and the furniture, for the same reason, restricted to such stark necessities as a wide, plain table, some book-cases, and a number of filing-cabinets standing flat against the walls. At ordinary times it also contained a couple of straight-backed chairs. To these a writing-chair had now been added for the superintendent's use.

He looked up at the sound of his name and said abruptly, 'You were quite right – he didn't do it.'

Miss Silver altered the angle of one of the upright chairs and sat down.

'If you are alluding to Mr Hazelton, Randal, I believe what I said was that it would surprise me to learn that he had returned here last night. He did not seem to me to be in a condition to pursue any course of action which would require premeditation. I suppose from what you say that he had an alibi.'

'An alibi!' He lifted a hand and let it drop again upon the table. 'It is more than that. It is a cast-iron physical impossibility. He was taken off to a nursing home raving with DT at about eight o'clock yesterday evening, and he's been there, strapped down to his bed and under a strong narcotic, ever since. Short of a criminal conspiracy on the part of a highly respectable doctor, the matron, a sister, and at least two nurses, it simply couldn't have been done. Holroyd saw them all. Saw Hazelton – took someone along to identify him. And there we are. You were quite right – it was too easy, too obvious. Now perhaps you will oblige by being right again and telling me who *did* murder Tanis Lyle.'

She said soberly, 'I don't know, Randal.'

He had a quick sardonic smile for that.

'You surprise me! Who had a motive then? Perhaps you can tell me that.'

She said, 'No—' in rather an absent voice.

'What! You can't tell me anything?'

'I did not say that. I think a good many people might have had a motive.'

'You mean she had enemies – a beautiful young woman like that?'

'Oh, my dear Randal!' She looked at him very much as she had been used to look when he broke down in the multiplication table. 'I mean that she made enemies. I would not go out of my way to disparage the dead, but you should, I think, know something of Tanis Lyle's character. She was brought up to consider nobody but herself. Agnes and Lucy denied her nothing. She was extremely attractive to men, but they only attracted her in so far as they ministered to her vanity and self-esteem. Her aunts were very anxious that she should marry again, but she did not wish to do so. She had just completed a film over here, and she was ambitious of a career in Hollywood. She was one of those people who have a violently disturbing effect on other people's lives and relationships. The French, I believe, call a woman like that *une allumeuse*. It is not difficult to imagine that this might have provided a motive for her murder.'

He said, 'Love – jealousy – well, it is possible. Do you know of anyone who was in love with her, or jealous on her account besides Hazelton, with his opportune DT?'

Miss Silver paused.

'If I answer that question, Randal, you must not think that I am accusing anyone. I am not. I am not even suspecting anyone. I am only informing you of the relationship existing between Tanis Lyle and some other people in this house and in the neighbourhood.'

He smiled.

'You are always scrupulously just. I won't read anything between the lines of what you tell me – if I can help it. I may not be able to help it, you know.'

'I do not ask for impossibilities. I can give you some facts, or what I believe to be facts, based partly on my own observation and partly on what I have been told. Alistair Maxwell has some understanding with Petra North. It is, I gather, of long standing, and until recently they were exceedingly happy. For this Lucy is my authority. They are now terribly unhappy.'

'On account of Tanis Lyle?'

'Just so. Miss North remained devoted – Mr Alistair was quite obviously infatuated with Tanis. That is one case. There are also the Madisons – Lieutenant Commander Madison and his wife, living at Grange Cottage about a quarter of a mile away. You probably have their names already, as they dined and spent the evening here last night. Mr Madison appeared to me to be head-over-ears in love with Tanis. She danced with him nearly the whole evening, and his wife and Mr Alistair were both in a state of jealous misery.'

'Yes, Maxwell left the house, didn't he – went for a solitary walk? It's in his statement. I thought it odd at the time. But he had returned, I think, before the murder was committed.'

'If you know when the murder was committed.'

'He is said to have returned at a little after one o'clock.'

She nodded.

'That is correct. I heard him come upstairs with his brother. My room is just across the passage.'

'And Tanis Lyle was last seen alive during the general good-nights at twelve o'clock. The time's not long enough. She had undressed and got into those fancy black pyjamas. They'd never have risked an assignation so soon. Practically everyone would have been still awake at half-past twelve, and you'd have to put the meeting some time before that – time for them to meet, for them to quarrel, for him to shoot her, to wipe the pistol, the door handles – there were no finger marks on either – and then find his way over her dead body and out through the ruins, and come in, as he did, by the front door. I say the time's too short. It couldn't have been done then. Besides, somebody would have been bound to hear the shot.'

She said, 'The wind was very high. But I agree about the time – it must have been later than that. And I have no suspicion of Mr Alistair. I am merely telling you that he was infatuated with Tanis Lyle.'

He said quickly, 'Miss Fane told me she was engaged to Carey Desborough.'

Miss Silver shook her head.

'I don't think so.'

'She was quite positive about it.'

'Agnes is always positive.' Miss Silver's tone was dry. 'She is unable to believe that circumstances may be too strong for her. If she sets her heart on anything, in her opinion the matter is settled. It is, I believe, what is termed wishful thinking.'

Randal March surveyed her with a faintly quizzical smile.

'Having been at some pains to describe Miss Lyle as such a dangerously attractive woman, why are you so sure that Desborough wasn't in love with her?'

'Because he is in love with Laura Fane.'

'Oh – and what makes you think that?'

Miss Silver coughed.

'Love and a cold cannot be hid. It is, I believe, a Spanish proverb.'

'You are sure?'

'Oh, yes. They really do not trouble to hide it. A most attractive couple.'

His smile became a little more pronounced.

'Your well-known partiality for lovers! Would it surprise you to learn that Desborough had a serious quarrel with Miss Lyle on Wednesday night, and that the quarrel was about Laura Fane?'

'It would not surprise me in the least,' said Miss Silver. 'I saw them leave the room together, and they were away for some time. But I would like to know who told you that they had quarrelled.'

He made a face.

'Perry – the complete eavesdropper. Well, I shall see Desborough when he comes in.'

Miss Silver got up.

'I should believe very little that Perry says,' she observed.

March laughed.

'I am not biased in her favour. What about Desborough? Is he to be believed implicitly?'

Miss Silver smiled too, with rather a charming effect.

'According to David all men are liars. I am afraid that our profession does not incline us to disagree with him.

But I may at least say of Mr Desborough that I do not think he has had much practice in lying, or that he would be able to do it at all convincingly.'

Making her exit on that, Miss Silver proceeded upstairs to Miss Fane's room.

She found Agnes Fane in the armchair by the fire with a book on her knee, but she did not think she had been reading it, for she had the impression that the eyes which were turned upon her entrance had been dwelling upon a still vividly remembered past. It seemed to her that Agnes came back from it with a reluctant effort.

She took the opposite chair and proceeded at once to her errand.

'I hope you will not consider me inopportune, but I think you ought to know, without any further delay on my part, that the work for which you engaged me has been done.'

Miss Fane regarded her with some surprise.

'Oh, that?' she said. 'It was not important.'

Miss Silver coughed.

'It is not always easy to say what is important and what is not. In this case the reliability of a witness may be in question.'

Agnes Fane said, 'I see. So you have found out who has been pilfering. Who is it?'

'Your maid, Perry,' said Miss Silver.

If she had expected denial or opposition she was to be surprised. Miss Fane's hand rose slightly and fell again upon the arm of her chair.

'How exceedingly tiresome,' she said.

'You are not surprised?'

The pale lips moved into a smile.

'I have known Perry for forty-two years. I don't think you could tell me anything which would surprise me. She dislikes my having evacuees here. I suppose she hoped I should blame them for the thefts and take steps to get rid of them. That would be quite in character.'

'Yes. May I ask you what you intend to do?'

Miss Fane raised her finely-arched eyebrows.

'I shall let her see that I know. She will not do it again. By the way I suppose you are quite sure?'

'Oh, yes. I talked to her about the thefts. She said you were distressed about them, and allowed a good deal of animus against the evacuee families to appear. She asserted that they came prowling into the bedrooms when the family was in the drawing-room and the staff at supper in the servants' hall. I told her that I intended to mark some money and leave it on my dressing-table. I let her see me do it. You will perhaps remember that on Tuesday night I left the drawing-room as soon as Dean had removed the coffee service. I went up to my room. The money was still on the dressing-table. I stood behind the curtains and waited. Presently Perry came in. She stood listening for a moment. Then she picked up the money and went out again. She will, I am sure, have found an opportunity of hiding it in one of the rooms occupied by the evacuees.'

Miss Fane said, 'I see.' And then, rather abruptly, 'This is Friday. Why didn't you tell me before?'

'I did not wish to upset you just as you were expecting a party of Tanis's friends. As they were only coming down for a couple of nights, I thought it would be better to wait until they had gone.'

'That was very considerate.' The deep voice had a note of irony.

Miss Silver drew herself up as she replied, 'I did what I thought best. But now that my professional engagement is at an end—'

Miss Fane interrupted her with energy.

'Who said it was at an end? I most certainly did not.'

Miss Silver coughed.

'I do not quite—'

She was again interrupted.

'Oh, yes, you do – you understand me perfectly. What? Do you think I take steps to discover a petty theft, and stand aside and do nothing when my niece has been murdered?'

Miss Silver contemplated her with calm.

'The police—' she began, and heard an angry echo of the words.

'The police! Grinding their own axe and keeping their mouths shut! Keeping me in the dark – *me*! Have you seen the superintendent? Do you know what he came up here to tell me not half an hour ago?'

'I think so.'

Miss Fane stared at her.

'He came up to tell me that Jeffrey Hazelton is out of it. He was fool enough to suppose that it would be a relief to my mind.'

Miss Silver said quietly, 'If you think of the child, Agnes, it *should* be a relief.'

The white face went rigid for a moment. There was some strong control. She said more quietly, 'It leaves us in a terrible uncertainty. I wish you to work upon the case as my representative.'

Miss Silver said very seriously indeed, 'Agnes, this is a murder case. I cannot be anyone's representative. I can only work to discover the truth.'

'That is all I am asking you to do. I am asking you to find out who shot Tanis. And why. You may work with the police, or you may work separately. I lay no obligations on you. I ask neither fear nor favour. I ask that the murderer should be discovered – and punished.'

Miss Silver looked at her.

'Have you considered that the murderer may be someone whom you know, with whom you are on terms of friendship, relationship even – a family connection, a member of your household? All these are included among the possible suspects.'

'I am not a fool. I make no reservations. The murderer is to be discovered. Do you accept?'

Miss Silver inclined her head.

'On those terms – yes.'

Agnes Fane relaxed slightly. That same ironic smile just touched her lips.

'If it is Perry, I shall have to find a new maid. It would be incredibly tiresome.'

'Agnes!' Miss Silver permitted herself a shade of reproof.

'And if it is I,' said Agnes Fane, still smiling, 'then Perry will have to find herself a new mistress, which will be almost equally tiresome for her.'

TWENTY SEVEN

THE CURTAINS WERE drawn in Miss Fane's study. They were of a handsome golden-brown damask, a shade lighter than the wood-work. In combination with the glowing fire – the police are always handy with a fire – they made the room a good many degrees less bleak. Light came from a bowl in the ceiling. It showed Superintendent March, pleasant but official, at the writing-table, and Carey Desborough facing him across it in as easy an attitude as a hard and upright chair allowed. March had just said, 'I believe you and Miss Lyle were engaged.'

The statement was a little disingenuous. Or perhaps that is putting it too politely, since he believed no such thing. He merely wished to observe Mr Desborough's reactions. They were displayed in a lifted eyebrow and a faint stiffening of manner as he replied to what he chose to regard as a question.

'Oh, no – that's a mistake. There was no engagement.'

The superintendent wondered whether this was a quibble. He said, 'You would prefer to call it an understanding?'

This time Mr Desborough frowned. The expression suited him very well. A fine-looking young fellow, if you liked them on the dark and gloomy side. This was of course not the moment to be wreathed in smiles.

Carey said, 'I don't know where you got your information. We were not engaged, and we had no understanding. We were merely friends.'

March moved some papers which lay at his right hand, bringing one of them to the top and leaving it there.

'My information comes from Miss Fane. She tells me that there was an understanding, and that the engagement would have been announced very shortly.'

Carey nodded.

'I thought so. It's what she wanted, and when she wants anything she makes up her mind she's going to get it. But in this case she was all out – we were just friends.'

'You knew that she had this idea?'

'Oh, yes.'

'Did you do anything to disabuse her of it?'

'No.'

'Why not?'

The eyebrow went up again.

'Not a very easy thing to do. As a matter of fact, I told Tanis she ought to do it.'

'And what did Miss Lyle say to that?'

'She didn't want to at first, but afterwards she said she would.'

'Why didn't she want to?'

Carey frowned. He was aware of delicate ground under his feet. He wanted to tell the truth. But how do you convey the truth about a very complicated situation to someone who knows nothing about it, without embarking on a three-volume novel? You have to eliminate, but what you eliminate is part of the truth. What he wanted to do was to eliminate Laura. Yet as far as he was concerned the whole situation pivoted on Laura. He did the best he could, saying after no more than a momentary pause, 'Miss Fane was very keen on our marrying. She hated the idea of a film career. She wanted her to settle down here and have a family. Tanis was dependent on her. She didn't want to offend her, but she definitely didn't want to marry me or anyone else. If she had told Miss Fane, it would have upset her very much.'

March put out his hand to the paper he had extracted. This time he put it down in front of him on the blotting-pad. 'I don't think you are telling me very much. You haven't, for instance, said anything about a quarrel with Miss Lyle on Wednesday evening,' he said.

'A quarrel?'

'On Wednesday evening at about a quarter to six you left the drawing-room together and went to Miss Lyle's sitting-room, where, I am informed, you had a violent quarrel.'

Carey sat back and put his hands in his pockets. The attitude was an easy one, but the unseen hands were clenched. Fatal to lose the temper. Under the pressure of a very considerable self-restraint his dark skin flushed a little. He said with quite a good effect of nonchalance, 'Violent is a bit strong. I wanted her to tell Miss Fane, and she didn't want to – for the reasons I have just given. We both lost our tempers a bit, but I shouldn't have called it a violent quarrel.'

'No?' March touched the paper before him. 'This statement does.'

The flush deepened.

'Someone listening in? Who was it?'

'Miss Fane's maid, Perry. She came down in the lift, meaning to go out through Miss Lyle's sitting-room to the hall on her way to fetch something or other from the kitchen wing. She says she always comes down that way to avoid the stairs because she's got a stiff knee. Anyhow, she was there in the octagon room when you were talking, and she seems to have heard a good deal of what you said. She says the door was ajar, and she doesn't deny that she listened. Would you like to add anything to your account of your relations with Miss Lyle?' The superintendent's tone robbed the words of as much offence as was possible.

Carey pushed back his chair and stood up. He walked a few paces, stopped, turned, and came and sat down again. There is a time to speak and a time to be silent. The voice of common sense became insistent that this was a time to speak. It is, in fact, better to go than to be dragged. He said, 'All right, I'll tell you the whole thing. There's nothing in it, but when it comes to eavesdroppers you never know how things are going to be twisted. You can have the facts. My people and the Fanes were old friends. My mother used to bring me here when I was eight or nine. Tanis and I were about the same age. My mother died, and I didn't come here any more. I didn't see Tanis again till last summer, then I saw a lot of her. I came down here once or twice when I had leave. Miss Fane was very kind to me. It ended in my asking Tanis to marry me.'

'And she accepted you?'

This was the difficult bit, because he had believed himself to be accepted. It was Tanis who had, a good deal later on, dealt summarily with that belief.

'I thought – I was – encouraged. Afterwards she told me I had been mistaken – she only wanted to be friends with me,' he said.

'How long afterwards?'

'I crashed in October – I was in hospital for a couple of months. It was after I came out.'

'And while you were in hospital?'

Carey was silent. The bitterness of that time came back.

'She came to see you?'

'No.'

'Wrote?'

'No.'

'I see . . . And after you came out of hospital you asked for an explanation, and you were given to understand that you were just a friend? Was there any quarrel?'

'No. We went on seeing each other. I had a lot of time on my hands.'

'I see. Perry says she heard Miss Lyle claim that there was an engagement between you. She says that you wanted it broken off, but that Miss Lyle was not willing to release you.'

Oh, well, it had got to come – he had known that all along. He said, 'That's what I meant when I said things got twisted. If I were Perry I'd swear to every word we said. As it is, I've only got a sort of general impression. I took Tanis out of the drawing-room because I wanted to talk to her. She had shown me as plainly as anyone can that she didn't care a rap for me, but it suited her to let her aunts think that there was some understanding between us. It didn't suit me, because I had fallen in love with someone else – with her cousin, Laura Fane. That's what she was angry about. She didn't want me herself, but she didn't want to let me go.'

Randal March turned a leaf in Perry's statement, glanced down the page, and turned back again.

'I think I had better read you some of this,' he said.

'"*Miss Tanis was talking to him very loving. She called him darling and said they were engaged, weren't they, and didn't he want to make love to her. And he spoke very hard, and said she was to tell Miss Agnes that the engagement was broken off. And she said that would be all on account of Miss Laura – and a bad day she came into this house, the same as her mother, breaking off other people's engagements."'*

March glanced up.

'The last bit is, I gather, Perry's own comment. I don't know whether you would care to add yours?'

Carey Desborough smiled. The smile changed his face quite a lot. He appeared for the moment to be genuinely amused.

'A most ingenious liar, you know. Because nearly all of that's true – with a twist. Tanis used pretty well those words but she wasn't being loving she was being sarcastic. And I certainly didn't ask her to tell Miss Fane we had broken off an engagement – because there wasn't any engagement, and I asked her to tell Miss Fane that there wasn't.'

March returned to the statement.

'*"They began to quarrel very hot about Miss Laura. Miss Tanis said she wasn't any better than she ought to be, and Mr Carey he fired right up, and he said, You'll go too far one of these fine days."'*

'Did you say that?'

Carey nodded.

'Something like that. I told you we lost our tempers.'

'But it wasn't a quarrel?' The superintendent's tone was pleasantly ironical. He went back to the statement.

'*"And Miss Tanis said, I suppose you'd like to murder me? And he said there was nothing he'd like better."'*

He looked up.

'Any comment on that?'

In a split second of astounded realisation Carey saw what those idiotic quarrelling phrases could be made to suggest. He kept his voice cool as he said, 'Perry's got her knife into me – you can see that.'

'Did you use those words?'

'Not those words. As far as I can remember, she said wouldn't I like to murder her, and I said it would be a pleasure. We were both being sarcastic – not quite Perry's line of country. I suppose she doesn't mention that after that I started to go away, and came back to try and make it up?'

'No, she doesn't.'

Carey squared his shoulders.

'Well, I did. We'd been pretty good friends, and we'd had some good times – I said something like that. I didn't want to quarrel with her.'

'And what did she say?'

The dark colour came to Carey's face. He took a longish breath before he spoke.

'She said something pretty foul. I expect Perry's got it down.'

March read from the statement.

'*"Miss Tanis, she up and told him he might have lost his nerve for flying but he'd got plenty when it came to treating her the way he was."*'

'Is that correct?'

Carey met his look.

'Near enough. It got me on the raw. I haven't lost my nerve, but I can't fly yet because I can't judge distances properly. It's coming right, but I've been feeling pretty badly about it, and when she said that, I told her that was about enough, and I went.'

Randal March put down the statement, observing drily, 'So Perry says.'

He was thinking that a woman with a tongue like Tanis Lyle's might very easily get herself murdered, and that it was a good thing for Carey Desborough that his quarrel with her had taken place in the early evening of Wednesday and not on the night of the murder. It would require a very revengeful disposition to brood for from eighteen to twenty hours over a bitter word and then shoot a woman in the back. Unless there had been some fresh provocation. He looked across the table in a meditative manner and said, 'I'm afraid I really can't accept your view of this scene as a mere exchange of sarcasms. On your own showing it seems to me to have been a quarrel, and a pretty serious one at that.'

Carey smiled again with disarming frankness.

'Well, I suppose it was. But it didn't mean a lot, because—' He hesitated and looked appealingly at the superintendent. 'You know, I don't like saying things about Tanis, but I think they've got to be said. As far as she was concerned she could flick that quarrel away, because there weren't any feelings involved. She really didn't care a scrap, but she saw her way to getting something she did care about, and she set out to make the best bargain she could.'

March began to wonder what was coming next. When it came, it surprised him considerably.

'She went to Laura's room that night and offered to do a deal with her. She would square things up with Miss Fane and get her blessing on our engagement if Laura would undertake not to sell the Priory.'

'*Not* to sell it!'

'Yes. She didn't want to be tied up here – she wanted to go to Hollywood. But she couldn't afford to offend Miss Fane.'

March found himself a good deal interested.

'And what did Miss Laura say?'

'She didn't like it. She hadn't made up her mind to sell, but she didn't like the idea of a bargain behind Miss Fane's back. She's about the most honest person I've ever met.'

Randal March had a momentary picture of Miss Laura Fane's steady eyes.

Carey went on speaking.

'She said she must talk it over – with me. Well, we talked about it, but we hadn't come to any conclusion. But I want you to understand that we were both on perfectly friendly terms with Tanis that last day – anyone will tell you that. I danced with her in the evening, and she told me that she wanted to be friends, and that she would tell Miss Fane there wasn't anything in the engagement idea.'

March looked at him.

'That was last night – a few hours before the murder.'

Carey said, 'Yes.'

'You were on friendly terms when you parted – when you said good-night?'

Carey met the look with composure.

'Yes – anyone will tell you that.'

'You said good-night to Miss Lyle in the presence of the others?'

'Yes.'

'Did you meet her again after that?'

'No.' There was the faintest half-hesitation before the word came out.

'Did you see her again that night?'

There was no half-hesitation this time, but quite a long pause. Then Carey Desborough said, 'Yes.'

TWENTY EIGHT

IT WAS SOME time later that Carey was called to the telephone. A woman's voice said his name, but it was so strained and choked that it took him a moment to recognise Sylvia Madison.

'Oh, Carey – is that you?'

'Yes. Good Lord, Sylvia – what's the matter?'

The voice shook, and choked again.

'Carey – I'm – so frightened.'

'What's the matter, my dear?'

She gave a helpless little sob.

'It's Tim – he went out hours ago and he hasn't come back. I'm so frightened.'

He got a vivid flash-back to Tim Madison going past them in the field above the Grange. How long ago? Three hours – three and a half? No great matter anyhow if it hadn't been for his face.

'Yes – I met him when I was out with Laura. All set for a good long tramp, I should say. I shouldn't worry, Sylvia,' he said.

There was a breathless 'Oh!' And then, 'Did he speak to you?'

Carey made his voice as casual as he could.

'Oh, no. He was a good way off. We were coming back. He didn't speak.'

Sylvia's voice became a wail.

'He doesn't. It – it frightens me. He sits and stares and doesn't say anything. And he's been gone for *hours*.'

Carey became uneasily conscious of the fact that a telephone conversation is not always private. If the girl at the exchange was at a loose end she might at this moment be hanging on Sylvia's every trembling syllable. He said, 'Look here, my dear, you've just got the wind up. Whatever it is, he'll walk it off and come home like a lamb. I tell you what, I'll give you a ring about half-past eight, and if everything isn't OK by then, I'll come over. Like me to bring Laura?'

'Oh, no – I mean, I liked her awfully, but – well, perhaps you'd better. Tim might think – oh, I don't know, Carey – perhaps you won't have to come – but do just what you think.' She sounded helpless and distracted.

Carey, a little tickled at the idea that Tim Madison might regard an unchaperoned visit with suspicion, found himself thinking, 'He'd raise Cain if he was jealous. A scene about Sylvia would put the lid on it. I'll take Laura.'

When he called up again, it was to hear that Tim had just come in. In a hardly audible whisper Sylvia said, 'It's all right. Bring Laura some other time. Good-night.'

It was a relief, though he had been looking forward to the walk in the dark with Laura. They had now a perfectly ghastly evening before them – Alistair staring moodily at nothing at all; Robin with a volume of the *Encyclopedia Britannica* in which he read with admirable pertinacity; Petra talking too much, too brightly, and then falling into a distressed silence; Miss Silver knitting placidly and conversing with steady cheerfulness; while he and Laura got what comfort they could from the fact that they were in the same room, and that occasionally their eyes could meet. Everyone was glad when ten slow strokes from the clock in the hall made it decently possible to go to bed. It seemed incredible that it was not yet twenty-four hours since those other good-nights had been said in which Tanis Lyle had had her part. It must have been in everybody's thought, but no one spoke of it – in fact, they hardly spoke at all.

Carey's hand rested for a moment upon Laura's shoulder. The hard pressure said more than words could have done. They went up slowly and in silence to their rooms.

Miss Fane and Miss Adams did not appear at breakfast next day, but by the middle of the morning both were downstairs again, taking up their accustomed routine. Miss Fane's chair made its way to the north wing, where she held her usual interview with Mrs Dean in the housekeeper's room. Tearful sympathy was graciously accepted and then set aside. After the first few minutes there was nothing to distinguish the conversation from that of any other Saturday morning. Miss Fane wished a couple of economy dishes recommended by the Ministry of Food to be substituted for those suggested by Mrs Dean.

'Carrots are extremely rich in vitamins, and this potato and onion curry should be palatable as well as nourishing. We're really most fortunate in having such a good stock of onions . . .'

Mrs Dean agreed as to the onions, but maintained a considerable reserve on the subject of the Ministry's recipes. The dishes, having been ordered, would duly appear, but – 'I'm sure I don't know how they'll turn out, ma'am.'

Miss Fane passed to another subject.

'How is Florrie Mumford doing? Do you find her satisfactory?'

Mrs Dean bridled a little, emphasising a double chin.

Her large fair face lost the look of passive resistance which it had acquired at the mention of an entrée made chiefly of carrots, and became human again.

'Well, ma'am, satisfactory is a lot to say about any girl these days. I've no fault to find with her work.'

'With what then, Mrs Dean?'

'Well, ma'am, it's the way she carries on outside. She's quick at her work, and she don't have to be told anything twice – I'll say that for her. But she's taken up a kind of a giggling friendship with that girl upstairs – Gladys Hopkins, Mrs Slade's sister.'

Miss Fane said, 'Oh, well—' with a dignified indulgence. 'They're only girls after all.'

Mrs Dean tossed a head whose abundant sandy hair was tightly and neatly coiled after a fashion long extinct.

'If it stopped at that—' she said darkly.

Neither of the girls was seventeen. Miss Fane considered it her duty to probe further.

'I don't like hints, Mrs Dean. I think you had better tell me what you mean.'

Mrs Dean responded with alacrity.

'That Gladys, she's off down to the village every evening and doesn't care who she picks up with. I've told Mrs Slade she ought to keep a tighter hold on her, but it's no good – she's a poor thing and the girl's beyond her. Florrie's afternoon out they go off together dressed up to the nines, rouge and lipstick and all. And Florrie's got into a way of being late back. Ten sharp is the rule, and she's been anything five to twenty minutes over it regular. And that boy of hers that brings her home, young Shepherd, he comes right up the drive with her and round to the back door, and the two of them there in the yard, giggling and whispering. If girls wasn't so hard to get, I'd have asked you to give her her notice. But there it is, we might go further and fare worse. And she's good at her work.'

Miss Fane observed that the Shepherds were respectable people, and that she disliked unnecessary changes in her household.

'I asked you about the girl because I passed her in the passage just now. There was something about her expression – I hope you don't find her impertinent?'

Mrs Dean's buxom form appeared to expand. In a few well-chosen words she gave Miss Fane to understand that impertinence from girls was what she never had put up with and never meant to.

This concluded the audience. Miss Fane departed as she had come, in her self-propelling chair. She betook herself to a room not as a rule in use. The study having being allotted to Superintendent March, she had given orders that this small morning-room, which was next to the dining-room, should be prepared.

She found Miss Silver reading *The Times*, and enquired, 'Where is Lucy? I hope she has come down. The longer she shuts herself away, the harder she will find it to come back to ordinary life again.'

Miss Silver assented.

'That is quite true. But it is not so long, Agnes. You must remember that.'

'Am I likely to forget it?' said Agnes Fane. 'But if I can appear as usual, Lucy can too.'

'You have great strength of character,' said Miss Silver. 'But as a matter of fact, Lucy came down just after you did. She is with the superintendent in the study. He wished to see her.'

As she spoke she folded and proffered *The Times*, which was graciously accepted. It was Miss Fane's invariable practice after glancing at the headlines to read first the correspondence and then the three leading articles.

She was half-way through a letter from a gentleman with whom she cordially disagreed, when the door opened and Lucy Adams came in. Like her cousin, she was in black, but in her case the garment had obviously done service before. Shapeless and unbecoming, it had the rusty, battered look peculiar to old mourning. Her auburn front sat slightly awry. Her brooch of Whitby jet was crooked. But her face, though still puffed with yesterday's weeping, was composed, and the reddened eyes were dry. She was straightening her gold-rimmed pince-nez as she entered. It occurred to Miss Silver that there was a faint tinge of triumph in her manner.

'My dear Maud, what a charming man your friend is – the superintendent. An extraordinary profession to choose, but he really is a very charming man. Don't you agree with me, Agnes?'

Miss Fane raised her eyes from the paper for as brief a space as possible.

'I have no doubt that he is an efficient officer,' she remarked, and returned to *The Times*.

It was observable that Miss Maud Silver sat up very straight. There was an unwonted tinge of colour in her cheeks. After pressing her lips together and saying nothing for a moment, she got up and went out of the room.

Across the passage at the half-open study door stood the charming man and efficient officer who had just been damned with faint praise by Agnes Fane. He beckoned to Miss Silver, and she went over to him.

'I was just wondering how I was going to get hold of you. Come along in and listen. I've got plenty to tell you.'

TWENTY NINE

MISS SILVER DID not hurry herself. She took a seat, but her carriage remained extremely upright. Her first remark appeared irrelevant.

'Really, Agnes Fane can be extremely rude.'

Randal March made a good enough guess. He could not help laughing as he exclaimed, 'What – has she been calling me a policeman?'

Miss Silver took no notice of this. She was opening her knitting-bag, from which she produced an embryo bootee. The wool was of the pale-blue dedicated to male infancy, and the pattern intricate. She busied herself with it for a moment before she said, 'Lucy considers you a most charming person, my dear Randal.'

He made a wry face.

'There are people whom I would rather charm. But I'm sorry for her, poor thing. Now listen. The ballistics man says there's no doubt at all that the bullet taken from Tanis Lyle's body was fired from the pistol found in the open drawer of her bureau. The medical evidence is that it was fired on the level from not less than a yard away, and that death must have been instantaneous. You see what that means – she was shot while she was standing at the top of that flight of steps leading to the church. If she had been on one of the lower steps, the bullet would have entered at an angle. She had opened the door, and she was standing there looking out. She could have been shot from the lift, or from the drawing-room, or from the doorway of her sitting-room. A variation in her own position would make any of these possible.'

Miss Silver knitted. Then she said, 'Why should the door have been open?'

'I think she opened it herself.'

'Probably. But why?'

'The obvious answer is that she was expecting someone.'

She nodded.

'And then?'

'I don't know. Someone came up behind her and shot her dead. I don't know who it was.'

Miss Silver frowned.

'She came downstairs to admit someone to her sitting-room – that is what you suggest?'

'Well, it seems obvious.'

'And someone else – I think you did mean someone else – came in through her sitting-room and shot her from behind?'

March nodded.

'Through the sitting-room or the drawing-room, or from the lift. I don't think the drawing-room at all likely – the door was shut and the handle had not been wiped. But there are those three possibilities.'

She shook her head.

'She would have heard the lift coming down. And what about the handle there?'

'Perry's prints all over it. She came down that way as soon as the alarm was given.'

'And the sitting-room door?'

'Dean's prints on the outside handle of the door from the hall. He came in that way. Fortunately he didn't touch the inner handle or any part of the door between Miss Lyle's sitting-room and the octagon room, or of the oak door to the church. The inner handle had been wiped clean. The other two doors had not been wiped. They both show Miss Lyle's own fingerprints. The same with the bureau drawer. She opened it and those two doors herself, but the murderer had wiped the pistol and the inner handle of the sitting-room door. You see the picture that gives – she comes downstairs in her pyjamas and dressing-gown—'

Miss Silver coughed. 'You say the stairs, Randal, but she might have used the lift. Unlikely, I grant you, as even the best-kept machinery will make some sound.'

'She used the stairs,' said Randal March. 'Desborough saw her.'

Miss Silver narrowly escaped dropping a stitch. She said, 'Dear me!'

'Ah! That interests you. It interests me quite a lot. I told you I'd got things to tell you. He says the wind kept him awake and he read till he had finished his book. Then he thought he'd go down and get another. When he came out on the gallery overlooking the hall he saw Tanis Lyle on the bottom step of the stairs. There is a low-powered bulb burning in the hall at night, and he could see her quite well. She was in her black dressing-gown, and she was just stepping down into the hall. She went across it, opened her sitting-room door, and went in. All this I am prepared to believe – he could have no possible motive for making it up. But here we come to debatable ground. He says he went no farther. He didn't want to meet her, so he gave up any idea of getting himself a book and went back to bed. He looked at his watch, and, he says, the time was five minutes to two.'

Miss Silver said, 'Very interesting indeed. But I find no difficulty in believing that he did, in fact, go back to his room. If he had anything to conceal he had only to hold his tongue about the whole episode. It seems to me that he had every possible reason for wishing to avoid an interview with Tanis at such a compromising hour.'

March looked at her.

'Some reasons,' he agreed. 'We know what they were. But there may have been others which forced him to an interview. We have only his own word for it that there had been a reconciliation. I don't know if I told you about that. He says they danced together on the Thursday evening, and that she gave in all along the line – promised to tell Miss Fane there was no engagement and all that. But, as I said, we've only got his word for it. A woman like Tanis Lyle would not allow an open quarrel to spoil her house-party. She might dance with him, play the perfect hostess, and yet be threatening him – or Laura Fane. Perry heard her say something on the lines of "Your Laura's name will be mud." By the way, here's her statement. You had better read it.'

She took it from him, read it through, and laid it down with an expression of distaste.

'The type of witness who would twist the most innocent remark into something sinister,' was her comment. 'It is curious and salutary that hatred should invariably betray itself.'

'Why should she hate Carey Desborough?'

Miss Silver shook her head.

'Not Carey Desborough, Randal – Laura Fane.'

'But why?'

'She has been with Agnes for forty-one years. She was with her when Laura's father broke their engagement to marry Lilian Ferrers. The present situation bears a misleading resemblance to that unhappy affair – she sees Laura as another Lilian. She hates her, and her hatred puts a twist on everything. As Lord Tennyson so truly says, "A lie that is half a truth is ever the hardest to fight." I do not think that Perry can be considered at all a reliable witness.'

He had a quizzical, affectionate look for her quotation.

'No,' he said. 'But Desborough admits to a good deal of what's in that statement of hers. They did quarrel, and he was pressing her to tell Miss Fane that there was no engagement between them. She *did* call him darling and invite him to make love to her. He says that this was sarcasm and over Perry's head.'

'That is very likely. Tanis Lyle had a cynical, sarcastic vein.'

Randal March made a kind of sweeping gesture with his right hand.

'Well, there you are. It's like that all through. He admits the bit about saying he'd like to murder her too, only he says it wasn't a threat, just a sarcasm.'

'I expect he felt like wringing her neck,' said Miss Silver placidly. 'He had considerable provocation according to Perry. But since he restrained himself at the time, I am unable to believe that he went downstairs more than twenty-four hours later in the middle of the night and shot her in the back. That would imply an assignation, and—'

He interrupted her.

'Not necessarily – in fact, not at all. He admits to having seen her go downstairs. Suppose he followed her down, pressed her again about this engagement business – the quarrel flared up. She had a very offensive tongue, you know. That bit in Perry's statement about Laura Fane, and the piece at the end where she twitted him with having lost his nerve – they got him on the raw all right.'

'I am not surprised.'

'Nor am I,' he said. 'Well, it might have happened that way.'

'My dear Randal!' Her tone was one of mild reproof.

'And why not?'

'The door,' said Miss Silver more in sorrow than in anger – 'the door into the church. If she were quarrelling with Mr Desborough, can you think of any reason why she should have opened that door and stood there on the top step with her back to him, looking out?'

He frowned meditatively.

'I can't think of one—'

Her needles clicked.

'Nor can I.'

'But neither you nor I are omniscient. We can't think of everything.'

Miss Silver pressed her lips together. It was not her place to reprove a man of thirty-six, but she considered this use of the word omniscient slightly profane. She allowed the silence to speak for her.

Randal March broke it.

'There's something else,' he said. 'And that's why I called you in. You know I have just seen Miss Adams. Well, she has made a statement which brings Laura Fane into the picture.'

Miss Silver said nothing. Her lips remained pressed together.

He said in good-humoured exasperation, 'Oh, I knew you wouldn't like it – but there it is. I've got to see the girl, and I'd like you to be here, if she doesn't object. She can, of course. Is she likely to?'

Miss Silver said, 'No,' and said no more.

They sat in silence after he had rung the bell. A maid came – a dark-eyed girl with a sidelong look. It was Florrie Mumford, the under-housemaid, the girl Agnes didn't very much care about. She was sent to ask Miss Laura Fane if she would come to the study, and presently Laura came, in the black dress which Agnes Fane had given her.

March said, 'Come in.' And then, 'I want to ask you some questions, Miss Fane, and if you have no objection, I should like Miss Silver to be here. You are not obliged to answer me, and you are not obliged to have Miss Silver here – you can do just as you please about that.'

Laura stood just inside the door, which she had shut behind her. She looked very white, and there were smudges under her eyes. She said in a young, defenceless way, 'Oh, I should like her to stay. And I'll tell you – anything I can.'

He pulled up a chair for her, and she came round the table and sat down there with her hands in her lap. He took up one of the papers which lay before him and said, 'Miss Fane, did you leave your room at any time during the night on which the murder took place?'

She lifted those beautiful candid eyes to his and said, 'Yes.'

'Will you tell me why?'

'Yes. I woke up and remembered that I hadn't brought my Chinese shawl upstairs. I went down to get it.'

'In the middle of the night?'

Something in his tone brought a little colour to her cheeks.

'I know – it sounds silly. But I couldn't get to sleep again. I kept wondering where I had left it, and then I remembered, so I went down.'

Miss Silver knitted steadily, but she was watching them both.

'And where had you left it?' said Randal March.

'Hanging on the newel-post at the foot of the stairs.'

He came in very quick with 'Right, or left?' But there was no hesitation in her reply.

'The right-hand side going down.'

He glanced at the statement in his hand.

'And you went down, and fetched it, and came back again?'

She shook her head.

'No, I didn't fetch it. It wasn't there.'

In a way he was relieved. There had been a moment when he thought she was going to lie, looking him straight in the face with those wide, truthful eyes. Because Lucy Adams had said that Laura Fane came back to her room at three o'clock in the morning, and that she came empty-handed. He said gravely, 'The shawl wasn't there—'

'No, it wasn't there.'

'But you went on looking for it—'

'Yes – in the hall, and in the drawing-room.'

'Not anywhere else?'

'No.'

'Not in Miss Lyle's sitting-room?'

All her colour went, but the eyes did not waver. She thought, 'If I had, I should have found that open door – and Tanis dead—'

He saw a shudder go over her. She said, 'No, I didn't go in there. I was thinking – how dreadful if I had – because I suppose – I should have found her—'

It was disarming, but he must not be disarmed. He said quickly, 'How do you know that you would have found her then? What time was it?'

She wasn't frightened. She was puzzled.

'The clock struck as I was going upstairs. I think it struck three.'

'Then how do you know that the murder had taken

place? How do you know that Miss Lyle was already dead?'

'I suppose I don't. I didn't think about that, but – well, I suppose we all thought – it must have been – earlier than that—' Her voice trailed away, like a voice that is being faded out. When it was quite gone March said, 'I see. You are sure you didn't go into Miss Lyle's sitting-room?'

'Yes, I'm quite sure.'

'You didn't open the door from the hall?'

'Oh, no.'

'Or the door between the drawing-room and the octagon room? You were in the drawing-room, weren't you?'

'Yes, I was in the drawing-room. But I didn't open the door.'

'Why didn't you?'

The question leapt at her, but she only looked puzzled.

'Why should I? I was looking for my shawl. I thought I had left it in the hall, but it might have got back into the drawing-room. I never thought of looking anywhere else.'

He leaned back in his chair.

'You say you thought you left this shawl hanging on the newel-post. Actually, where did you leave it? Where was it found?'

Laura leaned forward. Colour came into her face and into her voice. She said, 'I did leave it on the newel-post – I'm sure I did. And it hasn't been found at all.'

'What?'

Miss Silver's eyes became intent.

Laura repeated her words.

'It hasn't been found at all.'

THIRTY

WHEN THEY WERE alone again March turned in his chair with an abrupt, 'Well?'

During the whole of the time that Laura had been in the room Miss Silver had knitted peacefully. The blue bootee had made considerable progress. The needles had clicked without intermission, but Miss Silver's lips had not uttered a single word. She unclosed them now. 'What do you expect me to say, my dear Randal?'

He smiled.

'What you think. You always do.'

She gave her little dry cough.

'I hope so. But in this case I would rather hear what you think yourself.'

The smile became a thoughtful one.

'A disarming creature. One would say candour itself – or one would have said so if one hadn't taken up this horrid trade. Do you remember Milly Morrison?'

'My dear Randal, any woman would have seen through Milly at a glance.'

'She was a very pretty girl.' His tone was drily regretful.

'And a sadly deceitful one,' said Miss Silver. She picked up her ball of wool, which had rolled under the writing-table, and added, 'Gentlemen are quite unable to believe any harm of a young woman who has large blue eyes. If Laura Fane's eyes were blue, you would not be suspecting her now.'

He laughed.

'Oh, she's got lovely eyes – I grant you that. Easy to look at, and easy to trust. But here we are with a set of awkward facts on our hands. Desborough and his quarrel with Tanis Lyle – a quarrel which drove him into something uncommonly like a threat to murder her. His admission that he saw her go downstairs just before two o'clock on the night of the murder. If he wasn't the murderer he was the last other person to see her alive. But suppose he is the murderer. We don't really know what their relations may have been. We do know that he was breaking with her to marry Laura Fane. Just now when you asked me if I could think of any reason why she should have opened the door to the church, I said I couldn't. It was stupid of me, because there's a perfectly obvious reason. He was threatening her with the pistol, and she had lost her head and was trying to make a bolt for it.'

Miss Silver shook her head.

'If you had seen Tanis Lyle when she was really being threatened with a pistol you would not entertain that idea for an instant. It is quite absurd. She would have faced him without a tremor.'

He said, 'You can't tell – people lose their nerve suddenly – I've seen it happen. But that's just speculation. This' – he took an envelope from a drawer and handed it to her – 'this is evidence.'

She had laid down her knitting. She now opened the envelope and took out a folded piece of paper. It contained a couple of black silk threads about eight inches long. They appeared to be much discoloured. She looked at them gravely and intently. Then, without speaking, she raised her eyes to the superintendent's face.

He said, 'Those threads were found clutched between

the fingers of Tanis Lyle's left hand. The stain is blood. Do they suggest anything to you?'

Miss Silver took her time. Then she said, 'What do they suggest to you?'

The quizzical look just showed, and was gone again.

'Quite a lot,' he said. 'The silk threads . . . My mother had one of those Chinese shawls – she has it still.'

Miss Silver nodded.

'Oh, yes, I remember it. But hers was all white – a very beautiful piece of work.'

'Yes. It had a deep fringe all round it, about eight or nine inches long – in fact, about the length of those silk threads. But, as you say, my mother's shawl is white. Laura Fane's, I suppose, is not, and I suppose you can describe it to me.'

Her needles clicked.

'Oh, yes. It is black, very beautifully embroidered with coloured flowers and butterflies.'

'And it has a black fringe about eight inches deep?'

'Yes, Randal.'

He threw up a hand in an exasperated gesture.

'You can't refuse to look facts in the face just because you have taken a fancy to Desborough and Laura Fane! Desborough was out of his room, and the girl out of hers and downstairs, round about the time when the murder must have taken place. Threads from the fringe of her shawl were between the dead woman's fingers. They are stained with blood. And the shawl itself has disappeared. Why? The obvious answer to that is that it, too, was stained and had to be disposed of.'

Miss Silver looked up calmly.

'And how do you imagine that it became stained?'

'You mustn't think that I am convinced of Desborough's guilt, or of Laura Fane's. I only say they could be guilty.

They had motive, they had opportunity, and those threads from the missing shawl and the fact that the shawl *is* missing are nasty bits of evidence to explain away. As to how the shawl may have got stained, I think that is quite easy. There is a quarrel between the three of them. Laura Fane may have interposed. There may have been a struggle in which these threads were broken off. They were caught in the setting of a ring which Miss Lyle was wearing. Well, she gets frightened and makes for the door into the church. Desborough shoots her, and she falls, as we know she did fall, from that top step. Laura Fane is horrified – I'll grant you that. She runs down the steps, kneels beside the body – someone did kneel there – the grass was all pressed down. When she realises that Miss Lyle is dead she comes back. She is concerned to save Desborough. They wipe the pistol and put it back in the drawer. They wipe the inner handle of the sitting-room door – probably the outer one too, because there are only Dean's fingerprints on it. Then one of them notices that the shawl is stained. What are they going to do about it? What *did* they do? Burned it in the furnace most probably, in which case we may whistle for our evidence, though the disappearance of the shawl is in itself a damning piece of evidence. Laura Fane may have gone back to her room and left Desborough to clear up the mess, or they may have done it together. The only thing we know for certain is that she was neither wearing nor carrying the shawl when she returned to her room. She said so herself, and Miss Adams—'

Miss Silver interrupted, a thing quite against her code of manners. She did it quietly and deliberately.

'Oh, yes – may I hear what Lucy has to say about it? I should be interested.'

He said, 'Of course. It's quite short . . . Yes, here it is. I'll read it to you.'

'Thank you. I am just turning the heel of my bootee.'

He read from Lucy Adams's statement:

'"*It was such a terribly windy night that my sleep was very much disturbed. I kept on waking up. I have a constitutional dislike for the sound of wind.*"' He looked up with half a laugh. 'There was a good deal more on those lines, but I'm afraid I cut it out.'

'Lucy has always been inclined to think too much about her feelings,' said Miss Silver.

Randal March resumed.

'"*My rest became more and more broken. I could only sleep in snatches. No, no, no – I did not hear any shot, I only heard that terrible wind. I became too nervous to stay in bed, so I got up and walked about my room.*"' He looked up again. 'She explained at considerable length that movement and a drink of cold water had a soothing effect upon her nerves and usually enabled her to go to sleep again, but not on this occasion. After walking about her room for a time, she says, she opened the door. The idea was to walk up and down the passage for a change.'

'Lucy has very little self-control,' said Miss Silver.

March went back to the statement.

'Here we are. She says, "*I opened my door and heard a footstep coming from the direction of the stairs. I drew the door to, but left a crack because I wanted to see who it was. At the same time I switched out my own light because I did not wish to be seen.*"'

'Lucy is a prying old maid,' said Miss Silver.

He very nearly laughed. It might not have been forgiven him if he had. He went on reading rather hastily.

'"*I saw Laura Fane coming along the passage from the stairs. There was a light at the other end outside my cousin's room, and I could see her quite plainly.*"'

Miss Silver coughed.

'The bulb is a fifteen-watt, and the passage is forty-five feet long. The distance between the light and Lucy's door would be about thirty feet, I should think.'

He murmured, 'You are always accurate,' and went on reading: ' "*Laura's door is very nearly opposite mine. She came along the passage and went into her room. She was wearing her night-gown, and a dressing-gown over it. She had slippers on her feet. She wasn't carrying a candle, or a book, or anything. I couldn't imagine why she should be out of her room like that, unless she had been meeting Mr Desborough. I was very much shocked at the idea. She went into her room and shut the door. I was so much upset that I was quite unable to sleep.*" '

Miss Silver's lips were firmly pressed together. He looked at her with some amusement.

'Well, that's all.'

'Lucy ought to be ashamed of herself. That is, I am sure, a most unfounded imputation.'

He laughed.

'I'll take your word for it. I don't think Laura Fane and Carey Desborough were indulging in a lovers' meeting. I wish I hadn't to suspect them of anything worse than that.'

Miss Silver put down her knitting and looked at him earnestly.

'Do you really suspect them, Randal?'

He said very seriously indeed, 'I don't know, but I'm going to make it my business to know. And the first thing I'm going to do is to find out what has become of that Chinese shawl.'

THIRTY ONE

RANDAL MARCH HAD done his best to be as good as his word, but he had failed. The house had been gone through with the proverbial tooth-comb, but there was no discoverable trace of Laura Fane's Chinese shawl. With its gaily-embroidered blooms, its butterflies, and its torn fringe, it had vanished as completely as if it had possessed only the fantastic substance of a dream. Police superintendents do not readily believe in the fantastic. March set Sergeant Stebbins and Police Constable Pollock to the loathly task of sorting through the dustbins and the furnace ashes.

'They must have burned it,' he said, encountering Miss Silver in the hall. 'There's about a millionth chance of finding a shred or two.'

He put a hand on her arm and walked with her to the study. When they were inside with the door shut he said, 'We didn't find the shawl, but we did find something else. Look at this.'

He gave her a shred of crumpled paper. She smoothed it out, looked at it, and read aloud, her cool, prim voice making a strange contrast with the scribbled words.

'"*All right, darling, come down to my sitting-room as soon as the coast is clear. Not before one – Aunt A. reads late.*"'

He said, 'There's no signature. Can you identify the writing?'

'Oh, yes – Tanis Lyle's.'

'It's obvious, of course, from the context, but – you are quite sure about the writing?'

'Oh, quite sure.'

She gave him back the note. 'Where did you find it?'

'In the breast pocket of Alistair Maxwell's dinner-jacket.'

'Dear me!'

'It's undated of course. I am going to show it to him and ask him if he's got anything to say about it. You can stay, if he doesn't object. I will explain that you are representing the family.'

Alistair Maxwell objected to nothing. He had the dazed, half-stupefied appearance of a man who is exhausted from shock and lack of sleep. His usually fresh complexion was dull and patchy. His fair hair was rough and his eyes set in his head. They stared at the bit of paper which the superintendent offered him.

'Yes, it's mine. Where did you find it? I thought I had put it in the fire.' He spoke in a dry, toneless voice, standing by the table. His eyes never left the paper.

'This note,' said March – 'it was from Miss Lyle?'

He did not look up.

'Yes. It doesn't matter now – does it?'

'I think it does. We want to know who killed her. This note makes an appointment with you for one o'clock. The time referred to is undoubtedly the middle of the night, because she speaks of her aunt reading late. Have you got anything to say about this appointment? Did you keep it?'

'Yes, I kept it.' The words were drained of expression.

'Would you care to tell me what happened?'

'Oh, yes – it doesn't matter now. We quarrelled.'

'Oh – you quarrelled. Seriously?'

'Yes. She was tearing everything to bits – Petra – me – everyone. It couldn't go on.'

March was looking very grave.

'Mr Maxwell, is this a confession? I must warn you that anything you say may be taken down and used in evidence against you.'

He looked up then in a slow, bewildered manner.

'What do you mean?'

'I think you know what I mean. You can make a statement, or a confession, but it is my duty to make sure that you understand what you are doing.'

'But—'

March said quickly, 'This note has very grave implications – you must realise that. When you admit that you kept the appointment, and that you had a very serious quarrel with Miss Lyle, you come very near to incriminating yourself.'

Alistair's look of bewilderment deepened. He said, 'I don't know what you mean.'

'Mr Maxwell, I am not trying to trap you. I am here to discover who shot Miss Lyle. You have admitted to being with her, and to having a very serious quarrel. Miss Lyle was shot at some time between two o'clock, when she was last seen alive, and the early hours of the morning. The medical evidence suggests that her death took place not much later than three o'clock. You must realise that you are in a serious position.'

The study door was jerked open. Petra North ran in. She banged it behind her and stood against it, eyes and cheeks blazing. She said in a clear, angry voice, 'He isn't! He didn't touch her – he wouldn't!'

March turned.

'You were listening at the door, Miss North?'

She left it and ran to Alistair, linking an arm through his.

'Of course I listened! Can't you see he's ill? How dare you try and bully him? He's ill. I tell you – he doesn't know what he's saying. You might just as well say that I did it. I wanted to, and I said so dozens of times – I expect you could get any number of people to say they've heard me. Because I hated her like poison. But Alistair didn't hate her. Alistair loved her. He's breaking his heart for her this minute. He worshipped her.'

She was quite outside herself, passionate in defence.

Alistair pulled roughly away.

'That's not true!' His voice was thick and unsteady. 'I think I hated her. She'd got me, and I couldn't get away. That's not right – you've got to be able to get away if you want to. She won't let you get away. I expect that's why she was killed.'

March's voice broke in.

'Mr Maxwell, do you wish to make a statement, or – a confession?'

Petra called out in a high, shrill voice, 'No, no, no – he didn't – he didn't do it! I did it – I shot her!'

The whole thing had passed at great speed. They were all standing. Miss Silver had one hand on the edge of the table, leaning on it. At Petra's words Alistair Maxwell took a lurching step forward and slumped down in the writing-chair, his arms flung across the table, his head sunk upon them. The movement was so abrupt, it had almost the effect of a fall. March looked down at him before he turned to Petra.

'You had better sit down, Miss North. We seem to be a chair short. I'll bring one in from the dining-room. You must consider what you have just said, and whether you would be willing to make a statement. I have to tell you that what you say may be used in evidence against you.'

Alistair Maxwell's hands clenched one upon the other. A strong shudder went over him.

Petra said nothing. She remained standing till March returned with the chair. Then she sat down.

When they were all seated March said gravely, 'Now, Miss North – have you considered your position?'

She had lost a little of her look of a kitten at bay, but she was still very flushed, very tense. She said in a defiant voice, 'I shot her. It wasn't anyone else – it was me.'

'And your motive?'

'She was tearing Alistair to bits. I couldn't bear it any longer.'

'I see. Will you tell me just what you did? You went up to your room with the others on Thursday night?'

'Yes, I went up with Laura Fane. We didn't talk. We went to our rooms.'

'Then will you go on from there? What did you do?'

She sat up very straight and stiff with her hands clasped in her lap and said like a child repeating a lesson, 'I got into a dressing-gown, but I didn't undress. I knew it was no good going to bed or trying to sleep – I was too unhappy. I thought about all the things that had been happening, and I couldn't see any way out of them as long as Tanis was alive. I hated her, and wished she was dead. Presently I couldn't bear it any longer in my room, so I went downstairs. There was a light in Tanis's sitting-room. I remembered about the pistol being in the bureau there. I went in. She wasn't there. I got the pistol and went into the octagon room to look for her. I could hear her opening the door there. She had just opened it when I came in. I shot her. She fell down the steps. That's all.'

March said, 'Not quite, Miss North. I should like to

ask you a few questions. When you came down the stairs you were in your dressing-gown. Was it very cold?'

The clasp of her hands had relaxed. She looked at him with some astonishment.

'No – I don't think so – I didn't notice.'

Miss Silver had been watching her intently. A very faint smile now changed the line of her lips.

March said, 'You didn't feel the need of an extra wrap or anything like that?'

'No.' Her tone was a puzzled one.

'You are sure of that?'

'Oh, yes, quite.'

'Well then, you came down the stairs into the hall. What time was it?'

She hesitated.

'I don't know – I didn't notice.'

'You didn't meet anyone?'

'No.'

'Or notice anything at all unusual?'

'No – I wasn't noticing things.'

'You didn't notice whether there was anything hanging on the newel-post at the foot of the stairs?'

Her flush deepened.

'I tell you I wasn't noticing things.'

'You're quite sure you didn't see Miss Laura Fane's Chinese shawl, or handle it?'

'Of course I'm sure. What's the good of all these questions? I've told you I shot Tanis. Isn't that enough?'

The severity of his look had relaxed a little.

'Not quite, I'm afraid. You say that you came into the sitting-room and got the pistol. Where was it?'

There was hardly a pause before she said, 'In the bureau.'

'Yes – Miss Lyle had told everyone that, hadn't she?

But the bureau has a flap, and three drawers. From which of these places did you take the pistol?'

She turned wide, startled eyes on him.

'Come, Miss North!'

She said in a whispering voice, 'I don't remember.' And then, 'It was – it was under the flap – I think.' The last two words were so faint as to be almost inaudible.

March regarded her.

'Well, you shot Miss Lyle. What did you do after that?'

She said with obvious relief, 'I came back to my room.'

His quizzical look showed for a moment.

'As quickly as all that? You didn't go down the steps to make sure that Miss Lyle was really dead?'

Her eyes were wary now.

'I don't know – I might have done—'

'Come, Miss North, you must remember whether you went down the steps or not.'

'I don't know.'

'Well, what did you do with the pistol? Do you know that?'

'I – I put it down.'

'Just like that?'

'I don't know what you mean.'

He was smiling a little.

'You shot Miss Lyle, and you don't know whether you went down the steps or not. And you put the pistol down, but you don't know where you put it. Let me see if I can help you to remember. Do you think you put it back under the flap of the bureau?'

'I don't know where I put it.'

She was frightened now, and afraid of committing herself.

'Do you think you might have dropped it after you fired?'

'I don't know.'

'But you remember opening the flap of the bureau to take the pistol out?'

'Yes.'

'Do you remember opening or shutting either of the doors in the room – the door from the hall, for instance? You came in that way?'

'Yes, I came in that way.'

'Then you had to open that door.'

'Yes.'

'Did you shut it behind you?'

'I don't know.' Her voice had begun to shake.

'Well then, after you had shot Miss Lyle and dropped the pistol – can you remember whether you had to open the sitting-room door to get back into the hall?'

'I don't know. I've told you that I don't know. What does it matter? I've told you I shot her.'

Randal March leaned back in his chair. He said in his agreeable voice, 'Miss North, you've told me a number of things, and most of them are untrue. To start with, you say you saw a light in Miss Lyle's sitting-room. That would mean that the door into the hall was open. Later on you say you had to open this door. Both these statements can't be true. If we are to believe the first of them, we have to swallow the improbability that Miss Lyle had gone into the octagon room to admit a midnight visitor, leaving her sitting-room door open to advertise the fact. I can't manage to believe that myself. If, on the other hand, you opened the door, how do you account for its not having your fingerprints on it? You say you took the pistol from under the bureau flap. You left no fingerprints there either. You don't know what you did with the pistol afterwards, but the person who used it had taken good care to wipe it and put it back in the place from which it was taken, which wasn't under the bureau flap at all. Your trouble is that you're trying to confess to a crime without having the least idea of how it was committed. The person who shot Miss Lyle kept a clear head. Tell-tale fingerprints were all most carefully removed. If you had removed them you wouldn't have forgotten the fact, or where they had been – where the pistol was, or where the murderer finally left it. You did your best, but you couldn't tell me these things because you didn't know them. Fortunately for you it is extremely difficult for an innocent person to prove himself guilty. You see, he doesn't really know enough about the job.'

Alistair Maxwell's head had lifted. He was looking at Petra. She was pale now, her expression one of misery. Alistair said in a sudden loud voice, 'Petra – you *fool*!'

The tears which had been gathering welled up and began to roll down her cheeks. She sat quite still and let them fall.

Alistair got up and came to her. With an arm about her shoulders, he addressed himself to March.

'I'm sorry, sir – she's a damned little fool. But I suppose she thought I did it. I didn't, you know. I'm afraid I made an exhibition of myself just now. It's been a shock, and I haven't been sleeping. I'm all right now. And I can explain about that note. It wasn't for Thursday night at all, it was for Wednesday. If you look at it again you'll see that it couldn't have been for Thursday, because it said one o'clock. Well, the Madisons were coming in on Thursday night. We always dance when they come in, and they never go away until well after midnight – anyone in the house will tell you that. She would never have said one o'clock if it had been for Thursday night.'

Petra turned in her chair with a quick movement and hid her face against his arm.

Randal March got to his feet and opened the door.

'Oh, take her away and pick up the bits, Maxwell!' he said.

THIRTY TWO

AS THE DOOR shut behind them, March turned a half-laughing, half-vexed face upon Miss Silver and saw that she was smiling.

'Well?' he said.

'As far as they are concerned, it is the best thing that could have happened. I imagine that he has been under a very severe strain for some time, and the shock of Tanis's death came very near to sending him off his balance. The counter-shock of hearing Miss North confess to the murder seems to have had a most salutary effect. I am convinced that his attachment to her is of a deep and lasting character. He has been torn in two directions, and has blamed himself bitterly. Miss North is devoted to him. Her confession was of course made on the spur of the moment and is quite ridiculous. You handled her very well indeed, Randal.'

He made her a mock-serious bow, and then came back to gravity.

'You think Maxwell cleared himself.'

'Do not you?'

He shrugged.

'I suppose I do – as a man. As a policeman, I'm not so sure. His rendering of the note is possible, even probable. You know as well as I do that it isn't conclusive. She might have said one o'clock and yet meant Thursday night, if she intended to get rid of the Madisons early. I know they didn't leave till half-past twelve, but then

Maxwell himself had flung out of the house and hadn't come back. She may have meant to tantalise him by allowing the party to run on until after his return. It was Mrs Madison who definitely broke it up, wasn't it?'

'Yes. She had been looking ill all the evening. She was evidently very unhappy indeed about her husband's attentions to Tanis.'

He looked at her sharply.

'Now do you mean anything by that, or don't you?'

Her faint, colourless eyebrows rose a little.

'My dear Randal, I was merely answering your question.'

He smiled.

'So you were. Madison's attentions were marked?'

Miss Silver gave her little cough.

'Extremely marked. They danced together nearly the whole evening. I could see that Agnes was uneasy.'

'She didn't interfere in any way?'

Miss Silver coughed again.

'It depends on what you would call interference. She beckoned to Mr Desborough. I was so placed that I unavoidably caught some of their conversation. She asked him if he had quarrelled with Tanis, and when he said no she said Mr Madison was making her conspicuous and urged him to put a stop to it. It was after that that he did dance with her.'

'I see. Was Maxwell in the room at this time?'

'No. He had already left the house according to Miss North. They were away from the drawing-room for some time together, and then she came back and said that he had gone out.'

March looked up with a glint of humour in his eyes.

'You seem to have had a delightful evening – Madison and Maxwell about as pleasant as thunder, Miss North and Mrs Madison acutely jealous and wretched—' He broke off and came at her with a sudden, 'What about Desborough and Laura Fane – how were they?'

Miss Silver smiled.

'They were happy, and very obviously in love. Laura was radiant, and after he had danced with Tanis Mr Desborough looked radiant too.'

'That is capable of more than one interpretation. It might substantiate his statement that she had promised to set things right for him with her aunt, or it might be taken to mean that a reconciliation of a different kind had taken place, and that she had given him an assignation.'

Miss Silver corrected him with decision.

'Oh, dear me no – it wasn't that. It would be impossible for anyone who saw them together to believe such a thing. I cannot repeat too emphatically that Mr Desborough was most evidently and completely in love with Laura and that if he ever had been in love with Tanis it was entirely a thing of the past. I remember assuring Agnes on Wednesday evening that she was quite mistaken in imagining that there was any warmer feeling between them than friendship.'

March began to put his papers together.

'Well, I accept your judgement on that point. What remains to be disproved is my original theory that Desborough did have an interview with her on Thursday – at the time when he admits to seeing her go downstairs, and when Laura Fane also admits to having been out of her room. I am afraid that they still head my list of suspects, with Maxwell as second string.'

Miss Silver folded her hands and pursed her lips for a moment. Then she said, 'And where does Mr Madison come on this list of yours, Randal?'

He paused, then turned to face her.

'Madison?'

Miss Silver inclined her head.

March frowned.

'Well, the evidence is quite clear as to his having left the house.'

Miss Silver coughed.

'Tanis Lyle's appointment was not with anyone in this house, Randal – I have been convinced of that all along. The fact that the door leading to the ruined church was open is not subsidiary but integral. The door was open because she herself had opened it – and she had opened it because she was going to admit someone with whom she had an assignation. There is to my mind no other explanation of the fact that this door was open, and that she herself was standing there on the top step when she was shot. Now whom was she expecting? Not her former husband, because he was in a London nursing home, strapped down in bed and under constant observation. Not Mr Desborough or Mr Maxwell, because they were both inside the house, and if she had had an appointment with either of them he would have come down the stairs and entered her sitting-room by way of the hall. Then who was it? I do not see how we can avoid the conclusion that it was Mr Madison. I certainly do not assert that he shot her, but I think it is more than probable that he was the visitor she was expecting.'

March regarded her with interest.

'You don't exonerate either Desborough or Maxwell that way,' he said. 'I suppose you know that. In fact, you are providing them with a motive – especially Maxwell. A jealous young man who has followed the woman with whom he is infatuated, only to find that she is opening her door to someone else, might easily lose his self-control.'

'You forget that according to the finger-prints it was Tanis herself who opened the drawer in which the pistol was. The pistol had been wiped, but not the drawer. Tanis's prints were plain upon it. Dean says the drawer was shut when he went his rounds before going to bed. He found it open next morning, and the pistol lying in full view. If anyone except Tanis handled that drawer, it must have been done very cleverly and carefully by a gloved hand or one with a handkerchief wrapped round it, and great care must have been taken not to disturb the existing finger-prints. This would mean both an intention to murder and a knowledge of the exact whereabouts of the pistol. I cannot myself see either Mr Desborough or Mr Maxwell combining the sudden frenzy which prompts a man to murder with this skilful precaution against discovery.'

March made an impatient gesture.

'The fact is, we don't know what happened, and probably we never shall. As for what a murderer will do and won't do, you know very well that a man who is off his balance – and I suppose no one murders unless he is off his balance – is incalculable. You can guess at the actions and reactions of a reasonable human being because reason is a common denominator, but the madman is outside reason – there isn't a common denominator any more, and there's simply no saying what he may or may not do. He swings on to his balance, and he does a sane thing. You say, "Yes, that's in character – that's all right – I might have done that myself." He swings off it, and you say, "I can't fit that bit in – it's all wrong – he wouldn't do that." And yet it may be quite true. The sane, controlled self wouldn't have done it, but the criminal, unbalanced self has done it. There's your explanation.'

Miss Silver smiled indulgently.

'Able but fallacious, my dear Randal,' she said. 'What I was pointing out to you was that we have here the evidence of a controlled intention to murder and, having murdered, to avoid the consequences. I find this incompatible with either Mr Desborough's or Mr Maxwell's frame of mind, or even with what you suppose to have been their frame of mind, on Thursday night. And you do not account for the disappearance of the Chinese shawl.'

March half frowned, half laughed.

'You want to hoist me with my own petard. How like a woman! Because, as you very well know, I did account for it on the supposition that Laura Fane was an accessory either during or after the fact, and that the shawl became stained and had to be destroyed. That is, of course, presuming that Desborough was the murderer. If it were Maxwell, you may have your point – the shawl eludes me. But I am very nearly sure that it wasn't Maxwell, and that the shawl has been destroyed because—'

It was at this moment that a hesitating tap upon the door was followed by its partial opening. Florrie Mumford was disclosed. At Miss Silver's crisp, 'Come in!' she advanced into the room with an odd sidelong movement. Her cap was over one ear, she was smudged with coal dust, and she held a dirty, crumpled-up newspaper in her hand.

'What is it, Florrie?' said Miss Silver in her most governessy tone. Really the girl was scandalously untidy. Mrs Dean ought to pull her up.

Florrie sent a bright, uneasy glance in the direction of the superintendent. He repeated Miss Silver's enquiry.

'What is it? What do you want?'

She came edging up to the writing-table and plumped the newspaper down in front of him.

'If you please, sir, the sergeant and the constable have been going through the ash bins and things—' She paused, her eyes going to and fro, looking at him sideways, looking away again.

He said, 'Yes?' in an encouraging voice.

'They said as how it was Miss Laura's shawl they was looking for. And I didn't say nothing to them – I've nothing against Miss Laura – but it kep' on coming into my mind and I thought as how I'd better bring it along.'

March's hands were on the paper, unfolding it, spreading it out. It was grimed with coal dust. It contained a little ash and some charred fragments of stuff. The stuff was a thick, lustreless black silk with a remnant of ruined embroidery clinging to it here and there. One bright butterfly survived the flames. By some erratic chance his jewelled wings had kept their turquoise sheen.

Florrie pointed with a smudged finger.

'I thought it would be ever so pretty cut out and sewed on again on a ribbon or something, and seeing I'd raked it out of the fire, I didn't think there'd be any harm.'

March's question came sharply.

'What fire did you rake it out of?'

'The drawing-room.' She gave her head a toss. 'I've all the fires to do before breakfast – drawing-room, dining-room, Miss Lyle's room, and this.'

After a good deal of questioning the story emerged, such as it was. Florrie went round doing fires before the black-out was taken down. She was supposed to start at seven, but on the morning after the murder she had been late, very late indeed – so late, in fact, that she had only done the drawing-room and dining-room when the bell went for breakfast in the servants' hall. Shaking in her shoes, she had slipped into the study at a quarter past eight after Dean had admitted the daylight, and was doing the grate there when the alarm was given and the house raised. Because of her hurry in the drawing-room she hadn't taken very much notice of what she bundled into her pan, but it did cross her mind to think there was something odd about the ash, and when she came to turn it out, there were these bits of stuff, and she wondered whatever Miss Laura had been and burned that lovely shawl for, and she thought it wouldn't hurt no one if she was to keep the butterfly, seeing it was put in the fire to be burned and no manner of use to no one.

When she was gone March got up. Face and voice were grave as he said, 'The analyst must have these at once. They're stained – something besides the burning. If, as I expect, that stain is blood, we have the reason why they survived the fire. The wet patch wouldn't burn, and somehow it must have screened the butterfly. Queer how the little things survive, isn't it?'

Miss Silver was as grave as he. She said, 'Yes.'

THIRTY THREE

CAREY TOOK LAURA to the Grange Cottage to see Sylvia Madison after lunch. Tim, it appeared, had been out ever since breakfast – 'and then he only drank some coffee and went off'. Sylvia, on the telephone, was very, very worried.

'It's all a damned nightmare,' Carey said soberly as they walked down the drive – 'and nightmares are a bit outside Sylvia's form. She's rather sweet, you know, and they used to be most awfully happy, but she wants propping, and Tim has let her down flat.'

Laura gave a shaky laugh.

'Darling, am I a chaperone?'

He nodded.

'Tim's as jealous as they're made. If he found me propping Sylvia, there might be the hell of a row.'

There was a sound of tapping footsteps behind them. Turning, they beheld Miss Silver hurrying down the drive in an antique black cloth jacket shaped to the waist and a grey and black checked scarf which only partially covered the coat's own collar of nibbled, yellowish fur. A felt hat, from which she had removed a bunch of purple pansies, was secured by a jetted hatpin of portentous size. She came up with them, holding the scarf.

'Agnes very kindly lent me this, but the ends fly out so. I am not really accustomed to wearing a scarf. My fur collar keeps me very snug, but the colour is perhaps a little bright for present circumstances. May I join you as far as our ways lie together? I thought of paying a call upon Mrs Madison. I fear that she may be feeling very much upset by what has occurred.'

There was a slight dismayed pause. Carey's frown came down. He said bluntly, 'Laura and I were going there. If she is upset—'

Miss Silver broke in brightly.

'Oh, but I should not dream of staying. Do you know, I guessed that you might be going there, and I rather welcomed the opportunity of accompanying you. But I have no intention of staying. I have something of Mrs Madison's which I should like to return to her – that is all.'

Stepping out briskly between two silent young people, she discoursed upon the weather, the beauties of a winter landscape, the difficulties of providing sufficient workers for the land in wartime, the duty of growing as many carrots and potatoes as possible, and, without any appearance of being inconsequent, the loneliness of life in the depths of the country for those who have not been brought up to it.

'Mrs Madison now – she hardly seems to be a country type, if you know what I mean, Mr Desborough.'

Mr Desborough knew very well. Until things had gone wrong for her Sylvia had played at living in the country as charmingly as she had played at being Tim Madison's petted bride. Now the play was done.

He replied briefly, 'No.'

Miss Silver continued her bright conversation.

'No? I thought not. She has too sheltered a look, if I may say so. Of course it is all right when her husband is here, but how does she manage when he is away? The lane between the cottage and the village is a lonely one, and I think she only has daily help, does she not?'

This time it was impossible to be quite monosyllabic. Carey said, 'Yes,' and then added, 'Her sister comes when Madison is away.'

Miss Silver beamed.

'Very nice for her. An older sister, I presume. Mrs Madison looks so very young, and so timid – I really could not imagine her walking about these lanes by herself after dark.'

Carey couldn't either. He said so bluntly.

'She's always lived in a town. They were bombed out of their flat, and she hasn't really got over it. Things frighten her – loud noises, the dark, being alone, all that sort of thing.'

Miss Silver's smile became sympathetic.

'Well, that is just what I thought.'

She went on talking about life in the country until they arrived within a stone's throw of the cottage. Behind her flow of talk she was reflecting that Mr Desborough was a very good-looking young man in spite of a deepening air of gloom – just a little like Manfred, though of course one didn't really *read* Lord Byron's poems, so apt to be coarse, though undeniably witty – when he turned and addressed her.

'One moment, Miss Silver. I don't want you to think me rude, but—'

He paused, and she said, 'Yes?' in an encouraging voice. That this increased his difficulty in proceeding was plain. The dark colour rose. He plunged on in a determined manner.

'The Madisons are my friends – I've known them a long time. Sylvia is a nervous, delicate sort of girl – she can't stand up for herself. She's very much upset about this business. I can't help knowing that you've got some connection with the police—'

Miss Silver coughed.

'Not with the police, Mr Desborough – I am a private detective. Superintendent March is kind enough to allow me certain facilities. He is an old friend, and he is aware that I should not abuse his indulgence. But my position in this affair is that my professional services have been engaged by Miss Fane.'

'And you were going to see Sylvia Madison in your professional capacity?'

Miss Silver paused for a moment before she replied.

'To some extent, yes.' Then, seeing that Carey was about to speak, she stopped him. 'Mr Desborough, I appreciate your point. You are going to see Mrs Madison as a friend. I am paying her a visit of a different character, though I hope not an unfriendly one. You are naturally unwilling to appear to sponsor me in any way by arriving in my company. I propose, therefore, that you and Miss Laura should precede me. You can tell Mrs Madison whatever you please. If she does not wish to see me she has only to shut her door. I shall not force myself upon her. It is, however, my belief that it would be to her own interest to see me. I do not press the point, and I may be wrong, but that is my present belief. If she decides to see me, I should like it to be in your presence and Miss Laura's.'

As she spoke, Carey's mood cleared. He was experiencing what so many of Miss Silver's clients had experienced before, a transition from irritation and criticism to a sense that here was something extraordinarily solid and reliable. He said in quite a different tone, 'Very well, I'll tell her. But she may say no.'

'Dear me, I hope she won't,' said Miss Silver placidly. 'It would really be a great pity.'

Ten minutes later she was entering Sylvia Madison's

drawing-room, the old living-room of the cottage with a bay thrown out and a good deal more light admitted. The low black beams and the deep hearth remained, contrasting with Sylvia's pretty frilly curtains and pale flowery chintzes. Everything except the cottage itself was pathetically new. Lamps, a chromium clock, a shagreen cigarette-box, the ash-trays freshly inscribed, were obviously wedding-presents and of no long standing. Sylvia's grey-blue tweed skirt and hand-knitted pullover were certainly part of her trousseau. She stood, holding tightly to Laura, and gazed at Miss Silver out of terrified blue eyes.

Miss Silver came forward with a small tissue-paper packet in her hand. Look and tone were kind but grave as she said, 'I'm so glad that you have felt able to see me. I think this belongs to you.'

Harmless words and few enough, but they drained the remaining colour from Sylvia's milky skin. She took the packet, let go of Laura, and sat down suddenly upon the couch from which she had risen at Miss Silver's entrance. In a nervous, indeterminate manner her fingers plucked at the paper. A sharper movement tilted the contents into her lap – a stained and crumpled handkerchief with an elaborately-embroidered 'Sylvia' across a corner.

She looked at it. They all looked at it. The stains were of a pale brownish-red like washed-out blood. The sheer linen was a mass of crumples and smears.

Miss Silver sat down upon the couch beside her and said in a crisp but friendly tone, 'That is your handkerchief, is it not? I expect you knew that you had dropped it, even if you were not quite sure of the exact spot. The wind had carried it to where I found it, wedged into a hole in one of the ruined arches.'

Laura said, 'Oh—' It was more a sighing breath than a word. She felt behind her for a chair and sat down.

Carey said quickly, 'Don't say anything, Sylvia – don't say anything at all – don't speak!'

Miss Silver smiled faintly. Her eyes were shrewd and kind.

'I am not trying to trap Mrs Madison,' she said. 'If I were I should not have allowed you to prepare her for my visit.' She turned to Sylvia. 'There are questions that I should naturally like to ask you, but I will refrain. Instead I will tell you how I think you came to lose your handkerchief.'

Sylvia lifted desperately frightened eyes.

'My dear,' said Miss Silver, 'will you not try to be brave? I might have gone to the police with this handkerchief – strictly speaking it was my duty to do so – but I have brought it to you, and instead of trying to find you alone I have been careful to secure the presence of two of your friends. What I have to say will be painful, but it will be better for you, and I think for everyone, if you will control yourself, and listen to me.'

Sylvia's lips moved, but no sound came. She continued to gaze at Miss Silver with the look of a creature that is caught in a trap. She was most desperately afraid, and the thing she was afraid of was coming nearer and nearer. She could neither help nor hinder it. She had just to sit there and see the knife come nearer, nearer, nearer . . .

Miss Silver removed the crumpled handkerchief, wrapped it in its tissue-paper, and began to speak.

'On Thursday night, the night on which Miss Lyle was shot, you left the Priory with your husband at half-past twelve and walked home. You had been very unhappy all the evening because of Mr Madison's attentions to Miss Lyle. Gentlemen are liable to these sudden infatuations.

They seldom mean very much and are usually of short duration, especially when their object is a changeable and unprincipled young woman. But they can be, of course, very distressing. It is very natural indeed that you should be distressed. I have no means of knowing whether you shared this distress with your husband.'

Sylvia shook her head mutely.

'Well, you reached home, and you separated for the night. But neither of you went to bed – Mr Madison because he intended to return to the Priory, and you because you suspected this intention. Shortly before two o'clock Mr Madison left the house and you followed him.'

Sylvia gave a faint gasp.

Miss Silver continued.

'What I should very much like to know is just how much time elapsed before you followed him. I think – indeed I may say – that I myself am sure that the time was very short. I think you would have kept as close to your husband as possible. You are not, I should say, accustomed to being out alone in the middle of the night. I do not ask you to confirm this, I only state my own opinion. When you reached the Priory you had to grope your way into the ruined church. You may have had a torch, but you would have been afraid to use it except in an emergency. I think you most probably had one, and that Mr Madison certainly had. You reached a place from which you were able to see a faint light proceeding from the open door of the octagon room. There was no light in that room, but there was a shaded light in Miss Lyle's sitting-room, and the door between the two rooms was open. From an experiment which I made yesterday I should say that the light was sufficient to enable you to distinguish the figure of your husband. He was either bending over the body of Miss Lyle or kneeling beside it. He may or may not have had his torch switched on. I am unable to say what happened next, or how long you both remained in this situation, but eventually Mr Madison went away. He may have gone into the house first, or he may not, but I think you remained where you were until he had left the precincts. Then you too approached Miss Lyle's body. You may have knelt down beside it – someone did. You may have switched on your torch. All I know for a fact is that you used your handkerchief either to wipe your own fingers which had become stained, or more directly in an attempt to staunch the wound. When you realised that there was nothing you could do you found your way home. It must have been a most terrible and unnerving experience. Mr Madison had some considerable start on you, and you were to all intents and purposes alone. While you were groping your way out of the ruins the stained handkerchief, which was still in your hand, dropped and was carried away by the wind. A downpour of rain occurred towards morning and washed some of the stain away – some, but not all. You reached home exhausted and prostrated. Now, Mrs Madison, I want to give you a piece of information and a piece of advice. I should also like to ask you a question, but there is no need for you to answer it unless you wish to do so. Here is the information. You cannot be made to give evidence against your husband. Most people know that. What is not so generally known is that there is nothing to prevent your giving evidence in his favour. I can see you are afraid that your husband shot Miss Lyle. It seems to me that your testimony might exonerate him. Now for my question. Have you had any explanation with Mr Madison?' She looked shrewdly at the shrinking Sylvia and continued. 'I can see that you have not. Secrets between married people are very disadvantageous. My advice to you is that you resume a confidence which should never have been interrupted. Tell him exactly what you did on Thursday night, and invite him to do the same. That is all, my dear. I will now leave you with your friends.'

THIRTY FOUR

SYLVIA REMAINED GAZING at the door which had just closed behind Miss Silver. She had the look of someone who has seen or heard something which they are quite unable to believe. As Laura came to sit beside her, she turned a little and said in a whispering voice, 'Who is she – how does she know – was she there?'

Laura shook her head.

'She doesn't have to be there. She knows things. I don't know how she does it.'

Carey pulled a chair up close and sat down, bringing himself nearer to Sylvia's level. Her pale hair glinted like silver gilt between him and the light from the big new window – a grey light glancing in under old dark beams.

'Would you like to talk about it, Sylvia? *Was* it like that?' he said.

Her left hand had caught at Laura's. She put out the other to him in a childish gesture.

'Oh, yes! Oh, Carey, how did she know? She must have been there! How did she know about my following Tim and being afraid of letting him get too far ahead – and afraid of getting too near – and afraid to use my torch? Oh, you don't know how awful it was – you don't *know*!' Her hands shook, her whole body shook.

Carey said insistently, 'Look here, Sylvia – did you hear the shot? Don't answer unless you're sure. Take time to think. Did you hear it?'

The trembling ceased. She became rigid. Her voice

went strained and thin, like a fine wire stretched to breaking-point.

'I don't know. I thought – it was someone – shooting. They do. I thought it was that.'

Carey's grasp on her hand tightened.

'Sylvia, listen! Where were you when you heard this shot?'

She said, 'I don't know' again, in a mechanical fashion.

'Nonsense! You must know. You've got to think. Was it while you were in the lane?'

'No – oh, no – it wasn't.'

'No, you wouldn't have heard it with all that wind. You must have been nearer than that – a good deal nearer. Was it before you came to the Priory gate, or after?'

'Oh, it was before,' said Sylvia, coming to life a little.

'Good girl! Keep right on remembering! Where do you think you were when you heard it?'

She pulled her hand away.

'Oh, I remember. It was at the corner, just after the crossroads. Why do you make me remember it? I don't want to.'

Carey and Laura looked at one another. The corner beyond the crossroads . . . In a direct line it was only a few hundred yards from the ruined Priory church. A few hundred yards as the crow flies, but nearly double that distance by way of footpath and drive. And by footpath and drive Tim Madison and Sylvia would have to take their way, since the Priory grounds were enclosed by a high stone wall. Which meant that Tanis Lyle was dead before Tim Madison so much as set foot inside those grounds.

Carey turned back to Sylvia. Her face was working and she had begun to cry.

'Just one more question,' he said. 'Did you hear any

other shot – after you were in the grounds – quite near the Priory – when you were in the ruins?'

'No, no – I didn't. How could I? She was dead. Oh, please, please, *please* don't ask me any more!'

As she sobbed out the words, the door was flung open, and there strode in upon them Tim Madison, his red hair in a shock and his blue eyes blazing. His voice as he enquired what was going on in his house was forcible enough to have dominated a hurricane. That he was in a towering temper was evident. He stood over Sylvia and shouted at Carey.

'What the hell do you think you're doing here, frightening her into fits? You and your tame detective! I met her in the lane, and if I'd known what she'd been up to I'd have broken her neck!'

Carey grinned suddenly.

'That would have been a lot of help, wouldn't it?' he said. 'Don't make more of an ass of yourself than you can help, Tim. I didn't bring Miss Silver here – she came. And I think she came to do you a service. Also if anyone's frightening Sylvia into fits, it's you. We'll be going now. See you later. Come along, Laura!'

Laura had never been readier to go in her life. She pressed Sylvia's trembling hand and, true to her upbringing, sent a murmured good-bye in the direction of an unwilling host.

When the door had shut on her and Carey, Tim Madison swung round upon his wife.

'What've you been saying? Do you hear? What've you said? What've you told them?' The sentences were shot at her like bullets.

Sylvia stared at him, the tears running down. With a smothered ejaculation he caught her wrists and jerked her to her feet.

'Stop crying and answer me! Did you talk to that woman? She's a detective, I tell you! Did you tell her anything? My God, Sylvy – what did you tell her?'

Sylvia stopped crying. The awful silence which had hung between them like a piece of ice was broken. She didn't care how angry he was. He was thinking of *her* – angry with *her* – calling her Sylvy again, instead of making her feel like a ghost, unseen, unfelt, unwanted. His very anger warmed her. Life and loveliness flowed back. She looked at him, not afraid any more, and said, 'I didn't tell her anything. She knew it all. She told *me*.'

The angry colour went out of his face. He said, 'What!' in a voice that choked and failed.

Sylvia nodded.

'She did – really. You can ask Carey and Laura – they were here. And they didn't bring her, you know. They found out that she was coming, and she let them come on ahead and tell me. And Carey said I needn't see her, but—' Her voice began to waver. 'Oh, Tim – I dropped my handkerchief – so when they told me she'd got something she wanted to return to me – I knew – what it was.'

He said sharply, 'Where did you drop it?'

'In the ruins. She found it there. Oh, Tim – it's *stained*.'

'Where is it?'

'She took it away.'

His grasp tightened until it hurt.

'You might have dropped it any time – anywhere. With that wind, it could have blown in from the road. You must say your nose bled on Wednesday while we were out. I'll back you up.'

She shook her head.

'Tim, it's no use. She *knows*. She told me everything just the way it happened.'

'And what did you tell her?'

'Nothing.'

'D'you mean that? D'you mean you didn't say anything at all?'

'I couldn't – I was too frightened.'

'You didn't tell her she was right – anything like that?'

She shook her head.

He held her harder than ever for a moment, and then let go.

'Thank the Lord for that!' he said, and started for the door.

'Tim – where are you going?'

He said, 'To get your handkerchief back,' and went out of the room and out of the house, banging the doors behind him. The house shook and quivered.

Everything round Sylvia seemed to shake and quiver. She sat down again in the corner of the sofa and shut her eyes.

THIRTY FIVE

AFTER ENCOUNTERING THE tempestuous Mr Madison Miss Silver pursued a homeward way. 'Something accomplished, something done,' as she herself might have quoted, had earned, if not a night's repose, at any rate that inner sense of well-being which is the reward of effort.

Entering the Priory, she removed jacket and hat and descended to the morning-room, where she found Miss Lucy Adams sitting close to the window to catch the waning light. On this dark January day there really was little enough to read by after three o'clock in the afternoon.

Miss Adams put down her book in a somewhat self-conscious manner.

'Where have you been, Maud? Not out, surely? Such a bitter day. But of course it does make a break, though it wouldn't do for me to leave the house. People would talk – you know how it is in the country, and you always meet someone when you don't want to. There's a lot of gossip in a village. But you can't just sit, can you, so I took up a book to pass the time a little – but of course one can't keep one's mind on anything, and it's a stupid book really.'

Miss Silver's very serviceable eyes had already informed her that the work in question hailed from the Ledlington branch of a famous library, and that it was entitled *The Clue that Failed*. She remarked mildly that she found a good thriller very enjoyable herself.

'You always liked them, I remember, Lucy, and they have really improved out of all knowledge since we were girls.'

Miss Adams put the book down upon an already crowded table. There was something pettish about the action, and a tinge of the same quality in her voice as she said, 'Oh, I don't know about that. I don't remember caring for them specially. I read them – everyone does – there are such a lot of them. But as for caring for them *specially*' – she gave a jerky little laugh – 'it is Perry who does that. You wouldn't think it to look at her, would you, but if one of my library books is missing, I always know where it has got to. Perry will sit up to all hours to finish a thriller.'

Miss Silver had produced a ball of wool from her knitting-bag, and was casting on the right number of stitches to provide a pink bootee of the same size and pattern as the pale-blue pair which she had just completed. Without lifting her eyes she enquired, 'And Agnes – does she read them too?'

Lucy Adams tossed her head and set her pince-nez straight again.

'She wouldn't admit it if she did, though I don't see that there's anything to be ashamed of myself. Oh, no – Agnes reads all sorts of highbrow books. Dull as ditch-water, I call them. So we each have our own subscription, and if I do find that one of my novels has got into Agnes's room, well, of course it is always Perry who has left it there, and I have to look as if I believed that, which I don't. You know what Agnes *is*.'

Miss Silver cast on another stitch, and remarked in a soothing voice that everyone liked a change now and then.

'Agnes leads a sadly restricted life, poor thing.'

It was at this point that Dean opened the door and announced that Mr Madison would like to see Miss Silver – 'And I don't know if it was right, madam, but I have shown him into the study. He said he had come on a matter of business.'

Miss Silver said, 'Quite right, Dean.' She had a very alert look as she gathered her knitting-bag and her pink ball and crossed the passage.

She found Tim Madison pacing the floor and in no mood to be trifled with by an inquisitive old maid with a taste for amateur detection. Without any preliminaries he explained his presence, using a louder voice than is usual in a private house.

'I have come for my wife's handkerchief. She told me you were putting up some cock-and-bull story about it. I shall be glad if you will exercise your imagination on someone else's affairs. The facts are these. My wife is not strong. When we were out on Wednesday afternoon she had an attack of nose-bleeding. She felt faint, and I had to help her home. Afterwards she missed the handkerchief she had used. It seems that the wind had carried it to the Priory grounds.'

Miss Silver had remained standing, her knitting in one hand, her knitting-bag in the other. She now permitted a very faint smile to touch her lips as she said, 'Does it, Mr Madison?' And then, 'Will you not sit down?'

He was about to refuse, and in no measured tone, when something checked him. He didn't know quite how he had expected her to behave, but not like this. He had made a furious onslaught, and it was met with the complete calm, the poise, the hint of smiling superiority which swept him back to the schoolroom, almost to the nursery. Somehow – by what means, he had no idea – this little dowdy woman put him in his place, the place of a raging little boy confronted by authority. And the authority checked him. As she seated herself after a gentle, leisurely fashion, he jerked one of the upright chairs towards him and straddled it, folding his arms on the back and facing her.

She said, 'Thank you. I do not care to carry on a conversation for long in a standing position. Now, I think, we had better talk. Mr Madison – what makes you so sure that your wife shot Tanis Lyle?'

Only once before in his life had Tim Madison received so great a shock. For a moment his face went grey. The next the blood rushed violently to his head. His ears sang, and the room went round. Through this confusion came Miss Silver's voice, quiet and perfectly kind.

'You are quite wrong, you know. She did not do it.'

His head cleared. The drumming in his ears ceased. He said in a voice from which all the angry ring had gone, 'What did you say? Will you say it again?'

Miss Silver said it again – the same words, the same voice. She had begun to knit. Her manner was as composed as anything he had ever seen in his life. He gazed at her and said with the simplicity which comes after shock, 'How do you know?'

She smiled a little.

'Has she ever handled a pistol in her life? Would she know how to fire one? Would she in any conceivable circumstances have left her home in the middle of the night and come down that dark lane and through these grounds alone? Really, Mr Madison, you should know her better than that. No – what she did was to follow you.'

'She followed me?'

Miss Silver gave him the bright, pleased nod which approves a correct answer from a backward pupil.

'Exactly. She had guessed at your appointment with Miss Lyle. She followed you, keeping as close as she dared. I do not, of course, know how near the house you were when the shot was fired, but I think you must have heard it. In a country district a shot in the night is a common enough occurrence. You probably thought nothing of it at the time, but when you came to the foot of the steps leading to the octagon room you found Miss Lyle lying there dead. I think you must have turned on your torch. Your wife probably saw you there, kneeling over the body, or standing over it.'

He said in a hoarse, changed voice, 'Why do you say probably? Didn't she tell you?'

Miss Silver's needles clicked.

'I asked her no questions, and she has told me nothing. I am giving you the result of my own deductions, but they do not go all the way. I do not, for instance, know whether you went into the house or not. You had had a severe shock. There must have been a moment when you realised that your position was one of great danger, and you made your way home. When you were gone Mrs Madison nerved herself to approach the body. It must have cost her a very great effort. She did not know that Miss Lyle had been shot. She was past reasoning. She thought that she had been killed by you. I believe that it was a womanly instinct which made her overcome her fear in order to see if there was anything she could do. When she found that Miss Lyle was really dead she came away, in what state of helpless terror you can best imagine. She dropped the handkerchief which she had used in an attempt to staunch the wound. Fortunately the wind carried it to a place where it was overlooked by the police but where I discovered it. I say fortunately, because as soon as I found that handkerchief I was able to deduce from it the story which I have just given you, and to feel assured not only of your wife's innocence, of which I never had any doubt, but also of your own – a very different matter.'

He stared at her, his blue eyes fixed and straining.

'I'd like to know how you make that out.'

She was knitting steadily. Half an inch of pink bootee stood out from the needles like a little frill.

'It is very simple, Mr Madison. I have trained myself to observe character, and your wife is not hard to read. She is simple, gentle, affectionate, and timid. When I found her handkerchief I knew that she had been in the ruins shortly after the murder. Only one thing could possibly have brought her there – she had followed you. But she would never have allowed you to get far enough ahead to enter Miss Lyle's sitting-room, quarrel with her, and secure the pistol. You see, there must have been a quarrel, or Miss Lyle would not, after having admitted you, have opened that outer door again. She could only have done so if she had either become alarmed and was trying to escape – an explanation quite at variance with her character – or if she had lost her patience with you and was sending you away. In either case some time must have elapsed. A quarrel does not work up to the point of murder in a moment. By all accounts you were on the best of terms with her during the preceding evening. Now, admitting the necessity for sufficient time for such a violent quarrel to develop, what would your wife have been doing meanwhile? Can you believe for a moment that she would have stood outside alone in the dark? The emotion which was strong enough to induce her to follow you would, I am convinced, have taken her up those steps and into the sitting-room to confront you and Miss Lyle. She would not have stayed out there in the dark alone while you were in a lighted room with another woman – I am quite sure of that. Therefore, Mr Madison, you did not shoot Tanis Lyle. But when you reached home and discovered that your wife was not there and her bed not slept in, and when presently you heard her creep into the house – heard, as I am convinced you must have heard, her terrified breathing and her smothered sobs – you jumped to the dreadful conclusion that it was she who had done so. In your normal state of mind you would never have entertained such an idea. But under the influence of shock we are not normal.'

He said in a humble voice, and with evident emotion, 'I've been the damnedest fool.'

Miss Silver smiled at him kindly.

'Go home and comfort your wife. You will have to take care of her, I think. She has a fragile look.'

He got to his feet and stood there shamefaced.

'I was rude to you when you came in. I'm sorry. Carey said you had come to do us a service. He was right – you've done us a very great one. Thank you very much.'

He was going towards the door, when she called him back.

'Two questions, Mr Madison. You did hear the shot, didn't you? Where were you?'

'Just past the crossroads. I didn't think about it until afterwards.'

She nodded.

'Just one thing more. Did you enter the house?'

He shook his head.

'No – I never thought about it. I was knocked clean out, and then it was just like you said. I thought, "If anyone comes, I'm done."'

She rose on that and offered him her hand.

He said, 'What about Sylvia's handkerchief? Aren't you going to give it to me?'

Miss Silver coughed. Her hand felt small and firm in his. She withdrew it.

'Oh, no, Mr Madison. I shall have to show it to the superintendent. I could not be a party to concealing evidence. But I do hope that he will take the same view of the matter as I do. And now pray go home to your wife.'

A much chastened Mr Madison went home.

THIRTY SIX

RANDAL MARCH SURVEYED Miss Silver with a look which she found quite easy to read. It was, or would have been, severe, if severity had not hesitated upon the brink of expression. She was well aware that for no one else in the world would it have so hesitated. If she had been anyone but Miss Maud Silver, the superintendent would have been telling her very stiffly indeed exactly what he thought of people who concealed bloodstained handkerchiefs discovered on the scene of a murder, and then played a lone hand with two suspects instead of turning the whole matter over to the police. Being not without feminine tact, she showed no disposition to argue this point, presented, as it was, politely but firmly. She even nodded her head and said, 'Quite so' as the official view was expounded, and then addressed herself to turning the heel of the pink bootee. The official remonstrance went past her. Presently it ceased. Randal March allowed himself to relax.

'You seem very sure of the Madisons' innocence.'

'My dear Randal, of course I am sure.'

She spoke without lifting her eyes, and he replied with vigour.

'I wonder what a jury would say about it.'

She did look up then.

'I do not imagine that a jury will ever have the opportunity.'

He allowed himself an exasperated movement.

'Why are you so sure? You say that Madison would not have had time to commit the murder because the wife would have been too timid to let him get far enough ahead of her. But you know, there is an answer to that. He knew the pistol was in her bureau. Two of the statements agree that the fact was mentioned on Thursday evening when the Madisons were here. There may have been such a scene between him and his wife as to make him resolve to put a violent end to the situation. He is the type of man who might do a violent thing.'

Miss Silver shook her head.

'Bad psychology, Randal. Mr Madison would not shoot a woman in the back. He might strangle her if he was sufficiently provoked. It would, I think, require contact to rouse him to the point of murder. Besides, he was most firmly convinced that his wife had shot Miss Lyle. It was this conviction which was almost driving him out of his mind. No – you will find that my solution is correct. It springs from the characters of the people concerned. They are both simple types – he the vigorous, rather primitive male, and she his feminine counterpart, the timid clinging female. When you interview them – I suppose you mean to interview them – you will, I am convinced, find yourself believing in their innocence as firmly as I do.'

He thought it likely enough, but he did not say so. He made instead an impatient movement and said, 'Well, someone shot her, and I mean to find out who it was. If you won't have the Madisons, who is left? Let's get down to it. You won't be any better pleased if I head the list with Desborough and Laura Fane.'

He drew pen and paper towards him and wrote the names upon it in a small, forcible hand:

Carey Desborough. Laura Fane. Motive – to extricate Desborough from an entanglement to which he may have been deeply committed, and which had become intolerable.

Miss Silver's eyebrows rose.

'Is that a motive for murder?'

'It has been, time and again.'

'Men break such entanglements every day, my dear Randal.'

He nodded. 'That is true. But once in a while they break them violently – like this.'

He turned back to his paper and wrote:

Opportunity. They both admit to being up and out of their rooms long after everyone else had gone to bed. Laura Fane was seen returning to her room at 3.00 a.m. Desborough puts his time at 1.55, but we have only his word for it. LF's shawl disappeared that night. Two threads from the fringe caught on Miss Lyle's ring. Blood-stained fragements found among ashes of drawing-room fire.

Repeating aloud what he had written, he added, 'The stain was blood, you know.'

Miss Silver knitted unperturbed.

'So I supposed.'

'Well, it doesn't look too good for Desborough and Miss Fane – does it?'

'Appearances are often extremely deceptive. Pray continue your list, Randal. It is most interesting.'

He wrote:

Alistair Maxwell. Motive – jealousy. Opportunity – undated note making assignation 1.00 a.m. or later found in his dress clothes. Admits he kept appointment and quarrelled with deceased, but states it was on the previous night.

He looked up again.

'A case could very easily be made out against Alistair Maxwell. You saw the condition he was in. Are you going to tell me he mightn't have shot Tanis Lyle if he had come in upon her and found her on the point of admitting another man?'

Miss Silver unwound some of her pink wool.

'No,' she said. 'In those circumstances he might have shot her. But I do not see how they could have arisen. Tanis would not have invited Mr Madison if she already had an appointment with Mr Maxwell. The fact that she was expecting Mr Madison bears out Mr Maxwell's statement that her note to him referred to the previous evening. Added to this, if Mr Maxwell had been worked up to the point of murdering her he would have been quite past undertaking the cool removal of finger-prints – and, as I said before, the burning of the shawl is not explained.'

'Miss Lyle might have been wearing it. Say she felt cold when she came downstairs, and picked it up.'

Miss Silver's pink ball dropped and rolled. He bent to pick it up. She said equably, 'But why should Mr Maxwell burn it? I can see no motive at all. It would not compromise him.'

'No.' March laid a finger on the names at the top of the list. 'No. There it is – you've said it. The shawl could compromise no one except Laura Fane. Only she, or someone acting in her interest, had a motive for destroying it.'

Miss Silver said, 'I wonder. Pray go on with your list, Randal.'

He wrote:

Petra North. Motive – quite strong. Opportunity – the same as that of everyone else in the house. Obviously bogus confession – made on spur of moment to divert suspicion from Maxwell.

Tim Madison. Motive – none so far ascertainable. Opportunity – admits to having assignation with her that night. Says he found her already dead. Denies entering house.

Mrs Madison. Motive – jealousy. Opportunity – her blood-stained handkerchief found in ruins. Admits to being there and to having touched the body, but says she followed her husband and found Miss Lyle dead.

Miss Silver coughed slightly.

'That is not quite correct. Mrs Madision did follow her husband, did find him standing or kneeling over the body, and did touch it herself, afterwards losing her stained handkerchief. But she has not yet admitted to any of these things, though she will undoubtedly do so when you tax her with them.'

Randal March smiled.

'I'm merely being a little previous? I'll let it stand for the present. Well, I suppose that is about all. Miss Fane and Miss Adams could have no possible interest in their niece's death. She seems to have been the main object of their existence. There is no motive at all, and in Miss Fane's case at least, no opportunity, since she can only move about in her invalid chair.'

Miss Silver primmed her mouth.

'I agree with you that Agnes could not possibly have desired her niece's death, but had she desired it she could,

I think, have done everything that was done by the murderer.'

He made an exclamation of surprise.

'From an invalid chair?'

Miss Silver was silent for a moment. Then she said, 'She is extremely skilful in her use of it. She can go up and down in the lift without any assistance.'

'I didn't know that!'

She nodded.

'I thought perhaps you did not.'

'Could she have taken the pistol from the drawer and replaced it?'

'I think so.'

He frowned.

'There's something wrong here. Wait a minute – if Miss Fane came down in her chair by way of the lift, Miss Lyle must have both seen and heard her. The machinery is by no means silent. Even with a high wind blowing, I think it must have been heard by anyone who was standing at the door of the octagon room.'

Miss Silver said, 'The door was open, but the wind was on the other side of the house. That point has not been brought out. In my opinion it is an important one. The octagon room is screened by the south wall of the Priory. It is, in fact, so much sheltered that the door to the church had not blown to, but was still standing open when Dean discovered the body.'

March nodded.

'As you say, it is a point – and it bears out my contention that Miss Lyle would have heard the lift. Remember, she must have been on the look-out for Madison, and also for any sound from the house. I can't believe that she could have been taken by surprise from the lift. Also Miss Fane would have had no need to touch the inside handle of the sitting-room door, which was certainly touched and wiped by the murderer. It's quite incredible.'

Miss Silver shook her head.

'Nothing in human nature is incredible. Some things are harder to believe than others, that is all. But you must not think that I have any wish to direct your suspicions towards Agnes. I merely feel it my duty to tell you that her physical condition does not make it impossible for her to have done what the murderer did.'

He frowned again.

'If the shot had been fired from a sitting position, the course of the bullet would have been slightly upwards. Miss Lyle was a tall woman.'

Miss Silver looked at him seriously.

'Randal – when Agnes Fane commissioned me to discover who had murdered her niece she used a remarkable expression. I warned her that suspicion might rest upon a member of her household or of her family. She replied that she wished the murderer to be discovered, even if it were herself. Her maid Perry had been mentioned just before, and she said in that sardonic voice of hers, "If it is Perry, I shall have to find a new maid, which would be very tiresome. And if it is I, Perry will have to find a new mistress." '

'*Perry!*' March's voice had a startled sound.

'Yes.'

'And what motive would Perry have?'

'I do not know.'

'Do you think Miss Fane meant that she suspected Perry?'

Miss Silver shook his head.

'I do not think so. But Agnes has a strange character. She may have been hinting at some suspicion of her own, or she may have meant nothing at all – she is very secretive. There is something I feel I ought to tell you. I am in her employment, but on terms which in no way bind me to silence.'

March wondered what was coming. He was not at all prepared for her next words.

In a considerably lowered voice she said, 'You can leave the invalid chair out of it, Randal. Agnes Fane is not dependent on it. She can walk.'

'*What!*'

Miss Silver nodded.

'I have seen her. She has a pronounced limp, but she is perfectly active. It is supposed to be a dead secret. Perry knows of course, and Lucy – and, I suspect, the Deans. She sleeps badly, and likes to walk about the house at night when there is no one to see her. The doors to the servants' wing are locked by Dean before he goes to bed, so she feels safe from observation.'

'But why?'

'I told you she has a strange character. Her accident left her with one leg considerably shortened. She used to have a fine figure and a very graceful walk. She could not bear to be seen limping. She preferred the role of complete disablement, and she has kept it up for more than twenty years.'

He still looked startled.

'Do you mean that she could walk down the stairs?'

'Oh, yes – I have seen her do it.'

'When?'

'The night after I came here. She moves quite freely.'

'Does she know that you saw her?'

'Oh, no – I am sure she does not.'

He went on looking at her for a moment, and then pushed back his chair.

'Is this a red herring?'

She was putting away her knitting.

'I have no idea what you mean.'

He laughed a little.

'Haven't you? Look here, tell me frankly – do you really suspect Miss Agnes Fane?'

Miss Silver rose with dignity.

'I am quite unable to answer that question.'

'That means you do. But why? Tell me why.'

She shook her head.

'Would she have known how to use the pistol? Can you tell me that?'

She relaxed a little.

'Yes, I will tell you that. I have been thinking that you should know. When I visited here as a young girl Mr Fane, Agnes's father, had us all taught to shoot. He set up a target in the ruins, and we used to practise at it with his pistol. It was considered rather eccentric of him, but we found it quite enjoyable.'

He said, 'We?' on a sharp note of enquiry.

'Agnes, Lucy, and myself – oh, and of course Perry.'

'*Perry?*'

Miss Silver moved towards the door.

'Oh, yes,' she said soberly. 'Perry was a very good shot.'

THIRTY SEVEN

MISS SILVER WALKED out after tea to post a letter. Being Saturday afternoon, and the destination of the letter London, it might just as well have been posted next day, but Miss Silver was feeling a necessity for solitude accompanied by gentle movement. In fact, she desired to take a walk, and made the letter her excuse.

The evening was dark and still. The temperature had risen sensibly. The air, soft against her face, held a promise of rain. With the reflection that it was really quite pleasant out of doors, and that possibly a mild spell was about to set in, she turned out of the drive and made her way to the pillar-box at the cross-roads.

When she had posted her letter she walked back at a pace much slower than her usual brisk trot. Her mind was, in fact, busy with the train of thought evoked by her last conversation with Randal March. Perry – the name stayed in her mind – the name and what it stood for – forty-one years of devoted service to Agnes Fane, a relationship begun when both were young, and which had endured past youth, past the crash of Agnes's happiness and health, through many years of invalidism to this last tragedy. Search as she would, Miss Silver could find nothing in this relationship on which to base a motive for the murder of Tanis Lyle. If motive there were, it must lie elsewhere. But in what dark and secret places of a warped, frustrated nature? If there was one person in that household less unlikely than another to be capable of the hatred which is of the essence of murder, it was Perry. No hot rage or sudden impulse would prompt her, but some cold, fixed, implacable resentment might do so. But from what would such a resentment spring? There seemed no answer to that, unless – unless . . . A thought which had come to her earlier in the day now presented itself again and clamoured to be heard.

Miss Silver became so engrossed that she missed her way in the drive and found herself well away from it upon a path hedged by shrubs. A holly bush brought her up short where the path took a sudden turn. She received a slight scratch on the cheek, and immediately stood still to take her bearings. The shrubbery was dense, and it was extremely dark. She thought she must have skirted the north wing, and that she must be somewhere in the neighbourhood of the back premises, in which case it might be simpler to keep straight on until she came to the house.

She was regretting that she had not brought her torch, when the sound of footsteps and voices arrested her attention. The steps were cautious, and the voices lowered. There was a smothered 'O-oh!' as a twig snapped. A man spoke, low and gruff – 'Look out,' and a girl giggled and said, 'Can't look far in this blinking dark.' The word she used was not 'blinking'. It shocked Miss Silver considerably, especially from the lips of a young person of seventeen.

The girl was Florrie Mumford, and she had no business to be out in the shrubbery after dark with a man. Really Mrs Dean ought to know more about what went on. However that might be, there was Florrie, on the other side of the holly bush by the sound of her, and by his voice the young man was William Shepherd, one of the under-gardeners. 'And not the first time Florrie has slipped out to meet him,' was Miss Silver's conclusion. The sounds from the far side of the holly bush were suggestive of practice.

Miss Silver had been much too well brought up to indulge in eavesdropping. She had a moment's indecision as to whether it would not now be better to retrace her footsteps, when she heard something which translated her from the role of private gentlewoman to that of private detective. In this latter capacity her scruples about overhearing a private conversation ceased to be scruples at all.

What she heard was William Shepherd saying urgently, 'If you know who done it, Florrie, you did ought to tell.'

Florrie giggled.

'I'm not saying what I know, and I'm not telling neither, so there!'

'Then you shouldn't go hinting the way you been doing.'

'Who's been hinting?'

'You have, and well you know it, and if you don't mind out, your tongue'll be getting you into trouble one of these days.'

Florrie giggled again.

'Oh, will it?'

'Yes, it will. And you'd better shut your mouth on it and keep it shut, or you'll be sorry.'

'Sorry I took up with you!' Florrie's voice was pert.

There was the sound of a kiss, a slapped cheek, a scuffle, another kiss. Then William Shepherd, complacent over his smack.

'Silly – aren't you? Suppose I go off after another girl –

how'ud you like that? You be'ave yourself or you'll find out! And you drop this 'ere hinting, or you'll be getting both of us the sack.'

Florrie sounded pettish.

'Oh, well, you'll be getting called up anyway, so what's the odds?'

'Mother wouldn't like it if I got the sack, and no more she won't like it if you carry on the way you been doing, hinting and suchlike. If you got anything to say, you say it right out and ha' done, or you'll be getting trouble for your pains like I said.'

Florrie giggled and whispered.

'Suppose I was to get money. There's some people that'd pay proper for me to keep my hints to myself.'

'What are you talking about?'

Her voice teased him.

'Wouldn't you just like to know! Money – that's what I'm talking about. A word here and a word there, and maybe they'll bring me in a nice bit of money – enough to make you sit up and take a bit of notice. What'd you say to a hundred pounds?'

What William would have said can only be guessed at. From the distance Mrs Dean could be heard calling Florrie with acerbity.

'Florrie! Florrie! Where have you got to! It don't take half an hour to empty potato peelings, does it?'

Florrie giggled.

'There she goes! No, you can't – you've had enough. You lemme go! I'll be out tomorrow for my evening. Maybe I'll meet you, and maybe I'll have something in my pocket – there's no saying.'

Miss Silver stood where she was. Mrs Dean called again. Florrie rustled away. William Shepherd pushed through on to the path and went down it, passing so near that she could have touched him.

When all the sounds had died she made her way back to the drive, and so to the front door.

THIRTY EIGHT

AFTER A TIME spent in thought she proceeded to the study and, finding it empty, rang up Randal March.

'I have some information for you, and I think we had better speak French.'

This opening, delivered in the stiff grammatical French of his schoolroom days, roused him from the pleasant half-hour of relaxation which he had intended to take before allowing his mind to dwell upon the Priory murder. He replied readily, but with that indomitable British accent which exemplifies the ability of the English to withstand foreign influences.

Miss Silver continued briskly.

'I do not wish to incur any further censure for withholding evidence, so I think I had better communicate a conversation which I have just overheard. Just a moment first, if you please.'

She laid down the receiver and went noiselessly to the door and opened it. The wide passage was empty. From the morning-room almost immediately opposite came the sound of orchestral music on the wireless. With an approving nod she closed the door and returned to the telephone.

'Yes, that is quite all right. I thought I would just make sure that we could speak privately. Now I will tell you what I overheard.'

When she had repeated Florrie's conversation with William Shepherd she said soberly, 'I do not know what you think about it, but it appears to me that this girl may be in danger. It is a very risky thing to blackmail a murderer, and she is the light, silly type who takes a risk through ignorance and vanity.'

There was a pause.

March said, 'Have you spoken to her? Does she know that she was overheard?'

'Oh, no. I would not take such a step without letting you know.'

Ten miles away, the superintendent smiled. His Miss Silver had taken more important steps than this without informing the police. Her virtue amused him. At the same time he knew it to be an index of her concern. He said, 'Would you like to see her?'

Miss Silver coughed.

'I do not think so. She would not tell me anything. I know her type. She would not talk to a woman, though she might to a man. It is the same girl who brought you the fragments of the shawl. I do not know whether you observed her.'

'Not particularly.'

Her voice became severe.

'You should have done so. She was making eyes at you. Her manner to me was pert. She is that type. It would be useless for me to speak to her, but with your approval I will endeavour to caution her indirectly. She will be helping the butler at dinner tonight as the other girl is out, and if I could bring the conversation to the subject of blackmail, it might be possible to frighten her from pursuing a very dangerous course. I should also have an opportunity of observing the reactions of other members of the party. In fact, the whole thing might prove instructive.'

Randal March didn't see how it could do any harm. He said so, and Miss Silver rang off.

Passing through the hall, she encountered Carey Desborough and requested a word with him. As voices could be heard from the drawing-room which he had just left, she opened the door of Tanis Lyle's sitting-room and took him in there. It had the bleak, desolate look which comes so quickly to a room that has fallen out of use. It was clean and neat – too neat. Sofa and chairs undented; cushions that no one had leaned against; a carpet on which no one had trodden; ash-trays all clean, all set, each in its appropriate place; dead air in the room; no flowers. It might have been a designer's room in an exhibition of furniture. It chilled Carey to the bone.

Miss Silver appeared unmoved.

'Will you do something for me, Mr Desborough?' she said. 'It is really quite a small thing, but I should be glad of your co-operation.'

He said, 'Will you tell me what it is?' and saw her smile.

'You are cautious, Mr Desborough – have you any Scottish blood? It is really quite a small matter. I should be glad if you would assist me to introduce the subject of blackmail at dinner tonight.'

He was considerably startled, and showed it.

'Miss Silver!'

She came closer to him and said, dropping her voice, 'Has anyone been trying to blackmail you – or Miss Laura?'

Carey recovered himself. His manner was quite natural when he said, 'Not me. I'd have gone to the police – it's the only way with blackmail. And not Laura. She would have told me.'

Miss Silver nodded.

'Someone in this house is blackmailing, and someone

is being blackmailed. That is why I want to talk about blackmail at dinner tonight. Will you help me?'

He hesitated for a moment. Then he said, 'I don't like it very much.'

Miss Silver looked at him with gravity.

'I do not like it at all, pray believe that. But, Mr Desborough, consider the situation. We have had a murder here. A very foolish and ignorant person is now attempting to blackmail the murderer. Can you imagine anything more dangerous?'

'Frankly, no.'

'The conversation in which I hope you will assist is intended to deter the blackmailer. If it has that effect it will be worthwhile.'

Carey looked down the room. He wished that they could have talked anywhere else. It was so full of Tanis, and yet so empty. He remembered that he had loved her. And that the love was dead. And she was dead. He said abruptly, 'All right, I'll do it.'

THIRTY NINE

THE EVENING WAS not one upon which Miss Silver could look back with satisfaction. The Maxwells would be leaving next day, Alistair possibly returning for the inquest on Monday. Both brothers were silent and abstracted, though Alistair no longer appeared to be on the verge of a breakdown. Petra looked pale and exhausted. Her flow of talk had gone. Laura after a valiant attempt to engage Lucy Adams in conversation gave it up, her effort being requited by monosyllables and an air of complete inattention. But Miss Adams could, and did, engage in a discussion as to the relative merits of violas and pansies, a safe and pleasant subject introduced by Agnes Fane and maintained while they all partook of soup.

While the fish, which was the principal course, was being served, Miss Silver began a long, trickling story which culminated in an attempt at blackmail. The narrative had very little point, but it occupied the time required for handing round the fish, an office performed by Dean in his best manner and upon the heaviest silver entrée dish. If food was hard to come by, silver was not, and what was lacking in the one should to the best of his ability be made up by the other. He went round, and Florrie Mumford followed him, handing potatoes in their jackets, sliced and fried.

'So my friend very wisely communicated with the police, which was by far the best thing to do,' said Miss Silver, concluding her tale.

Carey Desborough, on the other side of the table, obediently took his cue.

'Blackmailing is pretty heavily punished.'

'Deservedly so,' said Miss Silver. She helped herself to the fried potato, remarked that it looked very good, and pursued the original theme. 'Sentences of seven, fourteen, or even twenty-one years have been given, and really when you think of the other risks which the blackmailer runs, it is surprising to find that anyone has so little sense as to embark on them. It may be an easy way of making money, but there is always the danger that the person blackmailed may either go to the police or take the law into his own hands.'

Florrie continued to hand fried potatoes without a tremor. She was a deft waitress. Miss Silver could not discern the least trace of discomposure. It might be that she was too securely wrapped up in her own conceit, or, what was just possible, that the word blackmail had no meaning for her. Miss Silver decided that this might very well be the case, and decided that she was wasting her time.

Lucy Adams said fretfully that she supposed there would be a great deal more crime after the war, and the conversation drifted by way of post-war farming back to the safer problems of gardening. The result of the experiment was exactly nil.

Retiring to her room rather earlier than usual, Miss Silver encountered Florrie going round with hot-water bottles. She came from the passage leading to the lift. Miss Fane's room, Perry's, Miss Adams's, Petra's, and Laura's had obviously been disposed of. She now carried a single bright-green rubber bottle which Miss Silver recognised as her own, and she wore an extremely self-satisfied look. 'Like a cat who has been at the cream,' was Miss Silver's mental comment.

She withdrew into her own room, leaving the door ajar. Florrie knocked, was told to come in, and proceeded to turn down the bed, insert the hot-water bottle, and lay out Miss Silver's nightdress, a garment over which she smiled and tossed her head. This impertinence, discerned by Miss Silver in the mirror, evoked a reproving frown. The garment, of cream Viyella, was in her opinion most comfortable and tasteful, being high in the neck and long in the sleeves, of a decent fullness, and very neatly finished with silk feather-stitching – very different of course from the skin-tight and transparent wisps in which the girls of the present generation attired themselves for the night.

Florrie, who considered the nightgown a 'sketch', was preparing to leave the room, when Miss Silver called her back.

'Just a moment, Florrie. And please close the door. I have something to say to you.'

For, after all, she was going to say it. To the relief of her conscience in time to come, she had made up her mind that she must speak to Florrie. Since the indirect warning had passed her by, she must be warned directly. If the warning were useless, as she fully expected, she would at least have done what she could.

Florrie stood there, fidgeting and looking pert.

'I've the hot-waters to put.'

There was a toss of the head which Miss Silver ignored. She said gravely, 'What I have to say to you will not take long. Your conversation with William Shepherd in the shrubbery this evening was overheard. You know, or pretend to know, something about the murder of Miss Lyle, and you are trying to use what you know to get money out of the person whom you suspect. That is what is called blackmail. You heard us talking about it at dinner. Perhaps you do not know that it is a very serious crime in the eyes of the law, and that it is always very heavily punished. Besides the punishment which the law would give you, there is the grave risk you would run. Your knowledge, if you have any, exposes you to danger. You should tell the police what you know or suspect without delay. They will protect you – and I must tell you that I think you are in need of protection. A person who has murdered once may murder again.'

As she spoke she was aware that it was to no purpose. Florrie's face was sat and defiant. She said rudely, 'I dunno what you're talking about.'

Miss Silver shook her head.

'I think you do. I shall not say any more, but I hope you will take my warning. That is all.'

The door was jerked open. Florrie bounced out, shutting it after her with something that was very nearly a bang. Miss Silver's warning had not disturbed her complacency nor altered her purpose by a hair's breadth.

'Nasty prying, nosy old maid!' and, 'A hundred pounds – a hundred pounds – a hundred pounds—' was all the burden of her thoughts. Anger, cupidity, triumph possessed her. There was no place for a warning, no place for fear.

She finished what she had to do and went to her room in the north wing. It was the smallest there, being in fact no more than a slip taken off the room next door, but it was a place of her own and a source of great satisfaction. If she had been obliged to share with Mary, the upper housemaid, she would have had to give up a number of things which she had no intention of giving up. The books which she read in bed – Mary's hair would have curled with horror if she had known what was in them. And she'd never have been able to slip out at night and meet Bert if she hadn't a room of her own. She giggled to herself as she thought what Bill Shepherd would say if he knew about Bert. A cut above Bill, Bert was. Butchers always made money, and his father had a fine shop in Ledlington, as well as the small branch at Prior's Halt. A cut above Florrie herself – and that was where the hundred pounds would come in so nicely. Bert wasn't thinking about marrying, he was just out to have his fun, but if a girl had a hundred pounds in her pocket, there was no saying but what he'd think and think again. And she was going to have a real white satin wedding dress too, and orange-blossoms, and a veil, and white kid gloves. She tossed her head and thought contemptuously about Miss Silver, who was an old maid.

She stood in her room with the light turned off and waited as she had often waited before. The back door banged. That was Mary coming in after her evening out. She would have a word with Mrs Dean and then up to bed, and quick about it. Mary liked her sleep. There were no sounds from the rooms occupied by the evacuees. Judds and Slades, young and old, they were hearty sleepers. That was a bit of all right too.

Mary came up, Mrs Dean came up, and now was Florrie's time. Dean would be going his rounds, and as soon as he had finished he would come through the ground-floor door which shut off the kitchen wing and lock it behind him, then up the back stairs to the corresponding door on the upper floor and lock that too. What Florrie had to do was to nip through and be out of sight before he got there. She had done it often enough before. You could hear him on the stairs, and that was your time – out of your room, through the connecting door, and into the empty room just the other side of it, next to Miss Silver's. If anyone saw you – well, you'd forgotten one of the hot-water bottles. It was as easy as winking, and Florrie could wink with the best. Then when you'd finished what you'd slipped out for you could sleep comfortable enough on the morning-room sofa and slip back to your room as soon as Dean unlocked the upper door, as he always did at half-past six sharp before he had his shave.

She heard Dean on the stair and ran for it. Easy as kissing your hand. She stood in the dark, empty room and waited. Now he was locking the door. Now he was going away down the passage to the room over the kitchen which he shared with Mrs Dean.

There was a comfortable armchair in the empty room. Florrie felt her way to it and sat down. It was dark, and she had to wait until midnight, but she wasn't at all afraid of going to sleep. She had plenty of things to think about – a hundred things – a hundred pounds – each pound a fortune. She had no idea of the value of money. She was getting seventeen and sixpence a week, and she had to give three quarters of it to a cross-grained father of whom she went in bodily fear. She had never had a whole pound in her posession to do what she liked with. A hundred pounds meant escape from Dad – security – perhaps marriage to Bert and a rise in life. A comfortable tradesman's wife would have a nice little villa on the outskirts of Ledlington and household help. She saw herself ordering a maid about, shopping handsomely in High Street, buying the red three-piece she had seen at Jones's last time she was in, going out Sundays in a nice little car with Bert. Because in her dream Bert's father was dead and Bert had come in for the shop in Ledlington. Ever so much better than the branch at Prior's Holt. Money in the bank too – money . . .

She had left the door the least little crack ajar. Presently she came out of her dream. The clock in the hall was striking twelve. As her sharp ears caught the sound she slipped out of the room like a shadow, along the passage, down the big staircase, and through the hall to the study. She had not gone more eagerly to any of her meetings with Bert. Here – now – in this room, she was to get her hundred pounds.

The light in the hall which burned all night, saw her to the corner of the passage upon which the study opened. The door was open now, but the room was dark. So she was there first. A cold draught met her on the threshold. Someone must have left the window open. As she hesitated, the door of the morning-room opened behind her and the voice which she was expecting said, 'Put on the light, Florrie. I've got the money for you.'

A hundred pounds! Her hand went eagerly to the switch. For a moment she stood outlined against the sudden light within the room, then a gloved hand came up and the study poker came crashing down. She slumped forward without a cry. The person who had wielded the poker examined its work and was satisfied. The poker was laid down beside the body. A gloved left hand switched off the light. There was a faint sound of retreating footsteps. After that no sound at all. Nothing stirred in the house. A small cold wind blew in through the open window.

FORTY

LAURA WOKE UP in the dark. It was very dark indeed, because though one of the windows was open the blackout curtain hung across it and no light came through. She did not know what had waked her, but she came up out of sleep with a sense of fear pressing hard upon her and only just escaped. Fear – blind, formless, dreadfully unknown – it hammered at her brain, her heart, her pulses. There was no other sound in the room.

She sat up stiffly in the bed, listening, trying to steady herself, and moment by moment the dark tide ebbed away, leaving her Laura Fane again, in control, instead of a hunted thing without a name driven by a nameless fear.

The relief was very great, but her throat was dry and her body shaken. She got out of bed, felt her way to the washstand, and poured a glass of water from the carafe. Its icy coldness made her shiver, but it steadied her. She set the glass back and went to the door, walking barefoot on the carpet, feeling before her with her hands. It was in her mind to turn the key in the lock, though why, she could not have told, because the fear had been in her own mind, in a dream she had forgotten. It had come up with her out of her sleep, and it was gone. Why then should it be in her mind to lock the door of her room? She had no answer to this, but all at once she opened the door and looked out.

After the even velvet darkness inside the room the passage with its one light burning at the far end seemed really bright. She looked to the right, and saw the wide corridor spacious and empty. She looked to the left, and saw Agnes Fane come from the gallery leading to the stairs.

The fear returned. It caught at her heart and held her immovable. She could not have moved for her very life, but she did not know why. Except that she was seeing what she was not meant to see – what no one was meant to see. Because Agnes Fane was walking. She was on her feet and walking, unbelievably tall. Her left foot dragged in an ugly limp. It was as if she fought the drag and defied it, for her body remained erect. She came so slowly that if Laura could have moved she might have drawn back into the safe darkness of her room and locked the door. Only she could not move. She could only stand and wait while Agnes Fane came on.

As she drew nearer Laura saw her face like a white mask, her hair still orderly, her pearls about her throat, a loose gown wrapping her, purple or purplish red. Her dark eyes blazed. They came to Laura and rested there. She put a hand to the wall and stood looking down from that great height of hers. When she spoke her voice was low and harsh.

'What are you doing out of bed?'

There was a compulsion on Laura to speak, and to speak the truth. She said, 'I was afraid.'

Agnes Fane looked at her, not with scorn or anger, but with a cold alien look. She said, 'What are you afraid of?'

'I don't know.'

The look changed a little, and the voice became harsher.

'Go back to bed! And lock your door – both doors!

Perhaps you can lock fear out – who knows. Go back to your bed and stay there! Do you hear?'

Stiffly, Laura obeyed, moved from the threshold, stepped back into the room, leaned upon the door with the flat of her hand until it closed, turned the key in the lock. From the other side of the door there was the sound of a long sighing breath. The dragging step went past.

Laura groped to the bathroom door and locked that too, groped for the bedside switch and put on the light, got back into bed, and lay there shuddering with cold, and something more than cold. She did not know that she had been near her death, but the nearness chilled her to the bone.

FORTY ONE

PRESENTLY SHE GREW warmer. She felt for the hot-water bottle and drew it up beside her. The light from the bedside lamp made a comfortable glow in the room. The dream was gone, the fear was gone. She could begin to wonder at them now, and to wonder at herself for being afraid.

And then, as she looked towards the door, she saw the handle move. Instantly the terror was beating at her heart again. The handle turned quite silently until it could turn no more. Then it stopped. There was the faintest of faint sounds as pressure came upon the lock – hardly a sound at all. Perhaps she had only imagined it. Perhaps there had not really been a sound. The handle slipped round again and moved no more.

Laura sat up in bed, a hand on either side of her pressing the mattress down. She watched the door and strained to listen, but she could hear nothing. She kept saying to herself in a horrified inner whisper, 'The doors are locked. The bathroom door is locked. This door is locked. Nobody can get in.' And then, behind her on the left, there came a tapping on the bathroom door.

She was out of bed and on her feet in a moment. The tapping came again, faint but insistent. Standing with her hand on the jamb, bending to the crack between it and the door, she said, 'Who's there?'

She had never felt so much relief in all her life as she did when Lucy Adams's fretful voice came to her ear.

'Are you awake? Let me in! Why do you lock your door?'

Laura turned the key with a shaking hand. But it was relief that made it shake. All that horrible fear – and then Cousin Lucy.

She opened the door, and Lucy Adams came in in a red flannel dressing-gown with the gold chain of her pince-nez pinned to it. It was, as usual, crooked. The auburn front was presumably on her dressing-table. Its absence revealed a wide, thin parting, and scanty locks done up in metal curlers. She wore a worried expression, and spoke in a whisper.

'It is Agnes – she is ill. Why did you lock your door? I don't approve of it. Suppose there was a fire. Your Cousin Agnes is ill, and I could not make you hear. We must get the doctor at once. You must help me.'

Laura caught up her green dressing-gown and slipped it on.

'What's the matter? Is she very ill? What do you want me to do?'

Lucy Adams jerked at her pince-nez.

'She has these attacks. They are very alarming. She cannot be left. Perry is with her. I must go down and telephone for the doctor, but I can't do it alone. It's all been such a shock. I can't go down there alone. You must come with me.'

The wind blew in from the open window. Laura went over and shut it. She was shivering as she came back.

'Of course I'll come down with you. But wouldn't you like me to call Miss Silver, or Carey?'

'No – no – no – *no!* You mustn't do that! Nobody must know. They are strangers – we mustn't bring them in. I came to you because you are family. We've got to keep it in the family. Nobody else must know.'

Her look darted at Laura and dropped away again. Her voice shook nervously.

'No one outside the family,' she repeated.

'And the doctor—'

Miss Adams jerked impatiently.

'Doctors don't count – they can keep a secret. And we must hurry. Put on your slippers and come!'

As they went down into the dimly-lighted hall, Laura was wondering, and trying not to wonder, about this illness of Agnes Fane's. 'One of her attacks—' What kind of attack? 'We must keep it in the family. Nobody must know—' What was there to know? 'Doctors can keep a secret—' What secret was there to be kept? An echo of her own sick fear came to her, and she remembered the dragging limp, the white mask of a face, the voice that had told her to lock her door.

At the foot of the stairs Lucy Adams turned, speaking low.

'You had better wait here. There is no need for you to hear what I have to tell the doctor. But you won't go away?'

Laura shook her head. She was puzzled. She felt a shrinking embarrassment. But she was not frightened now. It did not frighten her to stay alone in the hall while Lucy Adams went into Tanis's sitting-room and shut the door. It might have frightened her if she had known that Florrie Mumford was lying dead across the threshold of the study not so very far away. But she did not know.

She leaned against the newel-post, shivering a little, and hoping that Cousin Lucy wouldn't be long. From where she stood she could just hear the murmur of her voice.

Then the door opened. Miss Adams stood there beckoning, the lighted room behind her. Laura obeyed reluctantly. Wouldn't they go upstairs again now? It appeared that they would not. Cousin Lucy drew her in and pushed the door to.

'We must wait down here for him and let him in. I was quite right to send for him, and he will come at once. Such a relief! I said I would be here to let him in. I may not hear the car, but you will, I am sure. I am not deaf, you know, but I do not hear quite so well as I used to. Now you sit down over there on the sofa, and I will take the chair. The doctor will not be long.'

Laura sat down on the couch at the farther side of the hearth. It was wide, and deep, and low. She pulled a cushion down and leaned against it. Across the hearth, incongruous in a squat, wide-armed chair, Miss Adams sat stiffly upright in her red flannel dressing-gown and her tight metal curlers. Behind her the door to the hall, not actually ajar but not quite latched. As a little thing will sometimes stick in one's thought and prick at it, this trifle caught Laura's attention and pricked there. If she had not felt so tired she would have gone over to the door to latch it properly.

She heard Lucy Adams say just in her usual rambling voice:

'You realise of course that it was your Cousin Agnes who shot Tanis.'

Laura felt exactly as if someone had hit her sharply and suddenly. The impact made her blink. She stared at Lucy and said nothing.

Miss Adams said in an exasperated tone, 'Really, Laura, you can be very stupid! Didn't you hear what I said?'

Laura moved stiff lips and said, 'Yes.'

'Then why don't you say something? It seems to me that my remark called for some comment.'

It seemed to Laura that comment was impossible. What do you say when one elderly relative who is sensibly attired in red flannel tells you point blank that another elderly relative is a homicidal maniac? For that was what it amounted to. The attacks which must not be witnessed by a stranger – 'We must keep it in the family . . . A doctor knows how to keep a secret . . .' – all these things meant one thing and one thing only, that Cousin Agnes was mad, and that in a fit of mania she had killed Tanis Lyle. She heard Lucy Adams say, 'Of course she did not mean to kill Tanis. It was a most unfortunate accident. She meant to kill you.'

A kind of stiffness invaded Laura, mind and body. It rendered her incapable of speech or movement. Behind Lucy Adams she saw the sitting-room door move in an inch or two, and move again – four – five – six inches. She wondered why it had moved.

FORTY TWO

MISS SILVER OPENED her eyes upon the darkness of her bedroom. She did not know what had waked her from the uneasy sleep into which she had fallen. She thought it was a sound. She listened, and could hear nothing. She therefore sat up in bed and listened again. Unbroken silence, unbroken darkness.

She switched on her bedside lamp and drew about her shoulders a large knitted shawl with an openwork border. The new stitch which she had been trying out had not proved very successful. She had not, therefore, given the shawl away to the baby for whom it had been intended, her niece Letty's second child, but had kept it for herself. She found it warm and comfortable now.

The minutes slipped away. If there had been a sound, it was not repeated. She decided that she was becoming fanciful – she had sat too late and thought too long. Tomorrow would be a painful and difficult day. She must really try to get a little sleep. But the desire for sleep had left her. She took a book at random from the bedside-table and began to read.

Actually, it was the sound of Florrie Mumford's fall which had roused her, her room being over the study.

She read for about twenty minutes, and found at the end of this time that she had not the slightest recollection of what she had been reading. While her eyes perused the printed page, her thoughts wandered towards strange conjectures and horrifying conclusions. They reached a point where she could no longer pretend to read.

In her usual controlled manner she replaced the book, got out of bed, and put on a warm grey dressing-gown industriously trimmed with wide crochet borders of crimson wool. No garment could possibly have been less becoming, but it was warm and serviceable, and it concealed every inch of the voluminous woollen nightgown beneath. When she had fastened it at the waist with a long grey cord she crossed the passage and tapped lightly upon Carey Desborough's door. Receiving no answer, she turned the handle and went in.

The first that Carey knew about it was light slanting down on him from the lamp beside the bed. He blinked at it, and at the astonishing vision of Miss Silver with her hand upon the switch. Then he came broad awake. He sat up and said in a horrified voice, 'What is it? What's happened?'

Miss Silver gave her slight cough.

'Nothing, I hope, Mr Desborough. I am sorry to disturb you, but I cannot help feeling extremely uneasy. I was awakened some little time ago by a sound. That at least is my impression, but of course I may be mistaken – our minds are disturbed, and trifles are apt to be magnified. If it would not be too much trouble, I would be glad if you would make a tour of the downstairs rooms with me.'

He was out of bed and reaching for his dressing-gown.

'You thought the sound came from there?'

'That was my impression. If I was mistaken, we can return to our rooms and say nothing about it. If, on the other hand—' She got no further, because Carey broke in.

'You're sure it was downstairs?'

Miss Silver became a little distant.

'I am not sure about anything, Mr Desborough. I think we had better investigate.'

They came down the stairs and into the hall. In Miss Silver's mind the purpose of turning to the right and proceeding in the direction of dining-room, morning-room, and study had been clearly formed, but as her foot took the last step down, this purpose dissolved. Her ear had caught the sound of a voice which she knew very well. The sound came from the left-hand side of the hall, from Tanis Lyle's sitting-room, the door which showed a crack of light.

She immediately touched Carey on the arm and put a finger to her lips. They stood for a moment, listening intently. Then, quite noiselessly, Miss Silver led the way to the door and, coming to it, pushed gently against it with her hand until the crack of light had become a six-inch band. In the brief preceding moment she heard Lucy Adams say, 'Of course she did not mean to kill Tanis. It was a most unfortunate accident. She meant to kill you.'

FORTY THREE

CAREY DESBOROUGH HEARD the words with stupefaction. They seemed to be part of a conversation carried on without any particular emphasis. Miss Adams had uttered them in very much the same manner in which she might have commented on a mistake about the ration-books or the changing of a novel at the library. There had been a mistake. A person unnamed hadn't really meant to kill Tanis Lyle. She had meant to kill someone else. He looked round the edge of the door and saw that this someone else was Laura, sitting stiffly upright on the wide green couch, her face as white as death, her black hair falling on her neck, her eyes wide and staring.

Miss Silver's small, firm hand closed on his arm. He looked round and saw her, finger at lip, sternly forbidding sound or movement. He turned back again. They stayed like that, listening intently.

Lucy Adams went on talking.

'That was quite natural of course. She hated you before you were born, and she has gone on hating you ever since. You ought never to have been born at all. I suppose you realise that your mother stole Oliver away from us. She had no right to him – he was ours. He would have been here now – living here, going in and out every day – if it hadn't been for Lilian. And she couldn't even keep what she had stolen. She let him die. He wouldn't have died if he had stayed here – we should have seen to that. So really, you see, she killed him, stealing him away like that. And so it was quite a just thing that you should die – quite, quite just. Agnes used to think about these things, and when she knew you were going to come and stay here she thought about them a lot more. But she didn't quite know what to do about it, because it isn't really at all easy to kill someone without being found out. You have to be very clever and think it all out, and then you have to be very quick to take an opportunity if it comes your way. Agnes was very clever and very quick. When Mr Hazelton came here and made that fuss and shot off his pistol, she saw at once that that was her opportunity, because if anyone was shot after that, people would think he had done it – especially if you were shot with his pistol. Tanis told us all where she had put it, you remember, after she took it away from him. But she wasn't speaking the truth when she said he still had the other pistol – the other one of the pair – because she had it herself, upstairs in one of her drawers. I expect she wanted everyone to think that she was still in danger, and how brave she was. Tanis was like that.'

Laura had stopped thinking about the door. Her eyes were on Lucy Adams's face. It looked just as usual. She might have been talking about the weather or the black-out. The foolish, rambling voice went on, a little sharpened by her dislike of Laura. But then Laura had always known that Cousin Lucy disliked her. Always? How silly! But it seemed like that. It seemed like years, and years, and years since she had come into this house.

On one side of a curtain in her mind Laura had these thoughts. On the other side of it she listened to Lucy Adams, who had never stopped talking.

'Now I will tell you about Thursday night. You would like to know what happened, wouldn't you, and it will all be in the family – you won't tell anyone.' She repeated the last words with a curious tittering laugh. 'You won't tell anyone – oh, no, you won't tell anyone. Well, I must tell you what happened. Agnes went up to her room, but she could not sleep because the wind was so high. I never can sleep myself when the wind is high – I told the police superintendent so. It gets on one's nerves, and then one cannot rest. It got on Agnes's nerves, and presently she opened her door to come out and walk about the house. She often does that at night when she cannot sleep, but nobody is supposed to know.'

Carey turned an astounded look upon Miss Silver. She nodded briefly, and he turned back again. Lucy Adams was saying, 'When she came out she saw someone just going round the corner at the other end of the passage. She couldn't really see who it was, and she thought she would like to find out, because people ought not to be walking about the house at that time of night – I am sure you will agree about that. Of course, we all know now that it was Tanis who was going downstairs, but when Agnes got to the top of the stairs and looked down into the hall she thought it was you.'

Laura opened her lips to speak, but no sound came. They were too dry and stiff.

Miss Adams nodded.

'That is what she thought, and it was a perfectly natural mistake for her to make. The light in the hall is not at all adequate. I have often told Agnes so – now perhaps she will believe me. And you had been wearing a black dress. Very misleading of you – I suppose you did it on purpose. Agnes could not be expected to know that Tanis had changed out of her white dress and put on a black coat and black pyjamas. She saw someone in black, and she thought that it was you. You are about the same height as Tanis, and your hair is the same colour. Black hair runs in the family. Agnes has it, and so had Oliver, but I take after my father. He had auburn hair, but ginger whiskers. Ladies, fortunately, do not have whiskers. Agnes was really not at all to blame – anyone might have made the same mistake – because in addition to the black coat and the similarity in the colour of the hair, Tanis had picked up the shawl which you had carelessly left hanging on the banisters and put it on. I suppose she felt cold. It was that Chinese shawl with the flowers and butterflies – a ridiculous thing for a young girl to wear, but you evidently thought that it became you.'

Laura made a faint movement with her hand. It was as if she was trying to push something away. Carey moved too, but Miss Silver's grasp tightened sharply upon his arm and he stood still again.

Lucy Adams said, 'You can see how perfectly natural it was that Agnes should mistake Tanis for you. I do not see how she could be blamed in the least. She saw someone dressed in black and wearing that very noticeable shawl, and of course she thought that it was you. When she saw you go into Tanis's sitting-room she naturally wanted to know what you were doing there, and about half-way down the stairs she remembered about the pistol and thought how easy it would be to shoot you, and how certain everyone would be that Jeffrey Hazelton had come back and done it. So she came to the sitting-room door and opened it. She remembered about all the things in the detective stories – you know she is very fond of reading them – so she took care to take hold of the handle through a fold of her dressing-gown. That is why there were only Dean's finger-prints on it. When she came into the sitting-room it was empty, but the door was open into the octagon room and she could hear you opening the outside door. Of course it was really Tanis, but she thought it was you. She was remembering the pistol all the time, and she was remembering Oliver and Lilian, and that you had no right ever to have been born, and so of course you hadn't any right to be alive. And if that wasn't enough, there you were, setting yourself up, making difficulties about selling the Priory, and if Agnes had died, we should all have been turned out, and we shouldn't have had anywhere to go, because I haven't any money of my own. Agnes thought about all these things, and she took hold of the drawer where the pistol was and pulled it open with the fold of her dressing-gown round her hand, just as she had done with the door. But she couldn't do that with the pistol because of putting up the safety-catch and pulling the trigger. So she took it in her bare hand and went as far as the door into the octagon room. The wind was blowing in, and the outside door was open. She saw you standing in the open doorway. She was quite sure that it was you, because the light from the sitting-room struck on the coloured embroidery of the shawl. You were holding it round you because of the cold. She pulled the trigger, and you fell down the steps on to the grass. Only it wasn't you, it was Tanis, because she cried out, and the moment Agnes heard her voice she knew that she had made a mistake. Most regrettable, of course, but I do not see how anyone could blame her – I am sure you agree about that. She fully intended to kill you, and it was not her fault if she failed.'

Miss Adams paused for a moment, as if she expected Laura to make some comment. When none was forthcoming, she continued her narrative.

'Agnes was naturally very much disappointed and upset. She took Tanis's torch, which was lying on the sofa, and went down the steps just to make sure, and unfortunately there was no doubt about it. Really a terrible accident. She had shot Tanis, and Tanis was dead. Mercifully, nobody had heard the shot, and she kept her head. It occurred to her at once that the shawl must be removed and destroyed. No one would suspect her of shooting Tanis, but she might be suspected of shooting you, and if the shawl were left on the body, someone might guess that she had shot Tanis by mistake. So she took it off and burned it in the drawing-room fire, which was still quite nice and hot. It was very clever and resourceful of her, wasn't it? And she remembered to come back here and wipe the pistol and put it back in the drawer, and to wipe the inside handle of the door, because she had inadvertently touched it when she went out with the shawl. And she wiped the torch too, and slipped it into the back of the drawer, because she thought it just as well that it shouldn't be noticed. And then she went back to bed, but she didn't really sleep very well.'

Words had been forming themselves in Laura's mind – 'How – do – you – know?' They said themselves over and over, coming out of the dark places of thought and swelling up into sound – louder – louder – louder.

'*How – do – you – know?*'

She did not know that the words had forced themselves between her rigid lips, and that they had reached Lucy Adams, until she saw a look of triumph on the pale, plump face.

'I am just going to tell you about that, but you must not be impatient. Agnes has no secrets from me, you ought to know that. She didn't give up her idea of killing you – oh, dear me, no! She had it all very cleverly planned. You remember about the other pistol – the one which Tanis told us was still in Jeffrey Hazelton's possession. Well, Agnes knew where it was. She knew that Tanis had it, so she removed it. Shall I tell you where it was when the house was being searched for your shawl? It was hung in a shoe-bag round Agnes's waist under her petticoat. Wasn't that clever? And tonight she meant to kill you. She was going to shoot you from quite, quite close, and leave the pistol in your hand, and then everyone would think that you had killed Tanis and Florrie, and committed suicide. Of course you don't know about Florrie, but she was blackmailing Agnes, so she had to be got out of the way. Agnes thought it all out. She would dispose of Florrie, and then get you to come down here by a clever trick – a clever, *clever* trick. It is a very good room for a crime because there are so many doors – two here, and four in the octagon room if you count the lift – so that even if the shot were heard, one could always get away. Very well thought out – isn't it? And we need not talk about Agnes any more, because that was only part of the trick. Did you think I had really sent for the doctor? Why, that was the trick, Laura – that was the clever trick! That was the trick to get you downstairs. And it wasn't Agnes who thought of it, any more than it was Agnes who did all the things I have been telling you. It was I who did them all – I – I – *I*! And now I am going to shoot you, Laura.'

When Lucy Adams said the word 'trick' for the first time, two things happened simultaneously. Miss Silver's hand dropped from the arm she was holding, and Carey Desborough pushed open the door and stepped inside the room. He did not know whether Laura saw him or not. Her eyes were fixed and staring.

Miss Adams certainly neither saw nor heard. Her mind had no room for anything beyond its crazy purpose. As she said, 'And now I am going to shoot you,' she reached for the pocket of her red flannel dressing-gown and Carey Desborough's two hands came down over her shoulders and took her by the wrists.

Laura saw that, and then she saw nothing at all. The room was full of a confusion of noise and mist which swirled about her and would not let her see, or hear, or know. When it cleared, Carey was standing in front of Cousin Lucy's chair, and she was standing too. He was holding her by the wrists. Miss Silver was at the telephone table. She was saying, 'Yes, please ask the superintendent to come up at once. It is very urgent indeed. Will you tell him so from me. Miss Silver . . . Yes, that is the name – Miss Maud Silver.' There was a click as she replaced the receiver.

Laura gazed at the scene. There was a pistol lying on the floor, almost at her feet. It was quite unbelievable. A pistol – and Cousin Lucy had been going to shoot her. How can you believe a thing like that?

As Miss Silver came over and picked the pistol up, Lucy Adams said in an offended voice, 'Let go of my hands at once, Carey! You are really behaving very strangely indeed. Anyone would think that you had gone quite out of your mind.'

FORTY FOUR

'WHEN DID YOU begin to suspect her?' said Randal March.

Miss Silver's hands were busy with her knitting. A small pale-blue jacket was taking shape between the clicking needles. A fire burned brightly on the study hearth. A grey January sky obscured the low winter sun.

Miss Silver said, 'I cannot say, Randal. I could not accept either of the Madisons or any of the other suspects as providing a solution. There was an element of coolness and calculation which seemed incompatible with the theory that this was a crime of passion or jealousy. I did not think that Mr Madison, or Mr Maxwell, or Mr Desborough would have shot a woman in the back. It seemed to be quite incredible that they should have done so. You will remember my insistence upon the significance of the Chinese shawl. The threads from its fringe which were found entangled in Tanis's ring had to be explained. There were two possible explanations. Either Laura was wearing the shawl and there had been such a violent scene between them that the threads had been dragged out, or Tanis herself had been wearing the shawl when she was shot. I considered the first explanation extremely unlikely. You yourself suggested the second, my dear Randal, when you observed that Tanis might have felt chilly and have picked up the shawl on her way to the sitting-room. This theory was rendered likely by the destruction of the shawl. If Laura had been wearing it, it might have become stained, supposing she had descended the steps and bent over the body, but it would not in this case have been necessary to burn it. Every woman is aware that bloodstains come out very easily if the fabric is at once squeezed out in cold water. There was a bathroom next to Laura's room. She could have removed the stains and dried the shawl at the electric fire in her bedroom. The person who was cool enough to wipe off all betraying finger-prints would have been aware that the disappearance of the shawl could not possibly pass unnoticed. Its destruction must therefore have been an absolute necessity. A reason for this necessity presented itself immediately. A bloodstain can be removed, but a bullet-hole can neither be removed nor explained away. I became convinced that Tanis had been shot while wearing the shawl, and that the murderer had had the strongest possible reasons for removing and destroying it. At first I could not see why it should have been removed at all. If Tanis was wearing the shawl, and if she had been found in the morning still clutching it about her, there would have been no question of Laura being suspected, and therefore no reason why she or Mr Desborough should have removed it. Still less was there a reason why anyone else should have done so. Yet someone had done so, and I became convinced that the reason for the destruction of the shawl would give us the motive for the murder.

'I became more and more convinced that Tanis had been wearing the shawl. Consider how natural it was that she should pick it up as she went through the hall. It hung on the newel-post, a beautiful and conspicuous object. It was a cold night, and she was about to open an outside door and stand there waiting for Mr Madison. Those closely-woven oriental silks are warm. I was sure that she had picked it up and put it on. The murderer could have had only one reason for removing it – that it would endanger him unless he did remove it. It was not until late on Saturday night that I could see what this danger might be. If the murderer had seen Tanis cross the hall wearing the Chinese shawl he might have taken her for Laura Fane, and if it was Laura who was aimed at, the motive for the murder – and the possible suspects – had to be reconsidered. Tanis Lyle had many enemies. There were so many motives, so many suspects, that in her case it was difficult to select the most likely of them. But in Laura's case there was only one possible motive, an old grudge brooded over for more than twenty years, and only three possible suspects – Agnes Fane, her maid Perry, and Lucy Adams. I considered each of them in turn, and became convinced that it was Lucy who had shot Tanis.'

Randal March said, 'Why?'

Miss Silver coughed.

'I am sure you know the answer to that, my dear Randal. Agnes has remarkable eyesight, and so has Perry. But Lucy is short-sighted. She has worn glasses from a child. I think only a short-sighted person could have made the mistake that she actually did make.'

March said, 'I don't know. The height, the colour of the hair were the same. And with that noticeable Chinese shawl—'

Miss Silver shook her head.

'I am not thinking of those things, Randal. Laura had been wearing a black lace dress. Tanis had changed into black pyjamas and a heavy black silk coat. Only a very short-sighted person to whom all black materials look alike at a little distance could have mistaken that heavy silk for so different a material as lace.'

March smiled quizzically.

'How acute – and how feminine! That is where you will always have the advantage of me. I am only a man.'

Miss Silver smiled in return.

'Gentlemen always say that when they are feeling superior,' she said. 'It is still a handicap to be a woman, and they know it. You must not grudge us any of the slight advantages it confers.'

He laughed outright.

'Well, you made up your mind that Miss Adams was the murderer because of the difference between a bit of silk and a bit of lace. Anything else?'

The needles clicked. Miss Silver said, 'Oh, yes. It was the difference between the materials that made me suspect Lucy, but it was the behaviour of Florrie Mumford that confirmed those suspicions.'

'I don't see,' he said.

'Oh, *yes*, my dear Randal! I could not believe that she would have the temerity to blackmail Agnes Fane. Agnes is really a very intimidating person. I was sure that Florrie would not have had the courage to threaten her – so soon, and while she was still in her service. I think that if it had been Agnes the girl would have held her tongue until she could get away and do her blackmailing from a safer distance, if indeed she dared to do it at all. I was never able to consider Agnes seriously as the criminal, you know. She is a very efficient person, and if she had wished to murder Laura there would have been no bungling. Laura would have been murdered, and Agnes would never have been suspected, let alone blackmailed.'

'Well, that disposes of Miss Fane. What about Perry?'

'The motive was too slight, and as I said before, her eyesight is extremely good. And Florrie would never have expected to get a hundred pounds out of Perry.'

'So you arrived at Miss Adams.'

'So I arrived at Lucy. But I had no evidence – no shred or particle of evidence. I was, I may say, in considerable distress of mind. I did not know what to do. I thought of ringing you up, but the hour was late. I could not have mentioned my suspicions on the telephone, and you were in any case coming over early next morning in order to question Florrie. It seemed to me that our one chance of obtaining any real evidence was from Florrie.'

'I wonder what she knew,' said Randal March. 'That flapper friend of hers, Mrs Slade's sister, says she was in the habit of slipping through into this part of the house while Dean was locking up. Florrie may have heard the shot. She may have seen Miss Adams cross the hall. She may have stood behind the drawing-room curtains and watched her burn the Chinese shawl. We shall never know – unless Miss Adams tell us. She may, or she may not. All this girl Gladys can say is that Florrie was very pleased and excited and told her she knew something that was going to make her fortune, poor little wretch.'

Miss Silver laid down her knitting and folded her hands upon it.

'Randal, I thought she was safe, for that night at least. In spite of what I said to you I did warn her most seriously. And I knew that Dean locked the connecting doors at night. I thought she would be safe enough until the morning. Well, I was wrong.'

March looked kindly at her.

'You can't blame yourself – she asked for it.'

Miss Silver coughed.

'I do not blame myself, Randal. I committed an error of judgement, but it is easy to be wise after the event. I had no reasonable grounds for summoning you in the middle of the night, but my mind continued to be so much disturbed that I could not rest. I think it must have been the sound of Florrie's fall that roused me from a short, uneasy sleep. I had not consciously heard the fall, but I became more and more anxious, until at last I felt obliged to investigate. I then roused Mr Desborough, and we reached the hall in time to hear Lucy's extraordinary statement. She is of course unhinged.'

'Yes, I suppose she will be pronounced insane.'

Miss Silver looked at him gravely.

'A most unhappy story, Randal. I hope for Laura's sake that it need not all come out. You see, Lucy was just as much in love with Oliver as Agnes was. Everyone could see that. She made herself quite a laughing-stock over it, poor thing. And of course he never thought of her in that way at all. He used to laugh at her and call her "Poor old Lucy", and one day I am afraid she heard him. She never quite got over that. And then he ran away with Lilian Ferrers, and she and Agnes were left here together with nothing to do but to think how Oliver had treated them. Lucy had not at all a strong character, but like so many weak people she could hold on to a grudge. Even at school we used to say that she hoarded slights. She would treasure up anything unpleasant, just as other girls treasured up compliments – but then, of course, poor Lucy never had any compliments to treasure. After Oliver's marriage she just sat down here with Agnes for twenty-two years, while Agnes filled the house with hatred and resentment. Is it any wonder that Tanis Lyle grew up as she did, heartless and self-centred? Is it any wonder that Lucy became obsessed? Hatred is a deadly poison. For twenty-two years this house has been full of it.'

March nodded.

'That's grim,' he said.

'Yes, it is terrible. All those years Agnes was waiting for Laura to come of age. It was her most passionate desire to possess the Priory and to leave it to Tanis Lyle. Laura came of age, and came down here at Agnes's invitation. And her coming gave all that hatred a focus. But I still believe that nothing might have happened if it had not been for the violent disturbance set up by Jeffrey Hazelton. Into the already over-charged atmosphere of the house he introduced the idea of murder. He also introduced the necessary weapon, and there is no doubt that the scene in which he and Tanis took part excited Lucy's mind to the point of contemplating murder. Even so she might never have got beyond thinking about it if it had not been for what happened on Thursday night. A high wind has always had an upsetting effect upon her nerves. The gale, combined with the opportunity which she thought had been offered to her, was too much for the balance of her mind. It gave way, and from that moment she cannot, I think, be considered wholly responsible for her actions. When Florrie threatened her she behaved with great cunning. She must have known that the girl sometimes slipped through the connecting doors and got out of the house at night, so she made an appointment with her in the study at midnight, opening the window in order that it might be supposed that Florrie had been attacked by someone from outside. This, I think, goes to prove that she had not then conceived the horrible plan of involving Laura. I think that came later, when she had killed Florrie and had become completely insane. In that state she recognised no restraints and no difficulties. Having got Laura downstairs by a trick she meant to shoot her at point-blank range and leave the pistol in her hand. To her crazy mind it seemed quite certain that Laura would then be held responsible for both the other deaths. The Priory would pass into Agnes's possession, and the old score against Oliver Fane would have been paid. A dreadful story, Randal. And when I ask myself who is the real criminal, I cannot exonerate Agnes Fane.'

'How much did she know?' said March.

Miss Silver's eyes met his. They were steady and sad.

'I cannot say. I think that she suspected Lucy. I think so, but I cannot say. And she herself will never speak – I am quite sure of that. She will never tell us what she knew or suspected, or why she told Laura to lock her door last night. But I think – though this is only conjecture – that she found Florrie lying dead in the study and guessed at who the murderer must be. When she saw Laura at her bedroom door and told her to lock it she was obeying her conscience. She has a conscience, you know, and it would not permit her to expose even Laura whom she hated to what she knew to be a very real danger. I can respect her for that.'

March said, 'Yes.' And then, 'How has she taken it? Will it break her?'

'Agnes will never break,' said Miss Silver.

FORTY FIVE

CAREY AND LAURA drove away. Petra North had gone. The Maxwells had gone. The days they had spent in the Priory between Wednesday and Sunday were gone, joined with the dead days of dead, forgotten years. Perhaps some day they would be forgotten too.

Neither Carey nor Laura looked back, and neither spoke. They had seen Agnes Fane for a brief moment, rigid, indomitable – a courteous hostess bidding two guests farewell. Each in turn touched the ice-cold hand upon which there was still a fine glitter of diamonds. There was no word on either side of any future meeting. The inward shudder which Laura could conceal but not control still shook her as they drove on silently through the grey afternoon.

Presently when the road passed through woodland where great ramparts of holly rose shining and darkly green under the bare boughs of oak and chestnut, Carey drew in to the side and stopped the car. He put his arms round Laura and drew her close.

'Darling, you're so cold.'

She said in a forlorn whisper, 'I don't think I shall ever be warm again.'

'Oh, yes, you will – I'll make you warm. And you're not to shake – there's nothing to shake about now.'

She said, 'I can't stop. I don't feel as if I shall ever be able to stop. I keep seeing her.'

His voice sounded rough and angry.

'You won't see her again any more – ever. You won't see any of them again. We're going to be married on Thursday. Three clear week days – that's the quickest you can do it, unless you drag in the Archbishop of Canterbury and pay about thirty pounds for a special license. So I thought Thursday.'

'Carey, I couldn't!'

'You just see! You just stop thinking about a lot of bad old women and begin thinking about me, and you, and me – particularly me. We're going to be married on Thursday – you're going to be Laura Desborough. We'll go and set it all in train tomorrow morning. We'll have to get a wedding ring, you know, and you can choose your engagement ring at the same time – your aunt won't think it's legal without one. And you'd better telephone her to come up and give you away.'

'Carey, she won't!'

'Then we'll do without her. We're both of age. Darling, couldn't you stop shaking? It's all over. We're young – we're in love. You've no idea how tremendously I'm in love with you, but you're going to find out.'

He held her away and looked at her with something in his eyes which drove the cold shaking from Laura's heart.

'Snap out of it, darling, and kiss me! We're wasting time.'

PATRICIA WENTWORTH

THE CASE IS CLOSED

The Everton murder case has long been closed. The culprit has been charged with the murder of his uncle and has served a year of his sentence already. Or has he?

The evidence against Geoffrey Grey is convincing but his wife believes in his innocence. And so does her young cousin, Hilary, who decides to solve the mystery herself.

But when Hilary herself is nearly murdered she turns in desperation to her ex-fiancé for help. Fortunately he is acquainted with the singular Miss Silver, who is only too pleased to be asked to investigate.

HODDER

PATRICIA WENTWORTH

THROUGH THE WALL

There are bitter scenes in the Brand family when Martin Brand dies and leaves his large estate not to his widowed sister-in-law but to Marion, his young niece whom he had only met once in his life.

For Marion, the prospect of sharing her new home with Martin's predatory relations is not a happy one, and when a battered body wearing her coat is found on the beach her unhappiness turns to panic. Will Miss Silver find the murderer before the next killing?

HODDER

PATRICIA WENTWORTH

OUT OF THE PAST

James and Carmona Hardwick are spending the summer playing host to numerous friends and relatives in an old Hardwick family residence by the sea.

The arrival of Alan Field, a devastatingly handsome though shady figure from Carmona's past, lifts the holiday atmosphere from the ugly old house and replaces it with mounting tension, culminating in murder.

Fortunately for the Hardwicks and their guests, Miss Silver is present to unravel the secrets and lies and stop the killer in their midst.

HODDER

PATRICIA WENTWORTH

THE FINGERPRINT

When she found the body of her beloved Uncle Jonathan, Georgina's mind went blank. Instinctively, she stooped to pick up the revolver, thus becoming the prime suspect. Georgina stood to inherit a large fortune when her uncle died. But Uncle Jonathan had a second secret will and the beneficiary is the wide-eyed seemingly innocent Mirrie Fields.

But there was also the puzzle of the missing fingerprint. It was the showpiece of Uncle Jonathan's collection and he enjoyed telling the story of how he had acquired it from a self-confessed murderer, who was still at large. When the old man was shot, the print had been torn from its album.

Was the missing fingerprint the clue to the murderer's identity? Maud Silver is determined to find out.

HODDER

PATRICIA WENTWORTH

THE BENEVENT TREASURE

'The room was dark. She had pulled back the curtains and could just see the shape of the window. She sat up straight in bed with her heart beating fast . . .'

Somewhere among the dust and cobwebs of the sinister Benevent Mansion lies the legendary Benevent treasure. But a terrible death has been prophesied for whoever uncovers it.

When Candida Sayle is invited to visit her elderly maiden aunts, she dismisses such gloomy thoughts. But as Candida begins to discover the family's dark secrets she puts herself in grave danger. Thankfully Miss Silver has investigative skills of her own.

HODDER

PATRICIA WENTWORTH

THE CLOCK STRIKES TWELVE

New Year's Eve, 1940, is unusual for the Paradine family. Departing from tradition, James Paradine makes a speech that changes the course of many lives. Valuable documents have disappeared. A member of the family has taken them and the culprit has until midnight to confess and return the papers.

A few minutes after twelve James Paradine is dead.

It is left to Miss Silver to disentangle the threads that bind the Paradine family in a strange web of dislike, hatred and fear.

HODDER